John Dunloe Carteret

A Fortune Hunter

A Tale

John Dunloe Carteret

A Fortune Hunter
A Tale

ISBN/EAN: 9783744677776

Printed in Europe, USA, Canada, Australia, Japan

Cover: Foto ©Andreas Hilbeck / pixelio.de

More available books at **www.hansebooks.com**

A Fortune Hunter;

OR,

THE OLD STONE CORRAL.

A Tale of the Santa Fe Trail.

BY

JOHN DUNLOE CARTERET.

———◆———

CINCINNATI:

PRINTED FOR THE AUTHOR.

1888.

CONTENTS.

CHAPTER I.

CHAPTER II.

CHAPTER III.

CHAPTER IV.

CHAPTER V.

CHAPTER VI.

CHAPTER VII.

CHAPTER VIII.

CHAPTER IX.

CHAPTER X.

CHAPTER XI.

CHAPTER XII.

CHAPTER XIII.

CHAPTER XIV.

CHAPTER XV.

CHAPTER XVI.

CHAPTER XVII.

CHAPTER XVIII.

A FORTUNE HUNTER:

OR,

THE OLD STONE CORRAL.

Chapter I.

THE sinking sun threw its amber beams over the wide valley, rolling hills, and the dim buttes, wreathed in the blue haze of distance and looming with vague outlines in the wavering shimmer of the evening mirage.

A silvery stream, half hidden by fringing trees, wound through the prairie valley, but was lost to sight where a lofty butte shouldered boldly down from the highland on the south, as if to catch a view of the Eden-like landscape that dreamed below, while far away to the north a line of galloping hills bounded the vision, their mantles of tender green dappled by the shadow and sunshine of the fleecy clouds that floated overhead. On the south the level prairie melted away into the limitless distance, clothed in the tender grasses and flowers of early spring-time, while on every hand stretched away the horizon-bound prairies of the Western plains.

A wide meadow-land, made perfect by the hand of nature, but lacking that soul and animation which human occupancy alone can impart to any scene. No homes are visible; nothing but the blank page of nature, waiting to be written over with the histories of the people, which, something whispers to me, will soon invade this peaceful scene, over which now broods the unnatural calm of utter solitude.

Out beyond that blue line of hills, which flame up in the east, is raging the fierce conflict which we call civilization; but the shock and din, the roar and turmoil of the mighty battle die fitfully away long before reaching the quivering line of that dim horizon. I stand alone upon the crest of a breeze-kissed hill, listening to the moan and whisper of the wind sighing through the grasses at my feet, or the notes of a meadow lark, thrilling and sweet, as it flits by.

To the westward, on a lofty knoll, are visible the broken arches and ruined walls of the Old Stone Corral; rank vines now veil the loop-holes where once had flashed forth the leaden death-messenger for many a savage warrior that had tried to storm the impregnable inclosure, which had been built as a place of refuge for travelers on the Santa Fe Trail, that here crossed the Cottonwood on a stony ford. A giant elm, centuries old, stood amid the ruins, its drooping boughs of feathery spray weeping like a fountain of verdure over the spring that welled out from among its roots, then went gurgling away, a purling brook, to join the narrow stream in the valley.

The river here at the ruins had nearly encircled the hill on which they stood, and after half embracing the knoll in its timber-fringed course had wound away down the valley, but where the groves grew in masses of darkest green, there the stream had widened to miniature lakelets that flashed like silver in the slanting sunbeams.

On a low mound near by I see a great stone, like a rude monument, and drawing near I can barely decipher this dim and weather-worn inscription, carved on the red sandstone:

Erected to the Memory

OF

FIFTY-THREE VICTIMS OF THE CHEYENNES,

AUGUST 22, 1849.

NAMES ALL UNKNOWN.

Here is a dim, dark tragedy, buried within this grassy knoll, but within these pages all the mystery which haunts the flower-bespangled hillock will be cleared away. A difficult task indeed; but without those graves my story would never have been written.

I stand silent and thoughtful, gazing out over the tranquil landscape, which had once witnessed a scene of revolting horror here on this quiet spot; but all is peaceful now, the only sign of life visible being the long file of antelope that hurry by from the north. Halting on a lofty headland, they pause a moment, stretching their graceful necks to gaze back along their pathway, then with loud snorts wheeling and swiftly fleeing away.

At this moment the distant sound of hoofs was heard, becoming momentarily louder; then a group

2

of riders dash up on their sleek, superb horses, and draw rein at the rude monument.

"It must be here, Clifford, at this low mound," said one of the riders, a graceful girl of seventeen, with nut-brown hair and blue eyes.

"Yes, Maud, I recognize the knoll from father's and Uncle Roger's description. It was uncle who carved this inscription upon the stone, little dreaming then that we should all come here a quarter of a century later to secure a new home," replied a youth of near twenty years; handsome, golden-haired, and symmetrical, with eyes of pansy blue, and a look of pride and good birth about him which showed plain through the dust and tan of a long journey.

"Ah, dear Bruce and Ivarene! how sad to end their romance with such a tragedy!" said Maud tearfully, as Clifford dismounted; then, as he helped her to alight, they stood for a moment in mute sorrow while deciphering the inscription upon the stone.

"Maud, it is hard to believe that the heiress of grand old Montcluma, with her millions of gold and gems at command, who wedded noble Bruce in the great cathedral before the dignitaries and ambassadors of half Christendom with a pomp and splendor new to even luxury-steeped Mexico, is sleeping with her husband in the silence of this lonesome grave," Clifford said in a tone of deep sadness.

"Oh! how vivid the picture returns, of the silken and lace-robed heiress, who threw back the gilded lattice of her window, and with pearls glinting, and rubies burning in her raven hair, smiled as her handsome lover, in his uniform of gray and gold lace, swung himself up to her window by the passion-vines and fuchsias, that rained a shower of purple, white, and rose on his sunny hair. I can almost see the love-look in his blue eyes yet," said Maud with a flood of tears, as she leaned against the rude monument and covered her face with her hands.

"I have sometimes fancied that they escaped; for there was no one left but father to inquire, and you know how long he was covered with the stones of that old wall, remaining delirious for months after Uncle Roger found him," said Clifford, "and that million of their gold and gems, with father's store of gold, I have often fancied, Maud, was hidden near here; for there has never been a search made since the terrible massacre."

"That looks so improbable, Clifford. If the savages murdered them for plunder, as they certainly did, then it is idle to think that they would have left anything of value behind. Even the jewels would have been fought for, as savages are very fond of glitter and splendor," Maud replied.

"Yes, that very disposition of theirs to wrangle over their booty has given me a hope that the leader might have buried the gold, for the reason that it would have been impossible to carry away a ton of coin without first dividing it. I shall make the search at any rate, though it does look like a forlorn hope," he added with a sigh.

"Miss Warlow, there seems to have been a great tragedy enacted here in the past," said a young man of near Clifford's age, who had been silently regarding them from a distance, in company with a flaxen-

haired girl, younger than Maud, who still sat upon
her horse by his side.

"Yes, Mr. Moreland, and it nearly concerns us;
for our father, here on this spot, once lost a great
fortune, and at the same time those two friends
of whom we have been speaking. This all was long
before Clifford and I were born; but father has told
us so often of the tragedy that the names of Bruce
and Ivarene Walraven are dear and sacred to us all,"
Maud replied.

"Oh, Ralph! I wonder if Colonel Warlow would
tell us the particulars of that terrible affair?" said
the younger girl.

"It would be doubly interesting here upon the
closing scene of the tragedy," the young man replied.

"Will you ask your father, Maud, to tell us to-
night?" the young girl inquired eagerly.

"Yes, Grace: it will help to while away our
first Sabbath here, which will be a lonesome day
to-morrow," Maud made answer as they remounted
and rode down to the stream to water their horses.

"What a lovely camp-ground!" exclaimed
Grace. "Shall we not stop here, Ralph?"

"Yes, sister, if the others are willing. It is
not only a fine camping ground, but it is more:
This is a grand home-land, or will be when we
select our 'claims,' Monday. I never before have
seen a more beautiful or fertile valley than this."

Soon a long line of white covered wagons and
a comfortable carriage appeared, coming down the
Santa Fe trail, which wound its travel-worn course
over the hills from the north-east; and where soli-

tude had reigned but an hour before there now re-echoed the sounds of a busy camp, and ruddy fires leaped and sparkled, about which female forms flit-ted to and fro, preparing their evening meal. But while all was bustle and animation within the camp, a solitary figure could be seen standing at the long grave, bowed in an attitude of silent grief.

As he walked slowly back within the glare of the camp-fire, it was apparent that he was a man past middle life, of grave and dignified appearance; the lines of care, on his still handsome face, were deepened as if by grief as he seated himself by a tree, away from the glare of the light.

As he sat thus—lost in reverie—Maud came softly by, and, passing her hand over his hair in a caressing way, said:—

"What a lovely country this is! I am charmed with it already."

"Yes, Maud, my daughter, it is a fertile and picturesque region; but it will be hard to inure myself to living on this spot, for it is haunted by very bitter memories."

"Oh, it is sad, indeed, to think of the fate of Bruce and his graceful bride; but we will deck their grave with flowers, and I shall never cease to grieve for them," she said, dropping a kiss on her father's cheek, then hurrying away to the camp-fire.

He was roused from his gloomy reverie, a few minutes later, by his wife, who came to his side, and, as her hand rested fondly on his shoulder, she said, in a sweet voice of womanly sympathy, in which could be traced a sub-tone of strength and resolution :—

"George, dear, this is no time for repining; instead we should feel happy and grateful that we have found such a delightful country as this in which to select our future home. Oh, this valley is more beautiful than even my wildest dreams had ever pictured. I had felt apprehensive, husband, that your impressions of this place had been colored by your youthful enthusiasm of twenty, and own that I had made ample allowance for the quarter of a century which has passed since then; but it is certainly the most charming spot I have ever beheld."

"My dear, brave wife," he replied joyfully, "you lift a heavy burden from my heart; we will select a home near here early Monday morning, and begin building at once. I shall leave the selection with you, Mary, however."

"Oh, we are too late," she replied, with a cheerful smile. "Robbie has found the spot already; he has just returned from down the valley, where Scott Moreland and himself had driven the stock, and they report having found a perfect paradise. They are both boiling over with enthusiasm, and are bareheaded, having left their hats hanging on trees to mark the location of their respective 'claims,' and when I left the camp-fire they were inveighing against the injustice of a law that would not permit fifteen-year-old boys to take a 'homestead.'"

In a more cheerful mood the couple now sought the camp-fire, which was surrounded by more than a dozen persons of both sexes, all animated and

happy over the termination of their long and toil-
some journey.

The two who have just entered the circle are
Colonel Warlow and his wife, while the handsome
youth of fifteen, with hazel eyes and auburn hair,
which has a faint tinge of red, that accounts for the
reputation he has earned within the Warlow circle,
is Robbie, their youngest; while that golden-haired
young Adonis, who, in a fit of grave abstraction,
sits leaning against a tree, his white and tapering
hands clasped about his knee, the firelight glimmering over a small and well-shaped boot resting on
the round of his chair, is their oldest son, Clifford,
whom we have met before; while Maud, their only
daughter, is easily recognized as she flits about,
busy and graceful.

Next we see the family of Squire Moreland,
from the valley of the Merrimac—the squire himself being a representative Puritan, plain and grave;
his wife, a type of the live and thorough-going New
England woman, deeply imbued with the "thing-
ness of is," able to discuss apples or algebra, beans
or baptism, or in fact any subject down to zymol-
ogy. Then Ralph, principally to be recommended
for being "general good fellow." Next in their
family is Scott, quiet and grave, addressed by Rob
Warlow as the "Young Squire;" and their only
daughter, Grace, in whose make-up there is more
than a faint spice of the tomboy.

Colonel Warlow's family had left their old Missouri home, the tobacco and hemp plantation on
which the children had all been born, and, having

met the Morelands on their rout, bound for that
indefinite region "out West," they had journeyed
on together to this spot, attracted by Colonel Warlow's remembrance of its great beauty and natural
fertility, which had deeply impressed him when he
was here a quarter of a century before.

Learning, at Council Grove, that the valley was
open to homestead entry, they had hastened on,
miles ahead of other settlements, to locate here on
a spot that was beyond the utmost limit of civilization.

Soon the hungry travelers were seated at the
cloth that was spread on the downy buffalo-grass,
and were partaking of the broiled quail and antelope steak, the appetizing odors of which now pervaded the whole camp; but as the company ranged
themselves about the tempting repast, Maud and
Grace retired to a seat by the fire, declaring as they
did so, that they would not sacrifice their precious
lives by sitting at a table with thirteen other sinners.

"Give us a song, then," cried some one from
the table, at which Grace sprang up and brought
Maud's guitar from the carriage, and soon the sweet
strains,

> "Oft in the stilly night,
> Ere slumber's chains have bound me,
> Fond memory brings the light
> Of other days around me,"

re-echoed through the tranquil valley. As Maud's
tender soprano mingled with the luscious alto of
Grace's voice the listeners almost forgot the tempting feast spread before them, and cries of "Bravo!"

"Encore!" etc., greeted the close of the pathetic song, which was wholly lost, as to its sentiment, upon the younger members of the company.

"Pass the hat," cried Bob, whereupon Grace handed her sunshade around among the laughing group, but after inspecting the collection, she said with an air of contempt:—

"A wish-bone and five bread-crusts! Why, a *prima donna* would starve on such a meagre salary. I've a notion to play Herodias's daughter and dance off your heads;" and when Maud struck up a lively fandango, she shook her curls in a threatening manner, and then whirled off into an amazing waltz.

Jeers and hoots from the boys resounded at her last *pas seul*, and Clifford's voice was heard in the gay tumult saying: "Mademoiselle dis Grace must have learned her step at an Irish wake.

"Let us no longer serve an ungrateful public," said Maud, as they sat down to the table, where their gayety chased away all traces of care or sorrow. When the meal was finished, Maud and Grace begged Colonel Warlow to relate his early history. Their request was eagerly seconded by the other members of the company, who were anxious to learn the particulars of that tragedy, hinted at by the inscription on the mound, and how he came to be connected with the actors in that terrible drama, and to lose a great fortune on that spot so long ago. Then the colonel, after sitting for a few moments wrapped in serious thought, replied that it was a long story, and would require more than one evening to relate all the particulars of that great tragedy, that would always be fresh in his memory as long as life endured.

The company reminded him that it would be rather lonesome on their first Sabbath, and entreated him so eagerly that at length he consented; then, as the firelight leaped and sparkled, and the beams of the rising moon silvered the waters of the stream, moaning and fretting over the stony ford, they all gathered about the colonel, still and expectant. The quavering scream of a lone wolf died out on the hills in a plaintive wail; then only the faint whisper of the wind sighing though the willows was heard, and the colonel said:—

Chapter II.

COLONEL WARLOW'S STORY.

"WHEN a boy of twenty I joined the army that soon invaded Mexico, and carried victory with its banners into the Aztec capital—the world-renowned halls of the Montezumas.

"It was before Vera Cruz—when our ranks were swept by the iron hail, rained upon our storming columns by scores of cannon from San Juan de Ulloa—that I first saw Bruce Walraven, whom I was thenceforth to regard as a brother.

"An exploding shell had killed my horse, which had fallen upon me in such a way that made it impossible for me to rise without assistance; and while I was yet vainly struggling to extricate myself from the dangerous position, a squadron of cavalry rushed by, charging a company of Mexican infantry intrenched behind a light breastwork of sand-bags. I held up my hand with an imploring gesture—a human voice was lost in the wild thunder and roar of artillery—and the leader of the cavalry saw my sad plight. He wavered a moment as though struggling with discipline; but the sight of a fellow-soldier in distress seemed to outweigh all else, even the pride of leading his men, for he dashed to my side and helped me to rise; then, as a riderless horse galloped by, he caught its dangling rein, and by his help, in a moment more I was again in the saddle.

"By rapid riding we soon overtook the command, and were greeted by a ringing cheer from the soldiers, who quickly showed their appreciation of his humanity. Later in the war I would not have been so fortunate; but we were new, as yet, to scenes of bloodshed and carnage, which accounted for the laxity of discipline, but evidence of humanity, shown in this incident.

"After the successful storming of the enemy's slight earthworks, which, with their usual lack of military sience, had been but half manned and illy constructed, I had a long talk with young Lieutenant Walraven, and in a short time I had managed to be exchanged into his company; and we soon became inseparable companions, sharing the same blanket at night and rude fare during the day, or riding side by side through the battles of that glorious campaign, and finally reaching the valley of Mexico safely.

"Here, while engaged in a slight skirmish with the enemy, Walraven was wounded in the arm, and was immediately conveyed to the old hacienda of Monteluma, near by. At his urgent request I was detailed to stay with him as a guard. In the courts of that princely villa he rapidly convalesced; and one day, while seated by the great fountain, where myrtle and jasmine, oleander and roses, mingled their fragrance, he saw two beautiful Spanish ladies loitering near, and being concealed by the luxuriant foliage himself, he could see and hear all that passed without being discovered.

"He always afterward declared to me that at first he had no intention of playing the eavesdropper; but when he learned from their talk that it was himself they were discussing, then the temptation became too great to resist, so he sat very still while the following dialogue took place, and which, with his usual boyish frankness, he related to me an hour later. This was in Spanish; but Bruce was now quite proficient in that language, and readily understood all that was said:—

"'But, Ivarene, my dear, it does not become Don Rozarro's daughter and heiress—last, alas! of the proud line of Monteluma—to become infatuated with the blue eyes and golden hair of this wounded soldier; and if he is as handsome as a Norse king, to which you so foolishly compare him, he still is no less our country's enemy,' said the elder lady, who seemed to be a duenna, whose sole care consisted in keeping the younger and more beautiful lady hidden from the eyes of her unwelcome guests, but with what success you may readily perceive.

"'But, Labella, cousin dear, he is alone, wounded and ill in a foreign land—no mother, sister, or sweetheart near to soothe his long days of pain! (I wonder if he has a sweetheart in that cold Northland!) And then, Labella, does not the good Book command us to do good to those who hate us, and to love our enemies?' she replied with a mischievous smile.

"'Oh, the command, my darling, does not apply to every sunny-haired trooper who invades our country—'

"'No—no; not every one, true!' retorted Ivarene, archly, to which the duenna quickly replied:—

"'I fear, Ivarene, that your English education, and your much reading of those Northern books, have turned your head.'

"Here the ladies passed on through a latticed arcade, and their voices were lost in the distance; but my friend had seen and heard enough to lose his heart completely, and in the evening, as we sat on the balcony without, he was so quiet and thoughtful that I began to realize the fact that he was deeply entangled in the meshes of love at first sight.

"Leaving him to his reflections, I walked to the edge of the balcony to gaze out over the matchless landscape which the lofty mansion commanded.

"The tropic moon poured a flood of silvery radiance over the Vale of Mexico, while low down on the horizon burned the fiery Southern Cross. The bubbling domes of the great capital seemed to float upon the lakes which environ its walls, and her myriad lights twinkled and flashed back from their waters like stars on a frosty night.

"Old Chapultepec, with its castellated walls, towered out on the lofty headland; and the dark forests of cypress, that had witnessed the tragedies and pageants of Aztec splendor for a thousand years past, clothed the base of the hill in a sombre mantle, peopled by the spectres, I thought, of long dead princes and Montezumas that in the dim past had lived their lives of inconceivable luxury in those ancient groves.

"Over all loomed the old volcanoes, white and ghostly, with their mantles of eternal snow and hearts of hidden fire. Shrouded in mystery, they seemed a fit emblem of the Aztec past, whose buried histories still haunt this ancient land.

"Near by, at the foot of the lofty terrace, the groves of olive and orange were sombre in shade. In the soft wind the myrtle rustled faintly, and on the roses at our feet the dew-drops glinted in fitful splendor.

"In an angle of the old wall, where the murky shadows were deepest, the glow-worms burned in the damp grass, and the fire-flies glimmered incessantly. There I half fancied that I could see strange forms hovering; and when a figure flitted out into the moonlight, then was quickly lost again in the black shade of an aloe, I was startled for a moment; but concluding it was one of the peons belonging to the estate, I turned my eyes to again feast on the glorious view.

"There were numberless fountains pouring down their sheen of waters, that, after flashing a moment in the moonlight, rippled away in rivulets, which gurgled and sang as they leaped over the terraces in mimic cascades, where they joined the waters of the fairy-like lakes that slumbered in the grounds below. These tranquil sheets of water were the reservoirs which served to irrigate the vast estate, and were decked with floating gardens, on which were gilded arbors or lattices of white, with beds of bright-hued tropic flowers.

"On every hand lay league upon league of land, all owned by the young mistress of Monteluma. The long avenue of cypress only ending close to the walls of the capital, the villages of peons, the pasturages where the numerous flocks grazed, groves of orange and lemon, and the fields of wheat,—all these I knew were the undisputed estate of our hostess, of whom Bruce was now dreaming.

"I was aroused from my reverie by an exclamation from my companion, who had now sprung up excitedly and was pointing down toward the entrance, while he grasped the pistols that hung in his belt—weapons that were never lost sight of in this turbulent country. As I looked toward the spot where he was pointing I could see the long line of a hundred steps—which led up to the only entrance to the hacienda—lined and thronging with armed men.

"In a moment the situation flashed upon us: they were banditti or marauders, emboldened by the unprotected state of the rich villa, and were now attacking the great iron-studded door. If they effected an entrance, I shuddered with apprehension to think of the fate of its inmates; but we lost no time while we were thus speculating, but quickly barring the door on the balcony we rushed down into the court, and while I grasped the bell-rope and sent forth a wild alarm from the brazen bell that hung in the lofty tower, Bruce hurried on through the long hall toward the door of entrance.

" As he was fastening the chains and bars across the entrance a crowd of frightened peons came flocking into the hall, and while we were hastily arming them with the guns that hung upon the wall and directing them to guard the upper windows and doors that opened out upon the lofty balconies, the door of the great saloon was hurriedly thrown open, and Senora Labella asked in a trembling voice the reason of the commotion.

" When she learned that the bandits were at the door she fled back into the room, and as we followed, assuring her of our protection, we saw her fly to where the young heiress stood, her arm yet resting upon the gilded harp which she had but just that moment ceased playing, and the light from the silver chandelier falling softly upon her raven hair and the lustrous white silk that fell in graceful folds about her slender form.

" While the excited duenna clung to the more youthful lady, and gave way to incoherent cries of fear and moans of distress, we begged them to retire to a tower of great strength, and we would surely repel the attack; but Ivarene declared she would stay and help defend her home—saying she would not have it said that the last Rozarro was the first to flee from danger.

"After the senora had been given over to the care of a bevy of badly frightened maids, Ivarene hurried fearlessly out into the hall and showed Bruce where several loop-holes were concealed by slides of iron. These commanded the entrance, and while we rained a galling fire upon the enemy, she stood

3

in an angle of the thick wall and reloaded the guns for us, which we as rapidly discharged again with telling effect. The blows upon the door soon ceased, and we could see the marauders retreating down the steps; then, as a parting salute followed them, they could be heard galloping swiftly away.

" When all was still again, we accompanied the brave young heiress back to the saloon, where she thanked us earnestly for the rescue of her home from the hands of the marauders. Of course, we quickly assured her that the honors and glory of the occasion rested in her bravery and resolution. When she gave her hand to my handsome, sunny-haired friend, I think something stronger than admiration shone in his deep-blue eyes as he gazed upon the beautiful creole face, now suffused with blushes and lit by eyes of midnight blackness.

" The senora had now recovered from her agitation, and was voluble and profuse in her thanks and compliments. At a sign from her the servants brought great silver trays, loaded with cake of white and gold, with decanters of ruby wine, glittering in the flasks of cut glass like liquid fire. For an hour or more the dark-eyed young heiress sang songs of Spain in a voice of cultured melody, while her white fingers swept the gilded harp, that vibrated in tones of sweetest harmony under her skillful touch.

As a compliment to us she also sang several Scotch and English ballads, and we were pleasantly surprised to learn that she had received an education in England, and spoke our own tongue with remarkable fluency.

"From that night we were accorded all the privileges of honored guests in the great hacienda."

Here the colonel paused, remarking that as the hour was growing late his hearers would excuse him, which they promised to do providing he would continue his narrative on the morrow. As the party arose from about the camp-fire, Robbie said he felt heroic enough to eat several Mexicans, not to mention such relishes as wine, cake, and peons, at which very broad hint the tea-kettle was soon humming on the embers; and when the cups of the soothing beverage were handed around, Grace passed a basket, which, if not filled with such luxuries as those which had graced the Mexican saloon, were at least very acceptable to our friends.

Scott, whose attention was divided between a chicken-bone and reverie, suddenly inquired if they thought there would ever be another war with Mexico. As the party broke up with a laugh at his expense, the quiet of nature once more reigned over the valley, broken only by the hoarse croak of the frogs in the dark pools and the shrill cry of the cicada in the grass.

The moon threw a pale, silvery light upon the row of white tents, where our friends were soon dreaming of the new homes that they would build in this tranquil valley; yet no vision of the strange events which fate held in store for them came to prepare them for the life of trial and adventure which they were now entering upon.

One day more of quiet rest, then would begin a life new and strange for them all. They had left their old selves forever behind; their past was a blank; new faces and new friends awaited them here in their future home, which had never been even claimed as the property of any man since the dawn of creation.

Yes, fate is both unkind and compassionate in withholding a knowledge of the blessings and trials that await them here; so they slumber on, while unseen destiny begins to weave her web, checkered and mysterious as the veil of moonlight that wavers through the willows.

Chapter III.

COLONEL WARLOW'S STORY—CONTINUED.

THE morning of that Sabbath broke calm and serene. A warm haze brooded over the valley or danced in lines of quivering heat across the green prairies of the upland, and the dew had long since ceased to glitter on the rank blue-stem grass when our friends awoke.

The breakfast which followed almost caused them to forget the fact that they were out upon the borders of the "Great American Desert," and they might have fancied that they were once more but picnicking under the shade of their native groves; for it was a meal that had exhausted the culinary art of both matrons. Wild mushrooms, stewed in sweet cream, deliciously fragrant and hinting of the wild-wood near by, delicate brook-trout from the stream, mingled their aroma with the elder-bloom fritters which Maud was preparing; and on the snowy damask, spread on the grass, Mrs. Moreland's golden honey-comb vied with the War-low jelly and crimson marmalade, while the coffee would make one dream of Araby the blest.

An hour after the morning meal we find our friends seated under the shade of the great elm among the ruins, the sunlight struggling faintly through the verdant canopy and weaving a golden

veil over the ashen buffalo-grass, starred by daisies
and violets. The spring welled out with a sleepy
murmur, and overhead an oriole, near its swinging
nest, caroled forth a stream of bubbling melody.

"A month passed," continued the colonel, "and
we still lingered in the stately mansion, daily and
hourly meeting the young heiress, who was always
accompanied by her matronly kinswoman. But one
morning, as Bruce was loitering in the court, he
glanced up and saw the smiling face of Ivarene,
framed by the passion-flowers, fuchsias, and jasmine
which festooned the walls within the court and
wreathed the lattice above her balcony.

"With an impulse which he could not resist
our young hero swung himself up by the vines, and
stood, with his sunny hair and smiling blue eyes,
within the balcony. He wore the uniform of a
captain of cavalry—soft gray, with cords and lace
of frosted gilt over the breast—top-boots, embossed
with gold, and a hat half concealed by the drooping
plumes.

"She threw back the gilded jalousies which
guarded her window, and, smiling graciously, held
out her hand, which he clasped with all the rapture
of an infatuated lover.

"She was robed in soft, rose-colored India
muslin, embroidered in white lilies, and over her
breast and arms fell a cascade of lace, caught lightly
over her raven tresses, in that graceful manner
which the ladies of Spanish America wear the man-
tilla; gleaming through its filmy folds could be
seen the rubies which burned in her hair.

"Within that flower-entwined balcony was re-enacted that tender scene—old as the dawn of creation, still ever new. How he told the tale, or how she answered, I can not say, but may readily surmise from the brilliant wedding which followed in the old cathedral a few months later.

"Bruce had become very popular with the young officers of our army, and I have often seen him riding about the city with McClellan, and—"

"What! not our 'Little Mac?'" cried Squire Moreland, springing to his feet, transformed into an impetuous soldier by the magic of a name, and while the others regarded him with amazement, as he paced back and forth with clenched hands, he continued in a tone of repressed vehemence: "If there is one name that would cause me to leap from the grave, it is that of 'Little Mac,' the Giant of Antietam; and, as there is a God above, I believe it was McClellan who led us to victory at Gettysburg. Oh, can I ever forget that terrible day when the host of Lee beat and broke in thunder over the hills like the ocean on a rocky shore, drenching our ranks in a surf of blood—when reckless Longstreet charged like a whirlwind through smoke and flame, while our columns staggered under the shock? The scream of countless shells and the stunning belch and roar of a thousand cannon mingled with the trample of the Southern cavalry as it hurled its squadrons upon us like the throes of an earthquake, their storm of rebel yells rising above the notes of Dixie and all the din of conflict with the roar of a hurricane. Oh, Heaven! how then we longed for

one hour of 'Little Mac!' That day our Nation's
fate trembled in the balance; a few more shocks
and all would be lost; then this fierce army—another
such the world has never seen—would sweep over
the North like an avalanche! Every moment hurried myriads into eternity, wringing loving hearts
and breaking many a home from Maine to Texas.
But when the word, like an electric shock, flashed
along our hopeless ranks, '*Little Mac has come,*' can
I ever, ever, forget the shout of delight that burst
from the parched lips of threescore thousand men?
the rapid rush of marching ranks as they hurried
to death, shouting, 'Little Mac, Little Mac!' when
squadrons flashed by to the cannon's mouth, shaking the earth with their thunders of that mighty
name? Oh! the wild delight and glory of that hour,
when the fierce but baffled hosts of Lee broke and
fled! But at the battle's close they claimed that it
was only a ruse, and that McClellan was not there.
Yet I shall always believe he did lead us that day;
but, unwilling to impair the laurels of Meade, he
has kept silent all these years—only such a man is
capable of that grand heroism. I have interrupted
you, Colonel. Please excuse me, and proceed with
your narrative."

After a moment's silence, the colonel said:

"Bruce Walraven was descended from a noble
English family that had settled in New York in
the earliest colonial days, but their fortunes had
waned until himself and his sword were all that remained of that once powerful house. He was an
orphan, who had graduated with honor at West

Point Military Academy, and was utterly alone in the world, with no one to love but Ivarene and myself, yet no brothers could have been more deeply attached than we soon became to each other.

"I have never yet described him to you, from the fact that—that— Well, I feel a strange reluctance to say that Clifford, here, is the very image of that friend who died four years before my boy was born; but as I look at my son now, I almost fancy that Bruce is with me again, and that all my manhood's troubled years are only a fitful dream.

"Since his boyhood I have noticed Clifford's resemblance to Bruce, and as my boy grew older he seemed to almost take the place of my lost friend, which has resulted, you perceive, in a sort of companionship between us which leads strangers to take us for brothers, instead of father and son. But to my story again.

"The wedding-day dawned fair and serene, and at noon a company of young cadets from Chapultepec, all of whom were sons of the highest Mexican aristocracy, filed out on the avenue of cypresses that led to Monteluma, their snow-white horses trapped with gold and purple, and their steel helmets a mass of tossing plumes; their high top-boots of glossy black were embossed with gilt, and on the breasts of their white tunics the Mexican eagle flashed in silver, as two and two they galloped out to the great hacienda.

"An hour later Ivarene entered her low, open carriage, which was richly gilded and drawn by four white horses that were almost hidden by garlands

4

of bright-hued flowers. She wore a robe of white satin, while a tiara and necklace of pearls glimmered through the filmy veil that trailed like a mist about her form. Behind her, there rode in separate carriages, each drawn by two white horses, her seven bridesmaids, who were likewise dressed in white. Senora Labella sat by the side of Ivarene, and a grand dame also occupied each carriage with a bridesmaid ; their sumptuous toilets of satin, velvet, and brocade were of purple and cream-rose, emerald and lilac.

" As this brilliant company filed out on the avenue, four cadets riding in double file between each carriage, flowers were strewn in the road by long lines of peon children dressed in white. At the city gates a double guard of Mexican and American soldiers, riding white horses and gorgeous with military trappings, escorted them through the city to the grand plaza, where the old cathedral was thronged with the proud and great of two nations, while the ministers and foreign ambassadors of nearly all of Europe and the Americas, waited in pomp of state with their wives and daughters, all attired in the extreme of luxury. I shall not try to depict the splendor of the final scene when the cardinal in his robes of scarlet pronounced the solemn service, and pale, handsome Bruce, wearing his uniform of a colonel, received his bride from the hand of Don Hernando Rozarro, the Spanish ambassador.

" Haughty Santa Anna was there, and General Taylor looked happily on, while all around were

grouped our gallant officers, graceful and young,
whose names now thunder down the galleries of
fame linked with Antietam, Shiloh, and blood-
drenched Malvern Hill. Grant and Lee, those
slumbering lions, that in after years were to shake
the continent with appalling conflict, now stood side
by side, each carrying the wedding favor of their
friend.

"A scene of splendor ensued that recalled the
old pageants of the Montezumas, when a long line
of gilded coaches and prancing white horses filed out
in the twilight, along the avenue returning to Monteluma. The sun had set, but a parting gleam was
yet crimsoning the snow on the volcano of Toluco,
while the sombre cypresses were aglow with the
green and rosy light of torches, carried by the
double line of peons in their ancient Aztec garb.
Old Monteluma glimmered like a jewel from terrace to turret with colored lights, while out upon
the broad esplanades, where thousands of the peons
were feasting, the fountains flashed white and misty,
like the snow-storms of my Northern home.

"When Ivarene, leaning on Bruce's arm, walked
up the long flight of steps to the doorway of her
old home, the marble beneath her feet was hidden
by the rose-leaves strewn by peon girls in white,
while her train was borne by four small Indian
pages in feather costumes, gorgeous as humming-
birds. Within, the halls were blazing with light,
and garlanded by tropic flowers. Tables were loaded
with gold, silver, and crystal; wine flowed like
water; while the viol and harp, gay dance and song,

caused the hours to speed swiftly by, and the tired
but happy revelers only sought their homes when
the snowy summit of Popocatapetl was flushed with
rose, and bars of pale gold flashed out from behind
the dim crest of Orizaba.

" After a brief honey-moon, which was spent at
La Puebla, Bruce and his bride returned to Monteluma, and so urgent was the invitation which they
extended for me to make my home with them
until I should decide to return northward, that
I immediately joined them in their princely abode.

" My friend soon discovered that his rosy path
was beset thickly with thorns, for every day he was
made aware of the aversion in which his Mexican
neighbors held him; their cold neglect cut deeper
than their swords. So it was with growing alarm
that his wife beheld these symptoms, for she well
knew how the fine speeches and grave courtesy of
her countrymen often covered hearts of hate and
tiger-like rage; and when she saw the covert hos-
tility of her former friends she became apprehensive, indeed, for the safety of her husband.

" One day she startled us by proposing that we
should all go North to her husband's former home
on the Hudson, and she then proceeded to say that
she had grown to view her native land with something of the feelings with which it was regarded
abroad. She had resided in England several years,
and now longed again for the life and freedom of
the Anglo-Saxons.

" Although Bruce was overjoyed at the prospect,
he still said he would not insist on taking her from

her native land and kindred; but when she said that
her only relative living now was Labella, who was
soon to marry Herr Von Brunn, a merchant of the
capital, and that she had determined to sell Monteluma to an Englishman for seventy thousand doubloons, or over a million dollars, then he reluctantly
consented to the change, only stipulating that the
immediate park, grounds, and mansion should be
reserved, so that if she grew tired of her Northern
home they would find her old mansion awaiting
their return.

"Kissing him tenderly, she declared he was a
Rozarro in spirit, if not in name. It was decided to
leave the villa in charge of Labella, and in a short
time a sale of the estate was consummated for the
sum of fifty thousand doubloons, or seven hundred
and fifty thousand dollars in gold—the mansion and
park being reserved.

"Senora Labella was dowered by Ivarene with
a gift of several thousand doubloons on her wedding Von Brunn, after which event we set to work
earnestly preparing for our overland journey northward. A long train of wagons were loaded with
dry-goods for the markets of Northern Mexico.
The price of such articles there had been enhanced
enormously by the war, and Von Brunn shrewdly
advised us to pursue this course. When Ivarene
kindly offered to loan me money to invest in this
manner, I gladly accepted fifty thousand dollars,
with which I bought linen and cotton goods at the
port of Vera Cruz, which was then crowded by the
ships of all nations.

"I might be pardoned for digressing a moment while speaking of the strange belief in a future state which Bruce entertained. There was a vein of seriousness and grave, quiet religion running through the nature of my friend, and often, while we were stretched on our blanket with no canopy but the dewless Mexican sky, studded by the Southern Cross, and bespangled by constellations that were new and strange to our eyes—often, I say, he would talk of that weird belief, which then was very enigmatical to me, but which in my maturer life has recurred with a sweet solace to my declining years.

"Bruce believed that the soul was an individual, invisible as air and imperishable as time itself, and that the spirit was a progressive, rational being, which could never leave this earth until the great Judgment-day, at which time our planet would be as unfit for a human abode as the moon is at present.

"After death, which, he said, was only a wearing out of the outer garment of the soul or spirit, the animating principle, or life, would still inhabit the earth, invisible to human eyes, but yet an intelligent, observing being; subtile as air, yet powerful as electricity. Whenever the newly released soul chose to do so, it could take on a new form by being re-born. He thought that before birth we were possessed of a life akin to that of the vegetable kingdom, but at birth a spirit that had lived before took possession of our bodies, and used us as a habitation until our bodies became either worn through age, or distasteful to the occupant—death ensuing in either case.

"His highest idea of heaven, he said, would be to have the power to live again, and again meet those friends whom he had loved best in the prior life, guided to them unerringly by the mystic ties of love and affinity. Memory of the past life, he thought, was that sense which we call instinct, conscience, or- intuition, being only a feeble glimmer, as it were, of the previous state in which we had lived.

"I remember well, the night before the battle of Churubusco, how Bruce and I talked of these things; for he said, as we sat beneath a palm-tree, while the tropic moon flooded the earth with a dreamy splendor, that we were to fight the last great battle of the war on the morrow—a conflict in which one or both of us might perish—and all that reconciled him to such a fate was the belief that we should live again, and meet each other in this world, which was the only heaven we were yet fitted for.

"I would not have you entertain the thought for one instant that Bruce was skeptical or irreligious. On the contrary, his fearless piety was often commented upon; for I have seen him kneel on the bloody fields of Cerro Gordo and Contreras, and thank God in a trembling voice for his gracious preservation of my life and his own, while the rude soldiery stood by with mute respect, remembering his reckless daring and lion-like bravery in the hours of deadliest peril to which human life can be exposed.

"No; his creed was a very strange one, though one that is old as history itself; he appeared to

differ from the general belief only in his definition
of heaven and its location.   He often said that if a
man retrograded and became brutal he would meet
his punishment in the next life, for his brutal
instincts would seek their affinity after death and
he could only be re-born as a brute, in which state
he would remain until his new life exhausted the
brutal element from his soul.

"I fancy he imbibed his doctrines from his father,
who had been an officer in India.   It might have
been that the elder Walraven had there caught
glimpses of a belief somewhat akin to Buddhism.
When I pressed Bruce for his proof of this strange
theory he referred me to the Bible—Matthew xvi,
13, 14: 'When Jesus came to Cesarea Philippi, he
asked his disciples, saying, Whom do men say that
I, the Son of man, am?   And they said, Some say
that thou art John the Baptist; some, Elias; and
others, Jeremias, or one of the prophets.'   All of
which goes to prove how ancient the belief really
is; for it is apparent that people believed Christ to ·
be the reincarnation of a spirit of one of those people who had been dead many years.

"Ivarene soon became converted to Bruce's
creed, while I often find myself, even yet, taking
solace in this strange belief.

"Early in the spring of 1848, the long caravan
started northward, and when we arrived at Chihuahua, a ready market was found for the goods,
after disposing of which I found that I had more
than doubled the sum invested; so when the debt
was repaid to my kind benefactors, with the addi-

tion of a liberal interest for the use of the money, there was still left me, as clear profit, fifty thousand dollars in gold.

"We spent the winter in Santa Fe, but early the next spring resumed our journey, I having in the meantime bought a few wagon-loads of wool to take through to Independence, Missouri, which was then the eastern terminus of the Santa Fe Trail; but the money which I had saved from my speculation remained intact, and was deposited with fifty sacks of doubloons (which were the property of Bruce and Ivarene) in a large iron-bound cask of cypress-wood, each sack plainly marked with the name of its owner, and the whole tightly packed in wool within the cask.

"This vast treasure, more than half a million of dollars in gold coin, only represented a portion of my friend's wealth; for there were chests of costly silks, brocades, velvets, and priceless laces, all the accumulation of centuries of luxury and boundless riches; paintings by Murillo and Velasquez, that for ages had adorned the long gallery at Monteluma; books of vellum, and richly bound volumes from its marble-paved library, together with a dozen wagon-loads of carved ebony, mahogany, and rose-wood furniture from the same stately home.

"I shall never forget that glorious scene, the last evening in Chihuahua, when the sinking sun lit up the low room where we three sat, with an open casket before us and the stone table ablaze with glimmering gems.

"There were scores of great, pure diamonds,

flashing back a quivering glare of rainbow hues;
rubies glowing like fire with rose and crimson light;
white, frosty pearls, glinting beside the baleful
emeralds, that emitted fitful gleams of green and
gold. Over all flickered the wavering shimmer of
opal and blood-stones, mingling with the violet,
lilac, and purple rays of sapphires and amethysts.

"A great many of these gems had been purchased
by my friends through the advice and assistance of
Von Brunn; but the most precious of the lot were
heir-looms, of which Ivarene was justly proud, and
for an hour she recounted their histories:—

" The great blood-stone had once shone in the
war-club of an Aztec prince, who was slain in battle
by the first Baron of Monteluma, one of those ad-
venturous spirits that came over and shared the
glory of the conquest with Cortez.

" The carcanet of pearls was a gift from Queen
Isabella to the bride of the same brave knight.

"A diamond cross that had been bestowed by
Leo X. upon a cardinal of the house of Rozarro.

"A ruby dragon that carried in its mouth the
Order of the Golden Fleece. This was a mark of
the highest honor that a Spanish king could confer
upon his subject, a viceroy of Mexico, also a member of the same illustrious family at Monteluma.

" There was a chain of rose-colored coral, to
which was attached an enormous pearl of the same
delicate hue; this bauble had been bestowed by the
Doge of Genoa upon Don Arven Rozarro while
the latter was ambassador of Spain at that superb
though decaying city, and it was through this ele-

gant gift that the then all-powerful Spanish sword was induced to interpose its terrible edge as a shield against the aggressions of France.

"A pair of golden spurs, won long ago in the first Crusade by the Knight of Rozarro, and ropes of pearls that had adorned many a proud but long forgotten mistress of the great castle.

"All these were placed within the steel casket, and the only jewel that Ivarene reserved for her personal use on the journey was a locket with a long gold chain. This was the most precious *souvenir* in the whole collection, so she averred, for it was set in gems with the name of her mother, and contained the miniature portraits of Bruce and Ivarene.

"The precious casket was kept in the large carriage, where Ivarene, her two maids, and Bruce rode on cushioned seats, that were constructed so as to serve as couches when the inmates of the vehicle became fatigued. Everything that wealth and loving care could secure was provided by Bruce to lessen the tedium of the journey.

"The gold was placed in a large, strong wagon, drawn by twelve mules, and in addition to the treasure-cask, several barrels of wine and other liquors were placed in the wagon for the purpose of warding off suspicion. This vehicle was my special charge, and I carefully guarded it at night, but spent a portion of the day in sleep.

"We arrived in Santa Fe in the fall of 1848, and early the following spring our long caravan started out on the monotonous course across the plains, by the route to Independence, Missouri, the quiet routine of our journey only relieved by meeting with great trains of freighters on the broad trail, or when Ivarene would take her guitar and sit out in the starry evening playing the sweet airs of her home-land, old Spanish ballads full of pathos and melody. Thus we journeyed until we reached this very spot on the 22d of August, 1849. The night was dark and cloudy, while a strange silence brooded over all nature, broken only by the dismal howl of the wolf as it prowled on the lonely hills.

"We had remarked during the day that no teams were met—a most unusual occurrence on that great thoroughfare, the Santa Fe Trail—and we vaguely wondered why the corral should be silent and deserted; for it was a camping place that was renowned all along the trail for its safety and convenience.

"The corral was an inclosure of about an acre, surrounded by lofty stone walls that were pierced by loop-holes on every side; two large doors, or gates, opened to the north and south, which, after the teams of freighters had been drawn inside, were locked in times of danger. This fort-like corral had been built by the government as a place of refuge for travelers, but our long journey had been so free from trouble that we had become careless, and, as the night was very sultry and the air oppressive, we preferred camping outside the walls on the level land, where we are now sitting, near the bank of the Cottonwood.

"Ivarene had been feeling unwell that day, and we were all very solicitous for her comfort and welfare at that time; for it was known that an interesting event would soon occur, that would give my dear friend Bruce the title of father. In deference to her condition the usual noise and hilarity of the camp were not indulged in; but a sense of coming disaster, a foreboding of some great calamity, seemed to weigh on the spirits of our party on that fatal evening.

"How strange it is that when the sky is serene and clear we may feel the approaching storm! Who can explain that shock of repulsion we feel when we meet a secret foe? The same Providence whispered, that murky night, of the danger and disaster lurking near.

"But each one tried to shake off the feeling of apprehension; and as a storm was rising in the north-west we attributed our depression to that state of the atmosphere which precedes the thunderstorm.

"I did not sleep for several hours after retiring to the wagon, but remained wakeful and restless, listening to the jabbering of the wolves and rumble of the distant thunder. The fitful slumber into which I at length fell was pervaded by hideous dreams, and when I was awakened by the yell of savages it seemed, for a moment, only the continuation of the strange phantasms that had haunted my sleep.

"But I sprang out, a pistol in each hand, and was soon struggling in the whirlpool of confusion and terror that prevailed around. The crack of rifles and whistling of arrows, the shrieks of the wounded and dying, the blood-chilling whoops of the Indians, all commingled with the bellowing of the frightened cattle in hideous clamor.

"With a feeling of sickening dread I thought of Bruce and his wife as I dashed toward their wagon. As I neared it a vivid flash of lightning from the cloud which had arisen revealed a scene of such revolting horror that its remembrance causes me yet to turn faint and dizzy. More than a quarter of a century has rolled by, fraught with war and sorrow, but that scene of woe is burned deep within my heart, to rankle long as life endures."

Here the colonel's voice broke to a whisper, while the sobs of Maud and Grace mingled with their mother's soft weeping. Then, after a moment of silent anguish, while his hands hung clenched in an agony of intense grief, with bowed head and a voice so husky that it was barely audible, the colonel continued:—

"By the dazzling light I saw Ivarene kneeling in her white robe, a look of imploring agony upon her pale, uplifted face. Over her, with a poised tomahawk, glared a powerful, painted demon. Bruce, struggling in the grasp of two hideous savages, was driving his glittering dirk into the breast of one of his assailants. I fired at the heart of the wretch who stood over Ivarene. With a dying yell he bounded into the air. Then, as darkness was once again settling down over the scene, I felt the shock of a stunning blow—then a long oblivion."

The colonel was too visibly affected to proceed

further with the narrative, and as he relapsed into silence the listeners slowly dispersed, some to the duties of camp-life; others strolled out to the long, grass-grown grave, leaving Colonel Warlow alone, lost in meditation.

Chapter IV.

COLONEL WARLOW'S STORY—CONTINUED.

THE listeners had seated themselves on the buffalo-robes which Scott Moreland's thoughtfulness had provided, and the colonel resumed the thread of his narrative.

"The blow was followed by unconsciousness, and when I awoke, as it were, from a long and fevered sleep, I was seated in an easy-chair on a shaded veranda, and before me stretched the limitless ocean, its restless waves purling in foam on the sandy beach at my feet. Beside the porch on which I was seated grew luxuriant lime and orange trees, loaded with fruit and bloom, and the air was heavy with the sensuous' odors of tropical flowers.

"A ray of memory gleamed feebly across my confused and cloudy mind, and I vaguely wondered why my hands should be so wasted and thin. Then a wavering sensation swept over my mental faculties like a dark cloud. The glimmer of memory once again struggled and flickered, then flashed forth with a dazzling light, piercing through the fog and haze which had so long obscured the light of reason, and I felt as if the sun had just arisen.

"As I sat with closed eyes, gently rocking to and fro, I remembered dimly, like some half-forgotten dream, my long journey across the continent with Walraven, our camping beside the Kansas stream at the Stone Corral; and then with surprise I looked out on the ocean before me. Suddenly the memory of that night of horror came vividly to my mind, and with a loud cry I sprang to my feet; but a firm hand was laid on my shoulder, and a kind voice requested me to be calm, and pressed me to drink the glass of wine which was held to my lips.

"I obeyed mechanically, and as I drained the cup of its sparkling contents I glanced up at the bronzed though handsome stranger beside me, who, with joy and gratification beaming in his blue eyes, said in answer to my look of inquiry:—

"'Old boy, you will soon be yourself again; but you must not talk too much, nor ask questions just now.'

"'But where am I, and what does it all mean?' I exclaimed in a dazed sort of way.

"'You are near Los Angeles, and this is the Pacific Ocean which lies before you,' he answered slowly.

"When he had made this strange statement, I felt a wavering sensation once more cross my brain, as if madness were about to seize me.

"'You should not talk, nor think of the past,' said he anxiously, 'but brace up and recover; then we will go up to the mines, and dig out nuggets like nigger-heads.'

"'But at least tell me how I came here,' I entreated.

"'Well,' said he in a faltering manner, 'if you

5

will be composed I will do so; but you must not give way to your emotions.'

"I sank back in the chair, motioning for him to proceed, as the suspense was unbearable; and he then related the following, in soothing tones, like one who had long humored and tenderly nursed a suffering invalid :—

"My name is Roger ¡Coble, and my home is near Springfield, Ill., from which place I started to the gold-fields of the Sacramento River, which had thrown our quiet rural community into a great excitement by the rumor of their fabulous richness. Our train had only traveled a few days' drive westward from the Missouri, when we came to the Stone Corral on the bank of the Cottonwood. There we found you, wounded and delirious. I placed you on a canvas bed in one of my wagons, and brought you on to Santa Fe.

"'As you were still delirious and in a helpless condition, I could not bear the thought of leaving you at the latter place, but brought you along with the train to this place, where we arrived last week, and I am overjoyed to see you on your feet again.'

"'But what was the fate of Walraven and his wife?' I cried, in great excitement.

"Seeing the wild look again coming into my eyes, he said, with a saddened expression :—

"'Do not ask any more questions, my boy. When you become stronger I will tell you all. But now, my friend, do try to think of pleasanter themes. If you do not, you will surely relapse into your former deplorable state.'

"Therefore I took his kindly advice, and ignored the past with all its bitter memories, and
listened with growing interest to his hopeful plans
for the future. As he told of the great gold-fields
that had been discovered in the newly acquired
California, that were of such fabulous richness, he
said, that all the world was wild with excitement
and wonder, I began ·to feel the infection of his
enthusiasm, and almost forgot the fact that I was
penniless and two thousand miles from home.

"The next day I felt still stronger; but the
ugly wound on my head was not yet entirely healed,
being a painful reminder of the terrible blow which
I had received the night of the attack at the corral.

"As the days passed by I rapidly convalesced,
and erelong was able to walk through the orange-
groves, or sail with Roger out on the tranquil
water; but whenever I had nerved myself up to
the point of asking the fate of my friends, to my
horror I would find that same old sickening, wavering sensation steal over my brain that I remembered so well, and I would shudder to think that
I stood, as it were, upon the brink of madness.

"So in our long rambles on the sea-shore or
drives on the beach, we shunned all allusion to the
fateful past, tacitly ignoring the unexplained sequel
to that terrible tragedy; but the suspense and strain
were so great that it is a blissful thing that events
followed which diverted my mind from the painful
subject, or perhaps my reason may have been utterly overthrown.

"Roger had disposed of his teams, and, after

consulting me, procured tickets to San Francisco, a small village that had sprung up on the coast to the north, and as he gave me my ticket he said with a smile :—

"'We will be pards, George, and divide profit and loss up in the mines, and when you strike it "rich," why, you can repay me; and as for interest—guess we will smoke that out at your expense.'

"I replied, through my tears, that all the gold of this earth could not repay his kindness and generosity.

"Before sailing on the *Lapwing* I wrote to my friends in Missouri, telling them briefly of the disaster which had befallen me, but that I was with the best fellow alive; and in my letter to sister Amy I told her how nobly Roger had cared for me in my direst hour of trial and need, and I hinted that she must wait for me to bring him back, which I would do when I had regained my lost fortune by working in the mines, to which we were now just starting, full of hope and enthusiasm.

"Our first day out on the Pacific proved that body of water to be woefully misnamed indeed; for the weather was just as vile and fickle as I ever saw on the much maligned Atlantic. In the evening Roger and myself were seated on deck, watching the sun set in a pile of black clouds, which, as the broad streams of amber and violet flamed up from behind the sombre mass, slowly changed to purple, rose, and crimson, edged with gold.

"When the brilliant hues had faded, the dusky

clouds rested on a sullen sea, that was only ruffled by the fitful breeze, which rose and fell, then died away, leaving a death-like calm, oppressive as it was foreboding.

"The frightened sea-birds flew screaming by, flapping their broad white wings, then fading swiftly away. The captain now came on deck, and, by his quick orders and restless movements, we knew that he anticipated danger from the storm which we could see rapidly rising, and the rigging was soon in order to meet the heavy gale.

"A fiery moon rose in the pale eastern sky, and out to the south-west hung the bow-shaped cloud, black as ebony, save when veined by the blood-red lightning; but as the majestic mass towered to the zenith, it changed to green, edged by a roll of fleecy white, which rose and fell as if weaving a shroud for sea and sky.

"We lashed ourselves to the rigging, so we could get the full benefit, as Roger said, of our first storm at sea. We had not long to wait, for soon a wall of waves, like a troop of war-horses, came tossing their snowy manes on the gale, and when the mad surge struck us the old ship quivered in every timber. The clouds wrapped us about, and the blinding spray and rain drenched the deck; the lightning glimmered fitfully through the mist, or hissed in zigzag streams of molten gold along the surging waves. A lull, then again the blinding flash, followed by the bellowing thunder, crashing down, it seemed, to the caverns beneath, the wind shrieking through the rigging, the tumult of waves, rising in

hoarse clamor and deafening roar—followed again
by blinding stroke and maddening crash.

"I have stood on old Chapultepec's crumbling
wall, when mortar and cannon hurled their iron
hail; when screaming shells and belching roar mingled with the shrieks of mangled and dying men,
and the sullen boom of exploding mines shocked
and dulled the ear; but never had I known an
hour like this.

"The poor old vessel, like a hunted doe, bounded
away, followed by all the hounds of the gale, climb-
ing the dizzy cliff or leaping the yawning chasm,
and throwing the foam from off her sides; then
hiding in the gorges below, where the glassy wall
towered far above with combing crest, scattering
the spray out over the tossing sea. Again, as the
ship climbed the watery hill, she seemed to pause
one brief moment on the foamy height, then plunged
into the swishing whirlpool beneath.

"The night wore on, yet still our vessel staggered along in her wild flight; but the winds began
to abate their fury somewhat, and the flashes grew
more dim and fitful until the storm rolled away to
the east. Then the moon peered with white face
through the rift of clouds; but as her spectral light
only served to make more weird and appalling the
waste of heaving billows, she quickly hid behind
her fleecy veil, as if to shut the wild scene from
view.

"Although the wind had died to a gentle gale,
the frightened waves still galloped madly along as
though fleeing from a grizzly horror they dared not

face, and the ship labored like some jaded cavalry
horse, that staggers and reels after the fierce charge.

"The deck had been a scene of great confusion
ever since the storm had abated, and, although the
waves and spray broke over the vessel, the crew
were rushing about wildly, and to our surprise we
saw them launching the boats; so we unlashed ourselves and hurried forward—only to hear the despairing cry: 'The vessel is sinking!'

"I looked out upon the waves, which even now
seemed nearer, and with a clammy shudder compre-
hended what horror they were fleeing. Death rode
those cold waters, and every billow was a yawning
grave.

"What a dread alternative—to cast ourselves
out on that boiling, foaming sea, with only a frail
boat between us and eternity, or remain on deck
and feel the ship slowly settling under us!

"But the boats were quickly manned, and into
them were thrown a few casks of spirits and water,
with a small quantity of food; then we pushed off
from the fast-sinking ship, and in a moment were
riding the waves.

"We had left a light burning on the vessel, to
enable us to steer away from it, and thus avoid being
run down or ingulfed by the final whirlpool of the
wreck; and after tossing about on the troubled
waters for half an hour, trying to keep the boats
together, we heard a loud report, caused by the com-
pressed air blowing up the deck of the vessel; then
the light on the old ship went out forever, and the
sea closed over her shattered form.

"It may have been an hour before dawn, when suddenly we found ourselves among the breakers, and the coast looming dimly through the mist. Before we had time to realize our situation our boat was capsized and we were struggling with the waves.

"I shouted to Roger, but no answer. Then I saw a head appear above the water, and swam toward it, hoping it was he; but the form was carried around the headland by the rapid current, so I struck out for the frowning cliff.

"Diving under the largest waves, I saw, to my great joy, that I was gaining and soon was thrown on the rocks with terrible force; but I lost my hold on the stony ledge that I had clutched, and was being carried back to sea; but a thought struck me which I instantly recognized as being the only chance of escape, and to which I am certain I owe the preservation of my life: I dived to the bottom, and began walking toward the cliff, which was not more than a rod away.

"Oh, the horror and agony of those few moments under the sea! The seconds seemed to lengthen to hours. Brief as the time and short as the distance may have been, I've traveled many a thousand miles through the sandy deserts of the West and suffered less than in that one minute at the bottom of the ocean."

Chapter V.

COLONEL WARLOW'S STORY—CONTINUED.

"LET me see—where was I?" said the colonel, who had paused to light his pipe at this critical juncture of the narrative.

"Twenty thousand leagues under the sea," replied Grace Moreland, gaily.

"Well, I certainly could not have suffered more in the same time if I had been," said he with a grim smile. "But just when I had given up all hope, and thought my lungs would burst, I straightened up, determined to come to the surface at any risk. Lo! I had been groping along in four feet of water—and only a step from the shore!

"I had only time to plunge forward and clutch a jagged rock, when a mighty wave swept in, nearly tearing me from my place; but this time I held fast, and when the wave had receded I clambered up out of further danger, and there I lay, too utterly exhausted to move until dawn.

"I had hoped that daylight would reveal the presence of my companion; but the sun struggled up over a lone stretch of rocky, barren shore— nothing living was visible. I strained my eyes, gazing out over the long line of breakers. It was a fruitless quest; I was alone.

"Then I climbed up to the table-land. A sandy

plain, broken by patches of sage-brush and thickets of chapparal was before me, and out toward the rising sun rose a lofty chain of mountains, as though to shut me out from all the world.

"I walked around the promontory and along the coast for several miles, still hoping I might find my friend; in vain. I shouted repeatedly; no answer. So with a heavy heart I turned and walked inland.

"After assuaging my thirst at a cavity in the rocks, where the rain-water had collected, and satisfying my hunger with the eggs of a wild fowl, the nest of which I found near a sage-brush, I continued my explorations inland toward a pass which seemed to open in the mountains toward the east.

"As I neared the glen, trees, a brook, and a flock of sheep became visible. Then, to my great delight, a house showed through the trees; and when a woman appeared in the doorway, I hurried forward and addressed her in Spanish, to which she replied in the same tongue.

"I told my story of shipwreck, and the kind-hearted peasant woman bade me welcome to the humble dwelling, and proceeded to set before me a repast of omelet and frijoles. While I was still seated at the table, her husband, Pedro, came in from herding his flock, and we soon were on our way to the village to make inquiries regarding my lost friend and the crew of the *Lapwing*. But nothing could be learned of them; so I retired to rest, and that night slept the dreamless sleep of sheer exhaustion.

"In the morning I renewed the search, but with no better results; and although I traveled along the coast for more than a score of miles, nothing could be found but the bodies of three sailors that I recognized as having been among the crew of the ill-fated ship. At last, weary and heart-sore, I joined a party of miners, and proceeded to San Francisco; but as my inquiries there also proved fruitless, I immediately went to the diggings, where my fortunes soon mended, and I was able to send a small purse to honest Pedro.

"During my stay in the mines I had frequent letters from home, and sister Amy expressed great sorrow at the fate of my noble friend Roger; but I wrote that it might yet be possible he was living, and we still hoped on. The greatest comfort to me, however, were the letters from Mary, who urged me to return and not wait to acquire more gold; and as my luck was 'jes powerful,' as the miners averred, I found at the end of two years I had saved $50,000, and deciding to 'let well-enough alone,' set sail for home.

"As we were sailing out through the now world-renowned Golden Gate, the captain, to whom I had just intrusted my money, remarked that I did not seem to enter into the spirit of joy that pervaded the throng of returning miners; and in reply to his look of inquiry and tone of interest, I said that the last time I was on a ship I had witnessed a terrible storm, in which the vessel was wrecked, the crew and a dear, kind friend were lost, and I alone was saved; and now the sight of the ocean, once again, recalled it all so vividly that I was sad and grieved, even in the hour when I should rejoice that all my toil was over. I was too affected to talk further, but looked wistfully out over the cruel sea that had closed over Roger, my best and truest friend.

"The captain, after a few moments of silence, asked in a tone of sympathy:—

"'What was the name of the vessel that was wrecked?'

"'The *Lapwing*,' I replied.

"'But the crew and passengers were saved,' said he quickly.

"'Saved!—Roger saved!' I shouted, dizzy with joy; then as I sank into a seat, weak and unnerved, the officer continued:—

"'Yes, the crew was saved. They were picked up by a vessel bound for Acapulco. You can learn the particulars by calling on the American consul at that port, as I believe he took charge of them and assisted them on to their respective destinations.'

"'I'll give you a thousand gold dollars to put me off at Acapulco,' I cried impulsively.

"'Agreed,' said he, with a laugh. 'We always do stop there, and take a day to revictual and water. No, my friend, keep your hard-earned dollars; but if you find your gratitude burdensome, why, just name your next boy after me;' then he left me with a good-natured smile.

"I will say that I found it a very pleasant way of discharging the debt by naming my oldest son here after the good old sea-dog, Captain Clifford; and some way I always associate the name with the thought of that day when I heard the good news.

"How interminable seemed the long, bright days, as we sailed southward! I paced the deck for hours, and grew morose and nervous, chafing under the slowness of the stout craft. 'But all things have an end'—an adage, by the way, which my dealings and travel in the tropics has led' me to doubt—and when, one evening, we sailed into the long-wished for harbor, I was so impatient to land that only the thought of sharks prevented me from swimming ashore.

"After night-fall, however, I found myself in a crooked, winding alley, termed a street in the florid courtesy of that tropic land, and offering a coin to a villainous-looking native—the only guide I could procure—asked him to show me the way to the American consulate; and we were soon *en route* thitherward, I, meanwhile, taking the precaution to cover my vile-looking guide with a pistol in one hand and a bowie-knife in the other.

"For an age, it seemed, we tramped through the murky, unlighted streets, until at last we arrived before a fortress-like building, at the gate of which blinked one solitary lamp.

"At my request to see the consul, the servant informed me that 'his worshipful master had driven out this morning to dine with the noble Don Pablo de Zorilla, and that he would remain to the ball at the mansion of that illustrious senor,' etc.

"I could barely refrain from kicking the miserable flunky, and the air grew thick and maroon

with the expressions in which my disappointment
found utterance. Telling the porter that I hoped
his lazy master would not stop the 'wheels of com-
merce' to-morrow to eat garlic and capsicum with
the aristocracy, I returned to the vessel.

"Next morning I called again at the consulate,
and the scowling porter, after conducting me to a
room, said that his master was sleeping, but he was
instructed to say 'to the insolent American' that his
excellency 'was too lazy to see me until he had slept
off the effect of the garlic, capsicum, and other
kindred delicacies, of which he had been partaking.'
Then, grinning derisively, the servant left the room,
banging the door behind him.

" Well, I just stormed up and down that room for
two long hours, fuming, raving, and hurling invec-
tives at all the tribe of official sluggards. At length,
hearing footsteps without, I clenched my hands in
rage, vowing wrath and vengeance on the insulting
and self-sufficient officer; but when the servant
opened the door and announced, 'Senor Consul,' my
anger was all forgotten, and, instead of greeting that
functionary with a thwack on the ear, I sprang forward with a wild cry :—

"'Roger—Oh, Roger—am I dreaming?'

"'George—George—is it possible? Alive and
well? I've mourned you as dead for years. Thank
God—at last!'

"As I stood there wringing his hand and gazing
on his dear face through my tears, it is needless to
say all my belligerent designs oozed magically away.

" We were soon interrupted, however, by the

porter, who, at the first strange demonstration on my part, had fled shrieking 'Murder! murder!' his outcry bringing a whole brood of slipshod servants down upon my devoted head. They came swarming in, armed with gridirons, tongs, and gourds. One sallow, emaciated peon carried a crucifix, which he had evidently snatched as he flew to the rescue. A burly fellow was just on the eve of disemboweling me with a pot-metal poniard, when Roger hastened to explain that we were old friends who had not met for years, and as they retreated in a crestfallen manner, with many grunts and shrugs, we both smiled at the ludicrous phase of our meeting; yes, I believe that 'smiled' is a very mild term to apply to our hilarity on that occasion.

"Reminding Roger that the vessel sailed at four P. M., and my stay therefore was limited, I begged him to tell me the particulars of his happy escape, and when we were comfortably seated on the easy-chairs in the secluded court, he told briefly how he, with several others, clung to the capsized boat, and had been rescued by a passing vessel, bound southward. On reaching Acapulco he had called at the American consulate, but found the consul prostrated with yellow-fever, and (as Roger had passed through an attack of that dread scourge at New Orleans a few years previous to this) he had volunteered to nurse the stricken officer, who slowly recovered from the fearful malady.

"While that grateful invalid was convalescing, Roger had been intrusted with the accumulated business of the post. Having discharged the duties devolving on him to the satisfaction of his employer, that gentleman had deputized him as vice-consul, and then returned to the States.

" Finally the consul resigned, and Roger, on his recommendation, was appointed to the office as his successor, meantime receiving a hint from the home government to make himself as agreeable as possible to the natives.

" ' Which you see, George,' said he with a merry smile, ' meant to acquire a taste for " garlic and capsicum." '

" Then, at his request, I related my experience; how I had searched in vain for him along the coast; had gone to the mines and made my ' pile,' and on embarking for home had learned of the rescue of the crew and passengers of the *Lapwing;* the long days of suspense that had followed, and my impatience to learn something of his fate. I did not omit telling how narrowly he escaped a sound flogging at my hands after I had been kept waiting so long, which caused him great merriment.

" During our brief conversation I had been conscious of an undercurrent of burning anxiety to learn the fate of Bruce Walraven and his wife. The suspense and uncertainty which had haunted me for two long years—the mystery of their fate— would now vanish forever, I knew; but I shrank with a strange foreboding from asking the truth which my heart had so long been vainly seeking. My dry lips and parched tongue could only feebly articulate as I begged Roger to tell me the sequel of that terrible tragedy at the Old Corral.

" With a look of pain on his handsome face, he said, in a faltering voice:—

" ' I was journeying along on the Santa Fe Trail from Independence, Missouri, to California. Our large train had been delayed at Council Grove by a rumor that the Cheyennes were on the war-path; but nothing having been seen of the marauders, we started out, after a few days, trusting to our numbers for defense, and when we arrived at the Stone Corral, on the bank of the Cottonwood, a scene of revolting horror met our startled sight—a scene that will live forever in my memory.

" 'The stone walls of the corral had been hurled down, and near the side of the stream were the charred and crisped remains of at least fifty human victims, mingled with the irons of the wagons, which evidently had been fired and the bodies thrown into the blaze.'

" 'There were fifty-four persons in our train— How many bodies were found?' I asked, breathlessly.

" 'We counted the smouldering skeletons, and found that fifty-three persons had fallen victims to the diabolical fury of the Indians.'

" 'Oh, God—all gone!' I cried, hoarse with the misery of their certain destruction—' gallant Bruce and beautiful, kind Ivarene! What a terrible fate!'

" ' We were burying the skeletons on a knoll a few hundred paces westward from the Old Corral,' continued Roger, 'and were carrying stone from the confused mass of its ruined wall to place about the long trench, in which the remains were laid,

when moans, like some one in pain, were heard as
if issuing from the earth.

"'The mournful scene through which we had
just passed had so utterly shocked and unnerved
us, that it is little wonder we felt it might be the
spectres of the victims still haunting the scene of
the awful tragedy ; but a moment's reflection set us
to searching among the ruins, which resulted in
our finding you, wounded and delirious, buried
under the fallen wall.

"'Several large stones had rested against the
lower part of the wall, and thus, in a providential
manner, shielded you from the avalanche of stone
which had fallen when the savages had thrown
down the wall by prying with the wagon tongues,
that were still lying about as they had left them.

"'We placed you on a canvas stretcher, and put
you in one of my wagons. As there was a phy-
sician in our train, you did not lack for medical
attention; but that dreadful gash on your head was
very slow in healing. As your mind was completely
shattered, and you remained delirious all the long
journey to Santa Fe, we could not bear the thought
of leaving you there among strangers, but brought
you on to Los Angeles with the train.'

"'I never before have told you, Roger, that
there was more than one hundred thousand dollars
in gold and gems with our train ; but such was the
case ;' and as he sprang up in amazement, I told
him briefly the history of Bruce and Ivarene, and
how I had lost my fortune of fifty thousand dollars

in gold with that of my dear friends on that night of horror and despair.

"'It is needless to say,' replied Roger, 'that no trace of the treasure was found; but it seems incredible that so vast a sum could have been carried away by the savages! Did you have any liquor with the train?' he asked in a thoughtful manner.

"'Yes, several barrels of wine and brandy,' I answered.

"'Then that accounts for the blood on the grass, near several newly made graves close by. The Indians had found the brandy, no doubt, and the massacre ended in a drunken row among themselves, in which several of them had died a violent death. It is a mystery, though,' he added, 'how a pack of drunken, wrangling savages could have divided such an amount of coin without leaving some trace. And, George, I would advise you to make a systematic search on your return,' he continued; 'for it may have been that the treasure was buried there.'"

"Did you ever make the search?" asked Clifford Warlow of his father, in an eager tone.

"No; certainly not," replied the colonel; "it would have been folly to suppose that the band of pilfering, murderous savages would have left anything valuable behind."

But the answer did not satisfy his son, who looked out toward the knoll where the Old Corral, with its broken walls, cast long shadows in the slanting sunbeams; and as the colonel proceeded with his story it was noticed, by more than one of the group, that Sabbath afternoon, that Clifford remained lost in thought, and his eyes roamed from the speaker out over the scene of that tragedy of bygone years.

"At the end of that mournful story," pursued the colonel, " I was pressed by Roger to remain with him until the next vessel passed; but I declined, thanking him, and telling him that Mary was waiting for me on the banks of the Missouri, and I could tarry no longer than a few brief hours, until the craft would sail. Then, as we stood on the ship, whither he had accompanied me, I told him to remain in the cabin for a moment until I could return. Then going to the captain, I asked him for the money which I had deposited with him.

"The fifty thousand dollars was carried into the room where Roger was waiting, and when the sailors had retired, I said, in answer to his look of inquiry, that I was prepared to execute the compact which we entered into at Los Angeles, to be 'pards,' and divide profit and loss; and I tendered him there on the spot twenty-five thousand dollars, which was one-half of my savings in the mines. Roger would not hear to the proposition; he scouted the idea of 'robbing me of my hard earnings,' and all my pleadings were in vain,—he was obdurate.

"I reminded him how I owed my life to his care and kindness; but my entreaties all were unavailing, as he would only ridicule the offer, saying that he had now more than enough for an old bachelor. So I finally desisted, but told him that should he ever need assistance or the services of a friend, to call on me, for I felt a debt of gratitude which I could never repay him.

" I smile even yet to think how I blushed when I showed him Mary's picture; and while he was looking with undisguised admiration at the miniature of sister Amy, I told him how she had never ceased to regret his sad fate, and' that in her last letter, which I handed him, she had written that she still vaguely hoped he might some time return; that he may have escaped—' such things sometimes do occur—and she could yet thank him for his care and tenderness to her brother.' When the dear fellow beamed with such delight, I proceeded to say how delighted she and my mother would be to have him make us a long visit soon, which he readily promised to do within the year. As he still held the picture of my beautiful sister, and seemed so reluctant to surrender it, I ignored it entirely or pretended to do so, and as we proceeded with our talk, I saw, with half an eye, that he furtively slipped it into his pocket, at which I was so gratified, I had to pinch myself to keep from dancing a jig of delight.

" It was hard indeed to part with Roger, and not before he again promised to visit me within a year did I say farewell; then we were again sailing out on our homeward voyage. We tarried but a short time on the Isthmus of Panama; for, in fact, I had but an indifferent opinion of that little neck of land, made up, it seemed, of snakes, centipedes, and bad smells. Whew! it makes me faint, even yet, to remember how those nasty, vile, old swamps radiated their bad odors! There had just been an earthquake to roil up the concentrated filth which was packed away in those slimy bayous, and as every whiff of wind came loaded with its own peculiar stench, the variety became so wearying that I grew at length tired of the 'nasal panorama,' and vainly yearned for the friendly precincts of a glue factory.

"It always seemed to me that Nature had aimed to make a sea of the isthmus, but had taken the flux or cholera, and left her work but half completed."

Chapter VI.

COLONEL WARLOW'S STORY—CONTINUED.

"OUR ship touched at Havana, and in company with several other passengers, who lived in the Mississippi Valley, I decided to stop here until a vessel sailed for New Orleans, which would not occur for ten days yet; but years might be passed in that beautiful city of enchantment, the 'Queen of the Antilles,' and we found our stay one round of perpetual delight.

"A day was devoted to a sail around the sunlit harbor, environed by mansions, castles, and palm-decked hills—the sapphire sky bounded only by the purple mountains or pale-green sea. Then we visited Old Moro Castle, its portcullis, donjon-keep, and 'sounding barbacan,' its gloomy grandeur of turret and tower—

'Its loop-holed grates, where captives weep,'—

all recalling the feudal days of Scotland and Spain. Next we drove through the Prado of San Isabel, with its triumphal arches of snowy marble, its rose-decked alamedas lined with palm, cypress, and magnolia, its clear fountains foaming amid thickets of acacia and blooming oleander; and then on to the great theater of Tacon, where the evening was passed as if in fairy-land.

"Christmas-day we drove out to visit a coffee-plantation a dozen miles from the city walls. The dew was still glittering on the foliage as we whirled rapidly along in our easy volantas, and the air was rich with the odor of orange-blossoms and a myriad of other tropic flowers. We halted at the Bishop's Gardens for an hour, and I can but faintly describe their gorgeous floral wealth. These gardens are centuries old, dating back to the days of Charles V., when the Spanish banner of crimson and gold waved around the world.

"There were palm, myrtle, and mangoe trees growing beside canals where the clear rushing water rippled along over the bottom of gaily-colored tiles. Then there were plantations of yucca, the broad-leaved bread-fruit, lemons, guavas, and figs, with great basins of marble brimming with water, on which floated lilies white as snow. But, entrancing as were those avenues of whispering· myrtle, orange, and pine, we drove on through the warm sunlight until near noon, when we arrived at our destination.

"The coffee-plantation contained a league of land—three miles square—and was divided into innumerable plats by long avenues that cut each other at right angles, like streets, extending through the plantation. These avenues were lined on either side by palms of a hundred different species, and in their great width of full fifty paces, and three miles long, they were set in Bermuda-grass, mown like a carpet of velvet. The squares, however, were carefully cultivated, and no weeds were visible in the red, mellow soil.

"Next to the row of palms grew a line of orange-trees; then lemons, almonds, pomegranates, and olives, followed by a row of evergreens of infinite variety, the remainder of the square being planted to coffee-trees.

"It was a sight never to be forgotten that unfolded to our view as we drove down one of those long colonnades of palm, over which the parasites trailed, linking tree to tree with garlands of scarlet, rose, and golden blossoms—the snowy orange-flowers contrasting with its coppery fruit—gloomy pine, spruce, and cypress, with glimpses between of the coffee-trees loaded with their crimson berries.

"Thousands of birds flitted about, lending animation to the gorgeous tropical scene,—gaudy parrots, white doves, orioles, and blue-birds; while myriads of humming-birds of rose and emerald, gold and purple, wove and flashed among the trees.

"We, who live in these dull northern climes, can not fancy the pictures of life and color that adorn the forests of tropical America; but as I sat that Christmas-day amid the Cuban groves, and ate the most luscious fruits, fresh from the tree, the glorious sunlight sifting down through the feathery, fern-like palm-leaves, and over all the cloudless blue of the southern skies, I thought of the snow and ice which wrapped the hills and meadows of my northern home. But a feeling of longing stole over me for the brooks, bound by their crystal fetters and sheltered by the oak-clad hills, the merry jingling sleigh-bells in the frosty air, and, amid all this wealth of bloom and tropic life, my heart

turned back to the memory of rustic joys in my
boyhood's home,—the roaring fire on the hearth-
stone, when the frost-rime crept over the window-
pane; the rushing of the storm-king, as he piled
the ghostly drift without, or fled shrieking by,
shaking the gables in his wild wrath. Then fancy
came thronging on with dear faces of the home-
folk that I had not seen for years; and when I
awoke, with a start, to the thought that the ocean
rolled between me and my distant home, do not
blame me that a tear-drop went trickling down
through the sunlight of that foreign tropic land.

"After loitering for a few hours among the
coffee-trees, we ascended a mountain to drink of the
waters of a famous mineral spring, which gushes
from among the lofty cliffs; and as I stood on the
verge of a precipice, before me there spread a landscape of matchless grandeur,—the wide savannas
with their fields of cane, tobacco, and fruit, the dim
city, begirt with its walls and grim fortresses, and
the blue harbor, crowded with the ships of all nations; while far away to the north, stretching out,
it seemed, to eternity, lay the trackless ocean, dotted
with white winged ships and those gem-like islands,
' The Queen's Gardens.'

"Driving back to the city, we paid a moonlight
visit to the tomb of Columbus. I stood long and
silently by the urn where rests all that remains of
the Great Mariner—all save the Columbian spirit,
which will pervade the people of America as long
as this continent endures.

"Yes; you and I are actuated by the same

spirit that guided the illustrious pioneers out toward the setting sun—enterprise, ambition, and
energy. As I noted the humble monument, I
bitterly recalled the ingratitude and perfidy of
Spain; but when there rose to my mind a vision
of the grand and powerful nations, the splendid
cities and happy homes of the thronging millions
from Montreal to Buenos Ayres,—these, I mused,
are the monuments befitting the noble hero, and it
matters not that the lowly urn in the old cathedral
holds the ashes of mortality.

"Coming forth into the mellow moonlight, I
paused a moment to gather a spray from the roses
and passion-flowers, blooming in dew-drenched
clusters amid the orange and myrtle of the Paseo
hard by; and as I stood drinking, as it were, the
odors of that perfume-laden air, afar off could be
heard the sullen boom of the breakers as the sea
broke in thunder on the walls of Moro Castle,
while the faint, sweet notes of a guitar floated out
upon the night, mingling with the diapason of old
ocean's roar as it chanted its hymn of eternity on
the rocky beach.

"Two weeks later I drove up to my father's
gate, through the snow and ice of a Northern
winter. The white drift wrapped the hills and
meadows, and the gurgle of the brook in the sheltered valley sang faint and muffled within its crystal
prison; the dear old cedars bent low under their
white burden, and from the eaves of the time-worn,
red brick homestead, the icicles hung glittering like
spears in the frosty light.

"When I left home four years before, I was a smooth-faced boy of twenty, but while in the mines I had grown a beard like a Turk; and although in San Francisco I had passed under the sway of the barber, who despoiled me of more locks than Samson ever lost, yet enough remained to complete my disguise; and I was smiling at the surprise I had in store for the home-folks, when the door opened, and lo! Amy came flying down the path with such an outcry that all the family came rushing upon the scene, Amy saying, between smiles and tears:—

"'Oh, George, you thought we wouldn't know you; but I was watching, and when you paused at the gate and looked so wistfully towards the house, I knew—oh, it must be you!'

"Ah well—such a day will never come again! How I followed mother and Amy about, or sat in the kitchen with father on one hand and Dick on the other—all of us talking at once! Such a home-coming is known in all of its keen delight by only the long-absent miner or returning soldier. And the dinner which followed, where all the culinary treasures of earth, sky, land, and sea were laid under contribution, was a meal which caused me to say they certainly meant to stuff me as a curiosity, after the manner of a taxidermist.

"'There must be some means devised to keep you at home hereafter,' replied my mother.

"I said I was through with rambling; for I had brought enough money home for the whole family—unless we indulged in such dinners every day.

"Dick replied with a laugh that 'wealthy people could certainly afford salt for the potatoes.'

"'Oh, that is not a luxury, for I find it in both the fruit and coffee,' replied my father.

"In the evening I took Dick's grays and sleigh to drive over to Mary's home, and at starting was charged by Amy to be sure and bring Mary over to the 'wool-picking' at Widow Hawley's—a semi-festive meeting of the best society in that primitive but happy neighborhood. Promising to do my best to meet Dick and her that evening at the designated place of festivity, I touched the horses, and shot down the drive just in time to dodge the slipper, which, with a gay laugh, she hurled at my back; and as I rounded the curve of the stone wall into the highway, she and Dick cheered me very encouragingly.

"As I drove along the sparkling, crusted road, the west was still blushing faintly, and the moon peeped through the snowy tree-tops, that drooped in feathery sprays of frost and ice, sweeping the drifts below with their creaking, rattling branches, and the stars winked knowingly in the clear, cold sky as my sleigh-bells awoke the jingling echoes among the well-remembered hills that flanked the valley on either side.

"When I reached the door of Mary's dwelling the windows threw out a ruddy light from the great fire-place, where the flames leaped and crackled, and showers of sparks flashed up the wide chimney, while back and forth in the flickering light tripped Mary, singing as she spun on the roaring wheel.

"At my rap the wheel ceased its hum, a light footfall was heard, and—well, I'll just close the door, as it was only a private matter—but in a moment I was kissing her mother, who hugged me almost as hard—that is, she and the old gentleman did—no—no—I mean to say that Towser and all the rest of the— There—there I go again"—said the colonel, joining in the merriment of his hearers, who were shouting with laughter at the absurd flounders of the colonel's narrative; but when the last giggle of Grace and Rob had subsided, and cries of " hear, hear," resounded on every hand, then our friend Warlow resumed, as he cast a fond look toward his wife, who had been busy at the camp-fire preparing the evening meal while the shades of twilight were thickening among the trees.

" I only wished to say that I was highly gratified with my reception on that happy evening, and Mary and I were soon on the road to the residence of Mrs. Hawley, where we found a merry throng of old friends; and, after such a greeting as only one who meets his childhood's friends after long years of absence can appreciate, we were allotted a quiet corner, and our share of the evening's labor."

At this moment a summons to supper was heard, and the party adjourned to the camp-fire, to discuss the savory prairie-chicken and quail on toast, with which Mrs. Warlow celebrated the close of that Sabbath-day.

Chapter VII.

COLONEL WARLOW'S STORY—CONCLUDED.

AN hour later the party sat under the drooping boughs of an elm, near thickets of snowy elder and blooming wild-roses, which filled all the air with their delicious fragrance; the shallow stream murmured and gurgled along between its willow-fringed banks, glimmering like silver under the beams of the rising moon.

At the request of the group, the colonel resumed, as follows :—

"When the wool had been allotted to the captains, in equal proportions, the leaders divided the company in two parties. It was understood that the side first finishing its task of picking the burrs and other foreign matter from the fleeces of wool, should crown its captain and carry her in triumph around the room on a chair; then she should be awarded the honor of opening the ball, which was to follow in the wide kitchen.

"Mary and I were the last to finish, but were helped through our task by several smiling friends. Then our captain—wild, saucy Peg Sickle—bounded up with the cry, 'Crown the captain!' which was re-echoed by her noisy followers, who proceeded, with ludicrous ceremony, to carry the order into execution.

"The violins struck up a lively air, and the gay Peg, wearing her towering head-dress of wool, led off in the inspiriting quadrille; but the lively dance was watched ruefully through the open doorway by the other party, who still were at their unfinished task; but our hilarity was interrupted by cries of—

"'Fraud!—Shame!—Peggy has been hiding the fleece!'

"It transpired that the treacherous Peg had concealed nearly half the wool allotted to our party, and it had been discovered, in its hiding-place, under the bed; so poor Peg was dragged ignominiously from the unfinished set, and made to abdicate her woolly crown, which was quickly replaced by a diadem of cockle-burrs, with which her irate foes decked her brow, with the taunting reminder that 'uneasy *lies* the head that wears a crown.'

"We slunk back to our unfinished task, as our opponents finished theirs, and re-enacted the mummery; but we toiled faithfully, notwithstanding their jeers, and soon were allowed to join the revelers.

"I noticed, with gratification, that Amy appeared to still be heart-free; and as we were dancing together, later in the evening, I told her of finding Roger at Acapulco, and when she almost cried with delight at his escape, I began at once to build 'castles in Spain,' but prudently omitted mentioning the incident of the picture.

"Dancing and singing continued until a late hour, relieved, however, by huge baskets of hickory-nuts and apples, with supplementary pitchers of

cider. Of that ride home through the moonlight I'll say nothing, in deference to that lady by
the camp-fire yonder; but suffice it that she was
the heroine of that very happy occasion, and the
10th of May was set for our wedding, which, in
view of my four years' probation, I thought an age
to wait.

"Next day I bought the 'Nolan farm,' which
was only three miles from Mary's home, and at
once proceeded to put the place in thorough repair.
The premises were rather tumble-down, and 'the
bildin's a leetle shackelty,' as the fox-hunting squire
remarked; but I put such a force of workmen on
the old stone house and broken-backed barn that
the place was soon completely transformed.

"The fences were the most demoralized and dilapidated that I have ever beheld. In fact, brother
Dick asserted that the 'Nolan boys, Bill and Ike,
were never known to open a gap,' but rode their
horses at the rail-fence, knocking it down for rods;
then half of the next day would be devoted to re-
pairing the unpicturesque nuisance—said repairs
consisting of a load of brush, dumped where the
festive youths had make the floundering leap.

"Often I would come upon an unsightly place
in the fields—the squire's 'harrer,' a great thorn-
bush, spiked to the earth with brambles and thistle—
and I would smile at the vision of the sport-loving
farmer unhitching his team amid-field to chase the
venturesome coon or stiff-legged deer that had
caught his roving eye.

"My carpenters were finishing a stile and two
8

large gates in front of the house, which was tempo-
rarily occupied by its former owner, when Master
Dave Nolan, a scion of the old stock, came upon the
scene. He viewed the improvements with great
displeasure, and, crawling under one of the large
gates, he said, as he wriggled out, lizard style:—

"'Gates is all nonsense; aint half as handy as
a gap in the fence and a slick rail!'

"The 10th of May found the house thoroughly
renovated and furnished newly throughout; so, after
the wedding ceremony, when we had discussed the
dinner, Mary and I took a 'bridal tour' by going to
our new home, and in the evening our neighbors and
relatives gathered in to give us a house-warming.

"Soon after, I wrote Roger an invitation to
spend the summer with us, Mary and Amy adding
a feminine postscript, in which they expressed their
valuation of one who had proved so noble a friend
in my distress, and earnestly begging him to give
them an opportunity of thanking him personally.

"To which he responded that he would 'do himself the honor' of paying his respects in person the
following July—a visit which terminated in a wedding between my old friend and sister Amy. On
their bridal day I gave them the deed to the Maple
Dale plantation, which adjoined our own, and as I
handed the astonished pair the papers I remarked
that it was in fulfillment of the contract which
Roger and I had made at Los Angeles, and they
might charge it to 'Profit and Loss.'

"The newly-wedded pair left the plantation in
charge of an overseer, and returned to Acapulco;

but Roger resigned his position after a few months, and returned home to the quiet life of a planter.

"We enjoyed a long period of uninterrupted prosperity; but when the War of the Rebellion began, I raised a company and joined the Southern army. At the close of that terrible conflict all that was left me was my title and family, with the wreck of my once comfortable fortune.

"I shall hurry over the history of the struggling years that followed; how on returning from the war I found Mary and the children had fled to the city, and how I gathered them once more together on the farm, where the dear old homestead lay, a blackened ruin. But earnestly we tried to retrieve the lost years.

"The county in which I lived was 'reconstructed,' and from the bonds issued by the officers, and the taxes levied to run the costly, corrupt machine, there followed wide-spread financial distress.

"A treasurer had been appointed to finger our money. He was a hawk-nosed, black-haired little reprobate, named Toler, and the way he tolled all the grists which came to his tax-mill led us to believe that he was well named indeed. It was reported that he had once held the post of sutler in a regiment of Eastern troops. Whether that was true or not, he was undoubtedly the most subtle villain that ever sold scabby sheep or slipped a flagstone into a sack of bacon. Finally, this 'patriotic' officer, having stuffed his 'grip-sack' with county funds, one dark night took an excursion for his health, considerately leaving the county, which he only refrained from stealing from the fact that it was not portable.

"The reckless extravagance of that class of men, cursed and abhorred by both parties, led eventually to wide-spread ruin and bankruptcy; but out of the wreck of my once comfortable fortune I saved a few thousands, and, bearing favorable reports from the fertile Kansas prairies, we turned our steps westward toward the setting sun. Fate seemed to lead me here; so I will begin the life-struggle over again on the spot where I lost my friends and the gold doubloons here, near the shadows of the Old Stone-Corral."

When the colonel had finished the long and eventful history of his past life, a silence fell on the group—a silence tinged with sadness as they thought of the fate of Walraven and his wife; and as the camp-fire mingled its flickering light with the pale moonbeams, throwing an uncertain, wavering shimmer over the tangled vines and milk-white elder-blooms, a sense of their lone, isolated position slowly dawned upon them. They were far out on the verge of an untried, mysterious land, no evidences of civilization for miles around, and all the future, with its trials and struggles, looming grimly on the morrow. Is it any wonder that a feeling of dread, awe, and fear stole over the stoutest heart at the thought of the direful, tragic past haunting the spot with its painful memories, and the black veil of futurity hovering over them—hiding the joys and fears, the tears and graves, that lay beyond?

The colonel sat gazing, sad and thoughtful, out toward the knoll, where, resting in the moonlight, the victims of that horrible tragedy now slept their sleep of eternity in the lone, grassy grave.

The winds whispered softly among the trees; a song-bird twittered drowsily in its nest; then a long, mournful howl from a wolf on the distant hills broke the silence of the summer night. Maud, looking wistfully out to the west, where the great planets, those mute sentinels of time, kept their watch in the sky, repeated the sweet, pathetic " Dirge " of Tennyson :—

> " Round thee blow, self pleached deep,
>   Bramble-roses, faint and pale,
>   And long purples of the dale,—
>   Let them rave ;
>   These in every shower creep
>   Through the green that folds thy grave.
>   Let them rave.
>
> Chanteth not the brooding bee
> Sweeter tones than calumny?"

A wild cry from Mrs. Moreland startled the group from their reverie and broke in abruptly upon their musing. As they lifted their eyes or sprang to their feet in dismay, she pointed, with trembling finger, to where the uncertain moonlight flickered through the willows, and there they beheld a sight which froze them with horror, and haunted them with its mystery for long months thereafter.

But a few paces from where they sat stood the form of a strange, gray figure, in a loose, long robe, its locks and flowing beard of snowy white, its wildly gleaming eyes and snaggled fangs, showing dimly in the spectral light. With a long, bony finger pointed at the group, the figure stood for a brief moment; then, with a blood-chilling scream, it faded away amid the shadows.

Clifford Warlow and Ralph Moreland sprang after the vanishing figure, unheeding the wild shrieks of Maud and Grace, who begged them not to follow the frightful apparition. As the young men disappeared among the trees, Mrs. Warlow fell prone upon the earth with a low moan; and while all of the party that remained forgot their terror in their efforts to restore her from the death-like swoon in which she had fallen, the young men returned, reporting a fruitless search.

It was now proposed, as Mrs. Warlow had revived, that the boys—Clifford, Ralph, Scott, and Robbie—should make a more extended search with the three dogs; but they could not force the terror-stricken animals to leave the camp-fire, where they cowered trembling with fear. So the search again proved unavailing.

Chapter VIII.

THOSE were busy days which followed—days all too short for the years of labor that loomed so drearily before the pioneers; but they set to work bravely, plowing, building, and planning, and the manifold cares of their new, strange life left no time for repining over the events of the past, or even to investigate the nature of that strange visitant which had so startled them with its fleeting appearance.

Although a hurried search was made near the Old Corral, no trace of the lost treasure could be discovered; and whenever the subject was mentioned, or the hope expressed of the ultimate recovery of the princely treasure, the colonel would discourage it as delusive and visionary, and would say that the surest way to recover the lost fortune was to extract the gold from the soil through the medium of the plow and an application of good " horse sense " to their farming.

Several masons were employed from the nearest town, forty miles distant, and, after tearing down the walls of the Old Corral, the stone was utilized in building, first, a dwelling for Colonel Warlow in the grove in the river's bend; next, a cottage for Clifford on the site of the old stronghold, which had been entirely obliterated, save that portion which had fallen over Colonel Warlow years ago, and which had so providentially shielded him from death. The entire party had decided that it should remain as a monument of the past, and accordingly the stones which had been hurled down by the drunken fury of the Indians, were replaced carefully; so the wall now appeared as it did a quarter of a century before, on the night of that terrible tragedy.

Squire Moreland and his son Ralph also built, from the same confused stone-heap, comfortable dwellings a mile down the valley, but situated on the opposite side of the river from the Warlows; and, as all of the buildings were located near natural timber, they presented a very home-like appearance when completed.

But during all the while the plows were kept busily turning the fertile valley sod, which was planted in corn and millet, thus providing feed for the stock the ensuing winter.

Yet it must not be supposed by the reader that incessant toil alone occupied the time of the settlers, to the exclusion of all pleasure; for many were the pleasant fishing parties and excursions to the Sand Hills, far off to the north-west, where the delicious sand-plums crimsoned the low shrubs which clothed the hills, relieving, on these occasions, their life of monotony.

An occasional antelope-hunt on the Flats to the south was indulged in by the sporting members of the colony, varied by the excitement of a wolf-chase or the sight of a stray buffalo.

Then the ceaseless tide of travel on the Santa Fe

Trail, thronging with settlers bound for the rich prairies to the south, was in itself a link to the past and an endless source of interest to the colonists.

One of the first moves of the Warlow and Moreland families was to organize a school district, a proceeding which is never omitted by the first settler of the western prairies, who, the very day he " files," begins planning more or less secretly, to secure the location of a school-house on his " claim."

So, according to pioneer traditions, the district was organized, consisting of a territory ten miles square, and a meeting was called at the house of Colonel Warlow, at which assemblage of the settlers it was decided " to vote bonds to build a school-house immediately."

All the voters present agreed, with perfect unanimity, that " bonding " was the only feasible method of accomplishing the object which they had in view ; but when it came to specifying the time for which the bonds were to run, or, in other words, were to mature, then a stormy scene ensued, and with varying degrees of eloquence the subject was hotly discussed by the local orators.

It was proposed by one embryo politician— whose speeches were said by Robbie to be longer than his furrows—" that the bonds be made payable in one year," in which event the entire amount would have to be met by a direct tax on all the assessible property in the district ; and as the lands of the settlers would not be subject to taxation for the period of the next five years, the burden would fall upon the railroad land, which constituted one-half of all the territory embraced within the limits of the district; and the aforementioned "political economist" proceeded to demonstrate to his hearers the beauty and fitness (?) of making a company of friendly capitalists, who lived, as he averred, over in New England, not only pay the two thousand dollars which was to build their school-house, but, in addition to this, be taxed to maintain the school for the next five years; and he closed his brilliant peroration by asserting "that his policy was to make all bloated bondholders and corporation scamps squeal when he had the *chaince*."

The squire and colonel both opposed the measure, the latter replying in a speech of some length, in which he vigorously attacked the principles advocated by the "*chaince orator*," saying that it would be both immoral and unwise to take such a rascally advantage of a company that were doing so much to help the State and develop its resources. Then he warned his hearers of the consequences of so unjust a course, telling them plainly it was little better than highway robbery, and the railroad company would retaliate by raising the rates of shipping, whereby all would suffer alike.

But his appeal was disregarded by the rampant majority, and, although he pleaded with the audience to make the bonds payable in thirty years, which, he said, was but equitable, the motion to make the bonds payable in one year was sustained, and one ardent supporter of that *iniquitous* measure, a man in a coon-skin cap, was heard to remark, as he mounted his mule, which had one crank leg :—

"Good enough fur them railroad fellers; they just haint got no business a-comin' out hyur with their bulljine a-spilin' of our freightin'."

Although the free discussion at the meeting led to a feeling of animosity, the work of building was begun and rapidly pushed forward to completion, soon as the bonds which had been voted for the purpose could be disposed of to those same "bloated bondholders" of the East, and by the middle of August, the large stone school-house, with a bell-tower and rose window, crowned a knoll just across the river from the Old Corral.

THE GRASSHOPPER RAID.

A short time after the day on which the new school-house had been dedicated by a public dinner, in which all the colonists participated, a peculiar haziness was noticed in the air, and, on looking up at the sun, swarms of gauzy-winged insects were seen floating southward on the light breeze; but they were too high for Clifford and Rob—who stood in the barn-yard wondering what they were—to conjecture the terrible import of the phenomenon.

Thicker and more dense became the haze, now almost obscuring the sun, or again thinning out to a silvery mist, which quickly changed to fleecy clouds again, drifting overhead like the scud of a summer storm.

Mrs. Warlow, who stood on the latticed balcony that ran along the eastern front of the dwelling, and on which there opened glass doors, instead of windows, from the long range of dormer gables in the upper story of that picturesque homestead, was looking out to the north, and as she saw a dark, strange cloud quickly rising, she called to the boys to come in at once as a storm was almost upon them.

As the boys glanced out towards the north-west they could see the unnatural, black cloud stretching across the northern horizon, but momentarily growing nearer, like a dense shadow on a summer landscape.

Their father, who had been reading on the porch, laid aside his paper on hearing the unusual commotion, and stepped out in the yard.

" What can it be ?" said Clifford anxiously.

"A dust-storm, probably," replied the colonel, as the weather had been dry and parching hot for several weeks past.

On came the threatening cloud, filling the air from the earth to an incredible height, and a low muffled roar grew louder every moment; then, as the startled family sought the shelter of the dwelling, a seething mass of insects filled the air.

" Grasshoppers! grasshoppers !" cried Rob, dancing about in wild excitement.

" Locusts !" exclaimed the colonel in great consternation; but even then no one but himself realized the terrible disaster and wide-spread ruin which their visit portended; but as he said, gravely, that they were the dreaded locusts or grasshoppers which often laid waste whole nations of Spanish-America, devouring every vestige of the growing crops of those countries and in one day leaving the land like a desert, then the meaning of the appalling calamity slowly dawned upon them.

It was truly an awe-inspiring scene that met their sight, as they stood by the wide windows and looked out on the storm of insect life that raged by, darkening the sun itself as they swarmed along in countless billions.

One who sees the feeble "hopper" spring aside from his path through the Eastern meadows can but dimly comprehend the terrible sight—the cubic miles of winged pests that rush by with a hurtling roar, filling the air all that day like the drifting snow-flakes, through which the sunlight dimly glimmered, or rolling by like the rack of some fierce storm.

As the dew-drop that glints quivering in the morning may be a thing of beauty, but when multiplied by the waters of old ocean becomes grand and imposing, so it was with this feeble insect when re-enforced by his multitudinous kinsmen; and when our friends saw his hordes darkening the sun, and earth and sky swarming with his hosts, they realized, as Clifford said, "that neither corn nor cotton, but 'hopper,' was king," and thenceforth that once reviled insect was held in great respect, though still regarded as an unmitigated nuisance by all the members of our colony.

Next morning every tree, shrub, and building was covered by the insects in huge, dark masses, which flew up in disgusting swarms as the settlers walked along, and the fields of sod-corn were soon stripped clear of every ear and blade by the winged pests, and all the vegetables, also, fell victims to their rapacious appetites—save, perhaps, the warty old radishes, that stood bravely up in the ruined garden, rejoicing in their "strength." The woolly stems of the millet, likewise, defied their insatiable appetites.

The grasshoppers hung about until late in the fall, as if loath to leave such hospitable friends; and when it became apparent that the pests were depositing their eggs in the ground, honey-combing the roads, fields, and banks of the streams with their cells, then the outlook became truly discouraging; for it was known that the young brood, which the next summer's sun would hatch out, would work greater havoc and ruin than that which the settler had just witnessed,—all of which disheartening prospects only served still more to weaken the vertebræ of those settlers not endowed by nature with spines like an oak-tree.

Accordingly, near the end of September, this faint-hearted class inaugurated an hegira back to the Land of the Mother-in-law, and by their haste it was to be inferred that the much-maligned lady of story and song had changed her traditional spots, and now stood waiting to receive them with open hand, on the digital members of which no longer were visible the "claws" of malicious metaphor.

The long caravan, as it wended its eastward course, was headed by the "chaince" orator, and the coon-skin cap and crank-legged mule, of "bulljine" memory, guarded the rear of the retreating host.

It appeared as if the exodus of the settlers was

regarded as a signal of departure by the grass-hoppers also; for one fine morning they rose up in darkening swarms and departed to the south-west.

The Warlow and Moreland families, who had preferred to remain when their more faint-hearted neighbors left, now proceeded to sow their fields in wheat and rye, and the autumn rains and warm sunshine soon clothed the fields with a rank growth of the cereals, which, with the millet, prairie-hay, and the pasture the wheat-fields afforded, served to keep their stock in good condition during the mild winter that followed.

Our friends devoted the early winter to building stone barns and corrals, or pens for the stock, and so busy, indeed, were the energetic settlers that they could scarcely realize that March was with them again; but the way in which that wayward jade proceeded to demonstrate the fact left no doubt in the minds of those who tried to withstand her windy arguments. Although the weather was very dry, the wheat and rye fields were green and rank; but when April passed, and had neglected to shed the customary tears over the frolics of her wayward younger sister, and the drouth still continued, even the stoical colonel became alarmed and fearful for the future.

To add to the gloom of the outlook, the warm sunshine had so operated as an incubator that the earth fairly squirmed with the newly hatched brood of young grasshoppers; and as May came on still warm and dry, and the young pests began their

dread ravages on the tender young vegetables and
fields of grain, then grim famine, with all its horrors, stared the settlers in the face.

But on May 16th, a change was noticed in the
atmosphere. The barometer denoted a rain; and
as Rob limped about, he said that he could feel a
storm in his bones; but Clifford thought that was
owing to his tight boots.

A north-east wind began to blow, cold and
chilly, and a mist wrapped the earth in its foggy
folds until all the hills grew faint and dim; then a
fine, drizzling rain followed, which before noon
merged into a perfect deluge, and the rivulets as
they poured down from the highlands, mingled their
gurgling songs with the river's low bass, raging
and roaring over its rocky bed, all making sweet
music to the ear of the anxious colonist.

The Warlow homestead stood, as I have hereto-
fore explained, in a grove that grew in the river's
bend; and as the house was situated on low ground,
some apprehension was felt by the family lest the
river should reach the dwelling; and as the barn
was on still lower ground, on the bank of the stream,
it was suggested that the stock should be taken to
the upland pasture; a field that was inclosed with a
fence of barbed wire, and connected with the barn-
yard by a lane.

Accordingly, Clifford and Rob drove the horses
and mules, with the cattle, up to the pasture, and
after closing the gate started on their return through
the pouring rain; but when they reached the mar-
gin of what was, but an hour before, a shallow,

grass-bedded brook, babbling away through the meadow, they found now a wide glassy stream, to wade which they knew was impossible; so divesting themselves of their superfluous clothing, they tied their boots up in bundles to throw across.

Clifford's budget landed safely; but Rob was not so fortunate, he having undershot the mark, and he cried :—

"There go my Sundiest boots!"

At the rueful outcry, Clifford turned, just in time to see the bobbing bundle disappear in the muddy water.

The boys swam over safely (but Robbie's bundle was not recovered until several days had elapsed, but then found to be sadly water-logged), and as poor Rob stood shivering in the rain, Clifford gave him his overcoat.

"Oh, a fellow only needs a pair of sandals and a plantain-leaf to keep off the dew in this dry region," said Rob, as he buttoned the welcome garment around him.

The boys, after changing their wet garments when they reached home, went down into the parlor where Maud sat, twanging her guitar and singing :—

> " Oh, gentle, gentle summer rain!
> Let not the drooping lily pine;"

But Rob interrupted, and with an air of tragedy, sang :—

> " Oh, cats and pitchforks cease to rain
> And trickle down my chilly spine."

9

Then, his mother coming in, he proceeded to tell about their "cruise," and the sad fate of his bundle.

"Oh, you might have been drowned in that horrid stream!" said Maud, dropping her guitar in consternation.

"About the only way a fellow can escape such a fate out-doors to-day is to jump into the river," said Clifford, in high good-humor. "Talk about the 'dry belt,'" he continued; "I hope that geographical girdle will soon prove all too short to span this western 'waste.'"

The colonel, who had just come in, said with an anxious face:—

"I am afraid the only dry belt left by morning will be the upstairs, unless this flood ceases soon."

At this announcement Mrs. Warlow and Maud flew into a panic, saying they would all be drowned; to which gloomy predictions the colonel and Clifford replied with arguments to the effect that the house being of stone would resist any flood, and all that was necessary to insure their safety, would be to retire to the upper story of the dwelling in case the water rose into the house; and the feminine portion of the household was soon reassured, and busied themselves preparing an early supper, while the stronger members of the family were busy carrying the furniture up to that place of refuge.

The books, pictures, carpets, and other "household gods," were soon beyond danger; but the old rosewood piano was a load which nearly defied their united efforts, though it, too, was successfully drawn up the stairway with the aid of block and tackle, and finally the store of provisions—a very slender store indeed—was carried to the upper rooms.

After the hasty supper, Clifford and Rob went to the stream, lantern in hand, to take a survey of the situation. They found the river lacked now but a foot of reaching the upper bank, and as it was still raining in torrents they realized the gravity of their position.

It was a strange, weird sight—the sullen, roaring stream; but yesterday a silvery chain, scarce linking the shallow pools where pebbles and shells had shown in the clear, quiet depths—now a mad, dark river, boiling and swirling along in the red glare of the light.

When they had returned to the dwelling and reported the situation, the colonel looked very grave, and they began to canvass the prospect of a retreat. There was Clifford's dwelling, they remembered, at the Old Corral, situated high and dry; but to reach it they would have to cross a stream that was a foaming torrent, and the wild, swift river on the south completely cut them off from retreat in that direction; while away to the north stretched the limitless prairie, with not a habitation for more than a score of miles to shelter them from the cold and driving rain.

Chapter IX.

BUT when they thought of the wide valley and the vast quantity of water necessary to raise one foot after the river left its banks, they dismissed the thought of danger, and retired to rest.

The rain now poured down with greater fury than ever; the wind lashed the roof with the limbs of the old elm that drooped over the chimneys and gables of the dwelling; and the groaning and creaking added a gruesome feeling to the drowsiness which the plashing rain-drops caused to steal over the inmates of that danger-threatened household.

"It makes me think of spectres and shrieking ghosts," said Robbie, as he drew the cover up closer, and cuddled down by Clifford.

"Yes; it recalls the lines of 'Tam O'Shanter,'" replied his older brother, repeating a verse from that masterpiece of Burns:—

> "The wind blew as 't wad blawn its last;
> The rattling showers rose on the blast;
> The speedy gleams the darkness swallowed;
> Loud, deep, and lang the thunder bellowed.
> That night a child might understand
> The deil had business on his hand."

"If the Old Gent ventures from his fireside to-night, he'll get his tail wet," said Rob; then rolling over, the lad was soon in the "land of Nod."

But Clifford lay for hours listening to the hoarse

roar of wind, river, trees, and pelting rain; but finally he was lulled to sleep, though even in slumber he was weighed down and haunted by a sense of danger; and when the clock chimed the hour of twelve he arose, and stole down the stairs. As he reached the next to the last step his foot plashed in the water. He knew at once that the river was now out over all the wide valley, and had risen in a stealthy flow, invading the house, where it was at least two feet deep.

Watching the water by the light which he had returned and procured, he saw it was rising in an alarming manner; so he hastily dressed himself and went to the window, and opening the sash, which was all in one piece and hung on hinges, he looked out on the glaring, boiling flood below. As he stood thus, looking down on the terrible, raging whirlpool, he was rapidly revolving in his mind plans of escape from their perilous position; but every avenue of retreat seemed closed. As he cast his eyes about in despair, he started joyfully at the thought of the "Crows' Nest" up in the great elm—a place which could be reached by a flight of steps springing from the window ledge and leading far up into the forks of the tree.

Smiling at the fact that he had not thought of it before, he sprang up the stairs into the fanciful retreat, which Robbie in his boyish fancy had planned and built in the top of the lofty tree, and which, on warm, sultry days, had proved to be an aerial lounging-place as comfortable as it was novel. It was a stout platform about eight feet square, railed

about, and provided with seats, hammocks, and
even a rocking-chair. It was with a feeling of
relief that Clifford stood on the floor of the lofty
perch and glanced down at the glare of water.

Springing down the steps, which were also safely
railed, he went to the mark which he had made on
the wall and found the water had risen a full step,
and, knowing there was no time to lose, he ran to
the bed and awakened Robbie, telling him of the
situation, and in a few minutes that resolute young
chap was dressed and ready to lend a willing hand
in the plan which Clifford unfolded.

Taking a wagon-cover from one of the stow-
aways which flanked the room, and a piece of
scantling from the same catch-all, the boys cut the
ropes from the wagon-sheet, and after tying the
scantling securely to the limbs above the platform,
at a distance of six or seven feet overhead, they
next drew the canvas, tent-fashion, over it, then
brought the ends down in such a manner that the
rain was excluded from the "Nest," and tacking
the sheet to the floor and making a flap for the
doorway, the interior was quite impervious to the
rain, which still raged without.

Some blankets were next carried up and spread
on the floor, and then two beds were made hastily,
and the busy fellows did not omit the pillows and
sheets; so the place wore a very cozy appearance.
Then, when all was complete, they awakened their
parents and Maud, telling them of the safe retreat
into which they would be compelled to remove.

In a few moments they were all safely up in the

"Nest," and then the provisions and a few valuables were carried thither, Rob cautioning them not to forget a jug of water. Then the boys went down to the hall stairway and found that the water lacked but two feet of reaching the upper floor.

Alarmed and in great suspense, Clifford stood watching the flood, and was relieved to see that the water crept more slowly up the stair; then Robbie, coming up, said that the rain was about over and the stars were twinkling through the rifts above.

As the boys gazed at the water, a faint wet line became visible on the wall just above the flood. Breathless with suspense, they watched until the band widened; then Clifford shouted in wild excitement, "Falling—falling!"

"She's falling, falling!" shrieked Rob as he flew up to the "Nest" with the joyful news.

Yes; it was a blissful fact that the water was subsiding, and, that too, at a rate which soon promised relief from the danger which had threatened them with total ruin.

Clifford, ever thoughtful of the comfort of others, now built a fire in the warming stove which stood in his room, and proceeded to make coffee for the weary and chilly party that still remained up in their "Nest;" and as the young man remembered Rob's caution regarding the water-jug, he hastily tied a rope to a bucket, and reaching over the window-ledge, soon secured a supply of the necessary fluid. A steaming hot cup of the fragrant beverage was declared by the nestlings to be "prime and delicious" in the extreme.

Warmed and refreshed now, the family looked
out upon the strange scene which began to emerge
in the dawning light.   The valley was submerged
from hill to hill; but they could see the cattle
patiently grazing on the highlands, and the poultry
on the accustomed trees were roosting serenely, far
above the danger-line.

The surrounding country was quite rolling, and
the stream headed among the hills on the west, only
a few miles distant; so after the rain ceased, the
flood subsided as rapidly as it had risen—a pecu-
liarity of all Western streams.

The family watched the water subside until all
the old land-marks were once more visible.   The
fields were still covered in shallow water; but soon
the wild river shrank back into its narrow channel
once again.

There had been great anxiety felt for the safety
of the Moreland family, although it was known that
their dwelling was situated on higher ground than
the Warlow house; yet no sign of life was visible
at the homestead of their neighbor, and when a loud
halloo was heard from Ralph Moreland, who had
ridden over to the top of one of the hills which
shouldered down to the opposite side of the river,
a glad cry in response was raised from the inmates
of the "Nest."

It was amusing to see the bewildered way in
which he peered over, trying to discover their
whereabouts; and when he finally discovered the
aerial family, he eagerly asked after their welfare.

When he learned of their safety, he laughed in

a relieved and hearty way at their " elevated station
in life."

In answer to their inquiries regarding his father's
family, he said that the water had not reached the
dwelling; but he was too uneasy thinking of their
danger to wait longer than daylight to ride over,
and, although he did not mention the fact, they saw
that his horse was wet to the saddle-bow, and knew
that he had swam a dangerous side-stream to gain
the hill.

Maud begged him not to return until the water
subsided, and she kept shouting their experience
across the river, while the equally noisy youth replied in tones like a fog-horn.

Mrs. Warlow and the colonel had now descended
to the " lower regions," as Clifford termed the first
story of the dwelling, where he and Rob were removing a mountain of mud from the floor, and their
mother soon prepared a breakfast which those
hungry youths pronounced a royal banquet.

But Maud still carried on her loud flirtation
from the tree-top in tones which, Rob said, " could
be heard in the next county," and the way she
managed, with her lengthened description of their
experience, to detain Ralph until all danger of high
water on his return had passed, showed she felt a
greater interest in the rider than in the high-toned
subject.

After he had at length ridden away, Maud descended to the rooms below, where her mother was,
saying that " this inundation would be long remembered, and would become legendary and traditional."

"Yes," replied Clifford, gravely, "Rob and I will carry the memory of the event down to our 'remotest ancestors.'"

"Oh, I daresay it will lose nothing in the way of variations in the transmission," said Maud; "but here, you superior being, bring me a pail of water;" and Clifford marched off obediently to the muddy well.

"Why, madam," cried Rob, mockingly, as he scraped the mud from the floor, "have you regained your voice? I was afraid it was utterly lost;" and he giggled at the thought of how her tones had wandered away over the prairie.

"More scrubbing and less sarcasm, young man!" she replied, with a blush, as she vigorously attacked the wall, which was stained by the water, or frescoed with mud and slime; but as the plastering was of hard coat, it soon regained its wonted purity under the drenching which was administered by the energetic and busy workers, and long before nightfall the usual neatness and order reigned in the Warlow household.

The young brood of grasshoppers had all been swept away in the flood, or perished in the long, cold storm. Pious Mrs. Warlow said, "The hand of the Lord is revealed in freeing the land of those pests;" and indeed it appeared the work of Providence, which had so effectually destroyed them that no further trace was visible of the scourge which only a brief day before had threatened both the Missouri and Arkansas valleys with famine and desolation.

The weather, that for the past year had played the fickle jade, now tried to atone for her folly, and often would she burst into tears of remorse, and veil her face in summer clouds, at remembrance of the wild tantrums which had marred her equinoctial history.

In the propitious rain and sunshine which followed, the fields of grain emerged from their coat of rich sediment, and the lush, dank growth of the cereals ripened into great level fields of waving grain, the bronze and golden wheat and silvery sheen of barley and oats contrasting happily with the long rows of corn and emerald millet.

How often it is thus, that misfortune, on reaching a climax of superlative disaster, then assumes the form of diminutive comparison!

The migratory settlers, that had been sojourning in the Land of the Mother-in-law, now returned, re-enforced by cousins to a remote degree, and on their tattered old wagon-covers, on which had glared in letters of blue, black, and red, the legend "Kansas or BusT," and which on their subsequent flitting had been partially erased and the assertion "buStud by —" printed instead, now there glared the dauntless assertion, "kansiss is the bEsT lAnd unDur the suNn."

Chapter X.

ONE delightful day in June the Warlow and Moreland families, or the younger members of those households, attended a picnic which was held in a grove on the river seven miles below the Old Corral.

At an early hour Clifford, Maud, and Robbie drove down in their three-seated carriage, drawn by Clifford's iron grays, and at Squire Moreland's the party was re-enforced by Ralph, Grace, and Scott. Baskets and fishing-lines were stowed away under the seats, and the frying-pan, also, was given a place of honor in the same promiscuous stow-away.

The dew was sparkling like gems on the bearded wheat, so soon to fall before the reaper's stroke, and the tender grass and softly-fluttering trees were all bathed in the mellow sunlight, as they sped down the winding road.

When our friends arrived at the grove they found that the platform, which had been erected among the trees close to the river, was crowded with a well-dressed throng, who were merrily dancing to the music of violin, organ, and guitar. After the carriage-load had been deposited on the platform, and Rob and Scott had returned from caring for the team, the boys found Clifford, Grace, Ralph, and Maud busily improving the shining moments in the mazes of a cotillion.

When the music ceased, Maud was requested by one of the amateur musicians to second on the organ, which was a mere labor of love; and as she acceded to the request, she saw Rob and Grace spinning away in a waltz, dizzily gyrating about the platform with a full score of couples, all equally giddy and alike bent on extracting the most enjoyment out of the least possible time.

Clifford, who stood leaning against a tree, surveying the varied groups with that mingling of interest, amusement, and indifference, which we experience in viewing the movements of strangers who may soon become acquaintance, and possibly friends, was accosted by a handsome young man of near his own age, who greeted him very cordially.

The new-comer was Hugh Estill, the son of a wealthy ranchman who lived near, or at least but a few miles further down the valley. The two young men had become acquainted in a business way while Clifford had been buying cattle at the Estill ranch some weeks before, and it was to young Estill they owed the invitation to the picnic; so it was with a feeling of gratitude, not unmixed with respect in remembrance of the lordly ranch-house and its princely domain, that young Warlow shook hands and thanked the young ranchman for his thoughtful remembrance of them on this pleasant occasion.

Robbie had by this time surrendered his partner to a young cow-boy, a son of the greatest "cattle king" in the valley, and as the young "prince" led Miss Grace out through the changes of the quadrille he seemed totally oblivious of the fact that his leather

"leggins," jingling spurs, and silver-mounted re-
volver hanging from a cartridge-belt, were not
wholly in keeping with the festive occasion; and as
they paused in the dance, the bovine princeling,
after blowing a long breath and wiping his glowing
brow on his sleeve, observed :—

" That was a terrible swell—the young blood
with a biled vest, who just waltzed with you.   Ha!
ha!—a wild rose in his button-hole !   Guess I'll
have to get one also—by shot !"

But Miss Grace bluntly told him that a gourd-
vine would be far more suitable.

Robbie, who was happily unconscious of the dis-
paraging remarks which were being made at the
expense of his purple and fine linen, had joined
Clifford and been introduced to the new friend, who
passed some good-natured compliments on that urchin's dancing, to which Rob replied that he was
but re-dedicating his boots that so lately had been
resurrected ; and he proceeded to tell in his inimi-
table manner of the mishap that had carried his best
and dearly-beloved boots to a watery grave, from
which they were at length " resurrected," all filled
with mud and sand.   Laughing heartily, Hugh said
he hoped he would shine as brightly on the resurrection morn as those same " Sunday boots."

While Hugh and Robbie had been engaged in
the above frivolous and wholly unprofitable conversation, Clifford was improving the time in furtively
staring at a radiant and superbly beautiful young
lady who was playing the guitar near Maud ; and,
indeed, young Warlow might have been excused if

we had detected him in the rude act, for it was a face which once seen would never be forgotten.

Her eyes of softest blue were veiled by silken, jetty lashes, and a wealth of raven-black hair rippled low on a face of creamy olive. An expression of pride mingled with the spirited vivacity of her charming face, which he thought was the most fascinating he had ever beheld.

Every detail of her dress, from the wide straw hat with its drooping spray of lilies, the creamy grenadine with its tangled pattern of the same snowy flowers and cascades of foamy lace, the cross and chain of palest coral, with ribbons of the same faint rose-hue, evinced the taste and refined instincts of a well-born and cultured lady.

There seemed to be the ineffable charm of grace and elegance in her very attitude, as she stood by the organ and swept the guitar with white, tapering fingers, while through all the melody there thrilled the sweet, dripping notes, like the memory of some half-forgotten dream, which, though elusive and vague, still haunts our waking hours through all the turmoil of a busy day.

"Where have I seen that form and face before?" said Clifford, half audibly, as the last faint notes died away, and he awoke from a reverie, while a look of surprise and delight broke over his handsome face; then turning to young Estill he said, in an eager tone:—

"Who is that divine young creature who played the guitar until she set me to dreaming of old Spain?"

"Why, that musical divinity," said Estill, with a hearty laugh, "is my only sister Morelia; or Mora, as we have become used to calling her. I shall be pleased to present you, for I am truly relieved to find some one who can appreciate her music, which always sounded to me very much like cats fighting."

A moment later the young men were upon the platform, and young Estill said, in his easy, good-humored way: —

"Sister Mora, let me present my friend, Mr. Warlow, on whom your music has had the strange effect of setting him to dreaming, not of cats on the roof, but of castles in Spain,—which I have by his own confession."

She gave young Warlow a fair, dimpled hand, on which flashed one ring of rose-colored amethyst, and, after he had bowed very low, their eyes met in a swift glance of half-puzzled recognition and surprise, while a magnetic shock caused them both to tremble; but quickly recovering, she said, with a smile, while toying with a bracelet of carved Neapolitan coral: —

"My brother's criticisms are not of much value, for the sweetest sounds to his ears are the bellowings of beef-cattle."

Then, as she and Clifford sauntered out to a seat under a tree, he said: —

"How strange it is, Miss Estill, that I have never met you before, for it seems as though I have known you for years!"

"Why, Mr. Warlow, I was just trying to recall the time and place where I had seen you. It must have been while we were traveling that we have been thrown together for a moment; yet I can not now remember the circumstance," she replied, with a look of interest dawning in her blue eyes.

"If we had I would not have forgotten such a pleasant incident, Miss Estill. But I am puzzled to think why I remember even your tone and manner so well, for I can't recall any chance meeting with you in the past."

At that moment Grace and Hugh Estill came up, and proposed that they should repair to the river, near by, and spend an hour fishing; so they soon were seated under the shade of an enormous cottonwood-tree on the banks of a deep pool, while Hugh and Grace, who had been introduced at some former meeting, strayed along the stream in quest of a "better place," which they did not discover in *sight or hearing* of Miss Estill and Clifford.

After casting their hooks into the quiet water, they sat down upon the shady bank, and Miss Estill said:—

"Hugh has often spoken of you lately, and we had discussed the subject of calling on your sister and Miss Moreland, but decided that we would send you an invitation to our picnic, at which I hoped to become acquainted with them." Then, seeing a shade of disappointment flit over his face, she added, archly: "And you also. But I assure you that the call will not be deferred a great while longer; for I am delighted to find such charming girls for neighbors."

"The invitation was very kind and thoughtful

of you, Miss Estill. We had been longing to meet
congenial companions, and hailed the news of the
picnic with all the delight of people who have been
isolated from society for a year or more. I hope
you will believe it is no vain compliment when I
tell you that I have already met new friends here
that I value higher than any of my old ones,"
Clifford replied, as he knotted a bunch of elder-
bloom, snowy and fragrant, with the blossoms of
the wild heart's-ease, azure and gold, which grew
on the sandy stretch at their feet. Then, adding a
fern-like tuft of meadow-fescue, he held it toward
Miss Estill, while a look of undisguised admiration
shone in his clear blue eyes, saying :—

"In memory of my deep gratitude."

Fastening the flowers among the meshes of lace
on her breast, she busied herself a moment with
the fishing-tackle as she drew the hook from the
water with a dangerous movement. Then, with a
smile dimpling her face, she said :—

"If you feel such a deep sense of gratitude,
Mr. Warlow, you may discharge the debt by bait-
ing my hook, which some wary turtle or other
aquatic creature, has been investigating."

With ready alacrity, Clifford performed the de-
sired service; and as he let go the hook, Miss
Estill began a series of manœuvres with the fish-
pole that were as womanly as they were threatening. Finally, after the hook had performed for
some time around his head with a dangerous
"s-w-i-s-h," it fortunately landed plump into the

water, with a thud and splash loud enough to scare all the fish upon dry land.

They stood a moment, silently watching the widening ripple; then, as they seated themselves on the bank again, Miss Estill said, with a smile :—

"You are very brave, indeed, Mr. Warlow, never to wince. But perhaps you were not aware of the great risk a man runs who fishes with a woman. I never should have forgiven myself if that awkward hook had caught in your eye."

"Or my ear," he added, with such a look of comic distress that she dropped her fish-pole into the water with a merry laugh; then, as he joined in the merriment, the startled mocking-bird overhead hushed its song, and flitted away to some quieter nook.

"Now, if we are not more careful, we will have to dine on humility to-day," she said, as he recovered the fishing-tackle. "But do you really grow lonesome in your new home, Mr. Warlow?" she added.

"Yes, indeed I did," said Clifford, with an emphasis on the past tense that indicated the remoteness of those days. "But we were very busy until recently, and I did not fully realize what a hermit I had become until I came here into the crowd, and found myself growing hot and cold by turns, my heart palpitating, and my hands and feet getting heavy. Then I knew it would only be a matter of time when I should fly, like a South Sea Islander, at very sight of a human face, much less the presence of a fashionable young lady;" and he joined

Miss Estill's merriment at his charming candor, with an easy laugh.

"Oh, I appreciate the situation," she replied; "for when they sent me to Cincinnati to the boarding-school, where all was so strange, and the only ray of sunshine in the long weeks, months, and years was a flitting call from my fashionable aunt, or the yearly visits to my Western home, I felt desolate and miserable. Why, I was so shy, and possibly a bit wild, that I gained the name of Antelope among my school-mates;" and Miss Estill smiled somewhat sadly at remembrance of those past days.

"When you returned to your home, it certainly must have seemed lonely after the life in that 'American Florence,'" said young Warlow.

"Oh, it was paradise! I could scarcely believe that the old days of banishment were over; and indeed I half feared, sometimes, that they would pack me off again. It was such a perfect joy to be back at the dear old ranch once more with Hugh and my parents, that I vowed I should never leave again. But when I had been back a year I did sometimes long for a good, confidential chat with my girl friends, and would be a bit lonesome while Hugh was away; but our life is one ceaseless round of labor, toil, and care, so I have short time for repining. Would you believe, Mr. Warlow, that more than half the time all the duties of housekeeper, unaided, devolve upon me? Our house has been a constant panorama of 'domestic' weddings since I returned from school; yes, and for

years before also. No sooner would we begin to
appreciate some household treasure—a Nora, Ruth,
or Nelly, who had come from the East to lessen
our domestic burdens—than along would come some
spruce ranchman or handsome young homesteader,
and—presto!—our domestic was courted away in a
twinkling to brighten a new home. And what with
the wedding which mamma always insists upon,
and the bridal finery she bestows, the burden is
redoubled. My weary shoulders fairly ache as we
pass through the constant, or tri-yearly, recur-
rence of the same experience. Hugh says that
he believes the servant-girls of the East have
finally come to look upon our house as a matrimonial agency."

"Do you not think, Miss Estill, that the bright
new homes, which are a result of your charities, are
sufficient reward for your domestic martyrdom?"

"Oh, if you think our providing wives for the mis-
cellaneous ranchers, herders, and homesteaders could
be called a charity, I will have to say that our further-
ing of those matches has proved a mixed blessing
indeed; for I recall a world of conjugal infelicity
which has followed those hasty and ofttimes ill-
assorted matches. 'Marry at pleasure,' etc., is a
maxim true as it is trite, Mr. Warlow."

"Yes; it is undeniable that unhappy matings do
occur; but I can not see how a lonesome bachelor,
who eats his own vile cooking and goes through the
vain ceremony of laundry-work, could ever aggra-
vate his deplorable condition, Miss Estill."

"But the fact remains that he certainly does,"

she replied,. with a low gurgling laugh, like the ripple of some sweet, clear brook. "Why, Mr. Warlow, I recall a scene of which I was the innocent witness one evening last month. I was riding by the ranch of Mr. Blank, who had wooed and won our cook after a courtship that was as brief as it was fervid. I have reason to believe he pines for his former state of untrammeled freedom; for, in some argument which they seemed to be discussing that evening, she, his faithful help-meet, hurled the milk-stool at his head. I rode quickly away, mentally washing my hands of any further matrimonial schemes.

"Mr. Warlow! a fish, a fish!" she cried in a low tone, and he turned his eyes reluctantly to the sadly neglected fishing-tackle, which he had "set" by thrusting the poles into .the bank, and which they, in their long and absorbing conversation, had totally forgotten. There he saw the flash of a finny monster in the water, and the fish-pole violently threshing in the air above the pond, and as he drew the glittering perch from the pool, he found that it had become entangled in Miss Estill's fish-line also.

"It is our fish, is it not?—and a good omen," he said, as he secured the prize which fluttered at her feet.

"It is our 'luck,'" she replied gaily; "but we can boast of little skill in angling;" at which they both laughed, low but heartily, at the thought how far into foreign fields they had rambled, leaving their fishing to chance, and in that merry glance was laid the foundation of sympathy, appreciation, and friendship.

When they returned to the grove they were joined by Hugh, Grace, Maud, and Ralph, whose success had been most woefully indifferent. Those discomfited anglers looked with undisguised envy on the great piscatorial prize, and while it was frying on the fire, which Scott and Robbie kindled, they all lent a ready ear to the malicious story which the latter urchin told—"That Cliff had brought a mackerel to the picnic, and it was that same identical fish which they were frying."

When the cloth was spread on the grass, and the great fish, garnished with elder-blooms and wild-roses, was given the place of honor at the feast, Hugh Estill said:—

"Now, Mora, please pass the mackerel."

Only then was the fact made plain that Robbie was a boy, given to telling "fish stories," and could be trusted and relied upon only at the dinner-table.

Ah! it was a gleeful hour at that *al fresco* meal,— the soft breeze stirring the tree-tops, and the bright sunlight sifting down through the fluttering leaves on the silver and crystal, the frosty cake and quivering jelly, the crimson and gold, and, above all, the happy faces of our young friends.

Dancing and an impromptu concert, followed by charades on a temporary stage, served to pass away a few more blissful hours: then the revelers broke into groups and couples, sauntering into shady nooks, and engaging in those long and confidential

chats which are totally devoid of interest to any
save themselves.

Miss Estill and young Warlow were seated upon
a bank where the mingled sunlight and pale shadows
flickered softly over the lush and tender sward, and
their conversation steered away from the shoals and
quagmires of match-making and matrimony to the
vague and mystic fields of metaphysics.

"Do you know, Miss Estill, that I have—a dim
impression, shall I call it?—of having met you
somewhere before?"

"Yes; I remember distinctly of your having
not only met me, but also kindly helping me catch
a fish, before," she replied, archly.

Clifford said, in a laughing manner, that he was
not so ungallant as to forget that thrilling adventure, then he continued in an earnest tone:—

"I feel like we had met long years ago; and
somehow, Miss Estill, it all appears so natural to be
with you, to hear your tones and see your face, that
it is like the return of some dear friend whom you
have longed to see for years."

"You almost make me believe in the theory of
the transmigration of souls, Mr. Warlow. How
very possible it may have been that in some dim,
pre-historic age you and I were a pair of giant
king-fishers, who to-day were reunited on the banks
of our favorite stream after the lapse of untold
ages!—and what is more natural than we should
take to our antediluvian occupation at once?" and
she peered down into the pool with a sidelong glance
as though searching for her finny prey, while Clif-

ford shook with merriment at her happy imitation of that uncanny bird.

"I never was a firm believer in Swedenborg; yet the thought haunts me still that I certainly have met you before to-day, although, as you say, it may have been in some previous happy state, Miss Estill."

"Now, to be frank, Mr. Warlow, I confess to being a bit superstitious, which may be owing, however, to my living so isolated from society all these years that I even welcomed company of a supernatural nature, which, you know, is better than none."

"Why, it can not be that your vicinity is peopled by shrieking ghosts, too?" said Clifford quickly, as the memory of the spectre of the Stone Corral came to mind, which in the turmoil of their busy lives had been nearly forgotten.

"I can not see why I should revert to such a subject to-day; but some way the mention of trans-migration of souls brought the remembrance of the Gray Spectre to my mind," said she, glancing fur-tively over her shoulder; then, as she caught young Warlow's amused look, she smiled responsively, and continued :—

"You too have a skeleton in the family, I per-ceive; so let's unburden our souls and exchange confidences."

"With all my heart," said Clifford; "I am glad we have such a mutual bond of sympathy."

Then he told how the gray-robed figure had startled the group at the camp-fire, and fled shriek-

11

ing away, that memorable evening more than a year
before; and although all of their family had main-
tained an apprehensive outlook for a second visit
from his spookship, they never had been molested
further; and he concluded by saying:—

"But I hope, Miss Estill, your experience will
throw some light on the mystery."

"It is undoubtedly the same spectral being
which has haunted our ranch for the past twenty-
five years, and which has eluded pursuit on every
occasion, although papa, Hugh, and several herders
have endeavored, more or less bravely, to trace it;
but the mysterious apparition always vanishes into
the night without leaving a trace. Why, I have
become so fearful that, like the daughter of the
bold Glengyle,—

'Alone I dare not venture there,
Where walks, they say, the shrieking ghost,'—

and I often fly at the sight of my own shadow,"
said Miss Estill. "One evening, Mr. Warlow, I
was riding by a peculiarly lonesome spot near
home,—a lofty hill on which there is the grave of a
mysterious relative, who died near a quarter of a
century since, and of whose history I can learn but
little. Although Hugh and I often question our
parents about him, they seem to evade our inquiries.
I had reached a point close to the grave,—which is
all overgrown with thistles, notwithstanding the
fact that I had repeatedly planted flowers and roses
there that had always refused to grow,—when that
same hideous, gray-robed creature emerged from
the thicket about the grave, and as I halted, frozen

with horror at the sight, the gaunt wretch glared a moment, then fled shrieking away in the darkling twilight. Oh, I never paused to investigate, you may believe, but gave rein to my pony, which was as badly frightened as myself, and flew home like the wind," said Miss Estill with a shiver.

"Have you ever been up to the corral, Miss Estill?" Clifford asked.

"Not for three years, Mr. Warlow. Now, while we are speaking of supernatural things, I must tell you how strangely I always felt at that place. I can never go about the old ruin without being assailed by an uncanny feeling—something like one might be expected to feel who walks over her own grave, you know!" she added with a smile; then continuing she said earnestly: "It always seems that something terrible haunts the very air there, and I feel a weight of grief and misery that horrifies me whenever I pass the spot. If I had lost my dearest friend there, I should have very much the same sensation, I believe, at sight of the ruin. I struggle with my memory to recall some event with which I seem to have been connected there; but it is all in vain, for it is as intangible as a moonbeam."

"That is very mysterious indeed, Miss Estill; for I often feel very much that way myself there, but not in so marked a degree as when I pass that great hill three miles up the valley, known as Antelope Butte. I am often overpowered by a feeling of deepest melancholy and grief while only passing that hill. The first time I saw the place I was shocked to think how familiar it all seemed; for I found the spring near its base just where my instinct seemed to tell me that the water bubbled forth from the rocky cleft. But a feeling of unutterable longing and an uncontrollable yearning to see some one, the name even of whom I can not recall, always seizes me there, and I am both perplexed and horrified at the sensation," Clifford replied.

Gradually the tone of their conversation lost its gloomy hue, and rambled away into the realms of art, history, and song, of the fair foreign lands beyond that blue, quivering horizon; and as Miss Estill fluttered her fan of carved ivory and rose-plumes, talking in her sweet vivacious way, the sunlight threw a halo about the golden hair and Grecian face of the youth reclining on the bank, suffusing with rose the handsome features that even a western sun in all its fierceness could not rob of its fresh glow.

As the fastidious Miss Estill noted every detail of his faultless attire, neither old nor new, from the tips of his shapely fingers to his glossy boots bearing the undeniable stamp of gentleman, she thought how utterly effete was the comparison, " Rough as a farmer ;" and as admiration shone in his boyish face, illuminated with those honest blue eyes, fringed by their lashes of dead gold, is it any wonder that romance threw its glamour over the scene, and they half forgot to roam in fancy through foreign lands, thinking of the joyful present, which, alas! we seldom value until it has become a sweet memory only.

The long shadows which stole down from the

hill-tops warned our young friends that they would soon part, and reluctantly they returned to the platform, where preparations for starting were being made. Grace Moreland and Hugh Estill still appeared to be deeply engrossed with each other's society, and it was not remarkable that young Estill should hover about the vivacious and bewitching Grace; for. she was a sparkling, graceful creature, the picture of innocence and youth, in her dress of fleecy white.

As Clifford stood by Miss Estill at parting, he said, while his hand rested on the mane of her creamy horse:—

"Ah, Miss Estill, I little thought what this morning held in store. This has been a day that repays the many dark years of the past, and I shall treasure its memory forever."

"Yes; a blissful day indeed, Mr. Warlow; and it almost makes me sad to think I shall ever grow old," she replied, as she gave her hand, which he held longer—yes, I shall have to confess the fact, much longer—than the laws of conventionality demanded.

As the Warlow carriage drove up the broad valley, the coolness of twilight was brooding over the prairies, and the twittering songsters fluttered down from the highlands to the sheltering thickets which belted the stream, and the fire-flies gemmed the dusky groves and meadows when they alighted at their homes.

Chapter XI.

ON a clear, serene Sabbath following the picnic, Miss Estill and Hugh rode up to Squire Moreland's, excusing the call on that holy day by saying that they were too busy to spare one day of six; and after dinner at that hospitable home, they walked up to Colonel Warlow's, being accompanied by Grace, Ralph, and Scott.

They paused at the great latticed and arched gate to glance into the yard, which was inclosed by a low stone wall, over which the grapes and wild-roses clambered in heavy clusters of tangled foliage. Two gaudy peacocks were sunning their glittering plumage on the grass plat in front of the long stone dwelling resting so cool under the great elm—that same historical tree which had served as place of refuge during the "flood"—drooping low over the quaint gables, dormer windows, and chimneys wreathed by the transplanted wild vines which festooned the rough walls.

The colonel was asleep in a hammock, which was slung in the latticed porch, and his placid wife sat near, reading the Bible, as she rocked softly in the easy-chair. Clifford, clad in a cool white suit, was reading also; but I fear the work, in which he was so absorbed that he had not seen the approaching guests, was not of such a sacred nature as befitted the Lord's-day. Maud and Rob, swinging in a swing which was fastened to the limbs of the great elm, were likewise perusing the pages of some entertaining book, which Maud dropped with a little feminine squeak of delight as she saw her friends; then she flew down the path, and greeted the new-comers with unfeigned pleasure.

As she kissed Miss Estill and Grace in true girlish fashion, Rob, the handsome rogue, came forward and gravely offered to salute the ladies in the same manner; but his cordial advances were declined with thanks, whereupon he turned to the young men of the party and kissed them effusively, amid their merry peals of laughter at his sly way of ridiculing the feminine mode of greeting.

Mrs. Marlow said in her low, sweet voice, as she led the guests into the house, after they had been presented in due form by Clifford,—

"It is very kind of you, hunting us up this lonesome afternoon."

"We should have done so long before this if we had known what very agreeable neighbors lived so near," replied young Estill.

"You will smile, possibly, at our thinking twelve miles a neighborly distance, Mrs. Warlow, but I assure you it seems only a trifle when we remember that for years we have considered the people of Abilene and Lawrence our neighbors," said Miss Estill as she sank into an easy-chair, after Maud had relieved her of the jaunty black hat with its drooping white plume.

"We will freely forgive you, Miss Estill, if you

will atone for your past neglect," said Mrs. Warlow,
with a pleased smile. "The lack of society has been
the greatest privation attending our Western life,
and but for the unvarying kindness and sympathy
of Squire Moreland's family, I fear we should have
found it quite monotonous."

The room where they were seated was a wide,
many-windowed apartment, with cool lace curtains
sweeping the dark, rich carpet. The walls were
graced by a few pictures and portraits, and on the
brackets of walnut and mahogany were vases of
wild-flowers. A wide bay-window at one end was
half screened by the curtains of lace, and through
their filmy meshes could be seen the cherished ge-
raniums and fuchsias that were so dear to Maud as a
memento of the old Missouri home. A great
beveled mirror, framed in heavy gilt moulding,
reached from the mantel to the ceiling; and
strangest sight in this Western land was a wide
fire-place; but instead of the glowing coals and
crackling flames which one always associates with
the hearth-stone, there were banks of blooming plants.
The rich old piano and Maud's guitar occupied
one corner, and a low, velvet divan the other, on
each side of the mantel. It was a room which,
Miss Estill and her brother perceived, was redolent
with the refinement and harmony of the family, as
simply elegant and devoid of sham and pretense as
its owners.

Miss Estill gave a sigh of gratification as her glance
swept the apartment, and rested out on the shady,
well-kept lawn, where the hum of bees and songs

of wild-birds seemed so wholly in keeping with the
tone of happiness and industry which pervaded the
Warlow household.

"How strange it seems that you have been here
so short a time! It is almost like enchantment—
this evolving such a perfect home from the wild,
lonesome prairies and tangled woodland, where the
wolf and buffalo roamed unmolested not two short
years ago."

"We have to thank nature for the trees and
flowers, the vines also, Miss Estill; but you see we
had little else to occupy our time but the improvements of our new home; though I believe we can
truly say that we have not been idle the past year,"
replied Clifford.

"It is wonderful what a change your taste and
energy have made in that brief time. We can not
blame our Eastern friends, who never have beheld a
wide, desolate prairie transformed into such a charming home-land as this in a short year, if they do
vilify the average Kansan, and tax him with boast-
fulness and other vices not akin to truth."

At request of her guests, Maud was soon seated
at the rich, mellow-toned piano, and the strains of
"The Bridge" floated out through the open windows, as her sweet contralto rose, freighted with the
heart-throbs and regret which thrill through the
melody of that pathetic song.

"Ah! Tennyson never had heard this sad, weird
poem when he gave the title 'Lord of Human
Tears' to Victor Hugo, or our own Longfellow
would have won it," said Miss Estill with a sigh.

12

"Yes; Longfellow is the poet that seems nearest
in all our moments of retrospection. I never stand
at the crossing of the old Santa Fe and Abilene
Trails, on that hill yonder, without his lines re-
curring,—

> 'Like an odor of brine from the ocean,
> Comes the thought of other years;'—

and I must tell you, Miss Estill, that whenever I
meet you I feel that same remembrance, vague and
evanescent, of a time when you and I were very
happy, and were all—at least we were very great
friends: But it is so shadowy and indistinct that I
can not grasp its meaning. It is like the memory
of some half-forgotten dream or the dim recollec-
tions of a former life," replied young Warlow, in a
low tone, as the pulsing waves of music, the "Blue
Danube," throbbed through the vines and lace curtains of the bay-window where they sat.

"If you were less thrifty, Mr. Warlow, I would
suspect you were too fond of poetry to be practical.
But I should not throw sarcastic stones at your glass
house, for it has been no longer than a month ago
that mamma scolded me roundly for forgetting the
yeast in my batch of light bread. I had to lay all the
blame at the 'open door' of the 'Moated Grange,'
which I had been reading. Poor Mariana might
well have said, after looking on my leaden loaves :—

> 'I am aweary, aweary,—
> I would that I were dead!'"

While Clifford was making some laughing reply
to this bucket of poetical cold water, he and Miss
Estill were summoned to the piano, where our young

friends were floundering hopelessly through the in-
tricacies of a glee, in which Grace's alto would persist
in getting all tangled up with Hugh's baritone, and
the cat-calls of Rob's bastard bass and Scott's
frantic tenor only served to heighten the confusion,
that finally collapsed in subdued shrieks of laughter.
But when Miss Estill's dainty fingers rippled over
the guitar, and their voices blended with varying
degrees of melody as its twanging notes mingled
with the mellow tones of the piano, then something
like harmony prevailed again. Yet she and Clifford
would still exchange amused glances whenever Rob
gave vent to a more pronounced caterwaul than
usual, or Scott's gosling tenor squawked a wild note
of alarm.

"Miss Estill, I am longing to hear you render
a Spanish solo; for I never can help the picture of
a Castilian maiden playing amid the courts of the
Alhambra, rising whenever you take the guitar,"
said young Warlow, in a low tone.

"My broken Spanish would soon dispel the illusion," she replied, with a soft blush; "but I will
give you, instead, a poor translation of a Mexican
song;" and in a voice rich with melody and feeling,
she sang: —

> "There blooms no rose upon the plain,
> But costs the night a thousand tears,"—

while the guitar rained a shower of soft-dripping
music, veined with a thrill of sadness. As her
bosom rose and fell with the sweet strains, the ruby
heart which clasped the ruff at her slender throat

flashed rays of crimson and rose in the stray sunbeams that glinted through the room.

Clifford remained rapt in a reverie as the
dreamy music, with a low minor ripple, died away,
and the listeners sat in silence a moment, paying a
mute tribute to the graceful singer who now was
idly toying with the guitar.

One white arm was half revealed by the wide-
flowing sleeve, with its fall of creamy lace; a clus-
ter of fuchsias drooped among the waves of her
hair, and the wide ruff gave a graceful finish to the
close-fitting riding-habit of black velvet which
she wore.

Young Warlow was aroused by his mother
saying : —

"Miss Estill, the colonel, my husband."

He turned quickly, and saw his father standing
in the doorway, staring as if he had seen a sheeted
ghost. Yes; it was undeniable that the courtly
and urbane colonel was positively staring with a
white face at the beautiful guest, and as he came
forward he said, in an agitated voice : —

"Ivarene? No — no — impossible! Pardon,
Miss Estill; but your face reminds me so strongly
of a dear, kind friend, 'who passed over the dark
river long years ago,' that I was quite unnerved;"
and as he held her slender hand he looked hungrily
into the blue eyes that were regarding him with a
look of shy wonder. When Hugh was presented,
the colonel glanced keenly from the blonde, hazel-
eyed young man back to the creole face of the young
lady, and he again murmured brokenly, and in an

incredulous tone, "Brother and sister? Strange—
mystery!" and in the hearts of that group for many
a day echoed and re-echoed his words: "Mystery,
mystery!"

A constraint seemed to fall immediately upon
the inmates of the room, and Maud, perceiving the
traces of social frost in the atmosphere, suggested
that they should take a look at her flowers; and
the guests rose and followed in a confused group
out into the flower-garden, that was surrounded
with a low stone wall.

The paths, which divided the small plat into
four subdivisions, were interrupted at their inter-
section by a circular path, where a succession of
terraces of the same figure rose to the height of half
a dozen feet, the whole forming a circular mound,
crowned by a tiny latticed arbor, which was reached
by a flight of white stone steps, flanked by vases
of the same alabaster-like material.

The terraces were sodded with the dainty, short
buffalo-grass, and each offset was planted with a
profusion of flowers, now beginning to unfold their
blossoms. This unique ornament was the work of
Clifford and Robbie, who had in their "idle" moments thus transformed the unsightly pile of earth,
which had resulted from excavating the cellar, into
a "hanging garden to please Maud," and she felt
justly proud of the compliments which the guests
bestowed on the attractive feature of her trim garden,
with its wealth of lilies, roses, and gladioluses.

Although the group had emerged from the house
in a confused manner, it was remarkable how soon

order was restored, and the young people paired off into couples after the law of affinity—Maud and Ralph, Grace and Hugh, leaving Clifford and Miss Estill to either mate with Rob and Scott, or to choose each other for partners in the ramble; and it is also strange how quickly they chose the latter alternative, and sauntered away with appalling *sang-froid*, leaving those youths to their own resources without even the ghost of an apology. But the youngsters had ample revenge for this heartless, cold neglect, when, a few moments later, Rob was seen leaning on Scott's arm in a languishing manner, with a hollyhock perched daintily just above his nose, in semblance of a most coquettish hat, his bob-tailed coat embellished with an ·enormous petticoat of rhubarb-leaves, while Scott alternately cast admiring glances upon his frail "lady," or fanned the mock beauty with a catalpa-leaf fully half a yard broad.

And while Maud and Grace regarded their manœuvres with furtive scorn and ill-concealed disgust, this precious pair sauntered conspicuously after their friends, who could see "Miss Rob" mince along with exaggerated airs and graces, often pausing to sniff of the enormous water-pot, carried in imitation of a lady's scent-bottle.

Finally the party eluded the persecution of this devoted couple by going back into the house, and ascending to the "Crows' Nest" in the top of the old elm; and as Maud recounted the thrilling adventure of the "flood," she felt certain that Rob was too well acquainted with his paternal discipline

to venture upon any nonsense about the house. But
half an hour later, as they were strolling down to
the boat, the party, in turning an abrupt curve
in the path, surprised the infatuated Scott on his
knees kissing the hand of the shy he-damsel, who,
with affected modesty, was hiding her face in the
dainty fan and the last view our friends caught of
them while rowing up the river, the fascinating Rob
was sinking into the outstretched arms of his osten-
tatious lover.

Clifford rowed up the winding stream, which,
although only a few feet deep, was here several
rods in width. As they passed along, an old beaver,
which had built a dam below, stuck its snout up
through the tangled grass that trailed into the water;
then, after gazing a moment at the intruders, it
sank quietly from sight.

The pleasant ride suggested a boating song, and
a concert followed, which scared many a gray old
musk-rat to his den, and the frightened wild-fowls
scurried with whizzing wings out from the dark,
sedgy nooks, shaded by the elms and willows, as
the unwonted sounds floated out over the water.

Our friends walked up to Clifford's dwelling,
after landing and mooring the boat to a tree, and
while they rested on the pale ashen-green buffalo-
grass in the shadow of a mighty elm that smothered the gables of the stone cottage with its wide-
spread branches, Clifford pointed out the stone wall,
which was half concealed by the vines, where his
father had so narrowly escaped death a quarter of
a century before; and as they sat, he told of the

terrible tragedy that had here been enacted, which explained why Maud had so tenderly trained the roses over the ruined wall—the wall that had sheltered their father on that tragic night.

At the close of the mournful story Miss Estill exclaimed:—

· "Oh, what a cruel fate. Poor, ill-starred Ivarene! It was that unfortunate bride that I so strangely resemble. But how mysterious that it should be so! Now I do not wonder at your father's agitation at meeting one who reminded him of his lost friend and benefactress. That was why he gazed so pathetically into my eyes:—I recalled the days of his youth, his lost fortune, and the tragic fate of his dear friends."

Hugh Estill said :—

"Oh, this is not the first time I have heard the particulars of that tragedy. It was often talked of in the days of my boyhood; but I was a child at the time when it was still fresh in the memory of the few settlers in the upper valley of the Cottonwood. It was fully ten years after the event that I heard the version from one of our herders, who said it was whispered that white men were engaged in the massacre. Father was unnecessarily irritated, I thought, when I repeated what the fellow said, and he went so far as to discharge him, and forbade me ever mentioning the subject again."

"Your parents were living on your ranch at that time?" said Clifford, in a strange eager tone of inquiry.

"Yes; we have lived on the same place for the

past twenty-seven years, and both Mora and myself were born on the old ranch," replied Hugh.

After remaining rapt in silence a moment, Miss Estill said, as she and Clifford stood apart from the others, while he stooped to gather a spray of the sensitive-plant :—

"What is this strange, haunting sense of danger and grief that always assails me on this spot? It is like the dim remembrance of some tragic event connected with my own life—a half-forgotten nightmare, as it were—the very elusiveness of which is distressing to me. I feel that same sensation now which I mentioned having always felt on this spot, when you told me how strangely you were affected when passing Antelope Butte."

"I often experience that peculiar sentiment here, also, Miss Estill,—a kind of perception or impression of some dire calamity with which not only myself, but you likewise, have been connected here," Clifford replied with troubled face.

"I am afraid we shall mould if we stay in this gloomy shade any longer," cried Grace, springing up with a little shiver; but the bright look which young Estill beamed upon her showed plainly that he, at least, was in no danger of such a blighting fate.

It was a beautiful scene that burst upon their view as they emerged from under the low, sweeping boughs, and stood in the sunlight south of the gothic cottage. Around the knoll, on which they were standing, purled and gurgled the stream, fringed by feathery willows and stately elms, and, after half embracing the hill in its tortuous folds, winding away down the widening valley. Where the timber, which skirted the serpentine river, grew in groves of deepest green, there the stream had expanded into placid lakelets, which flashed like silver in the slanting sunbeams.

On the south, in the smooth, level valley, were fields of ripening grain,—wheat of coppery red or creamy gold, silvery sheen of rye and oats, set in a frame of emerald where the wild prairies came sheer up to the clear-cut fields, that were *innocent* of fence or hedge. Then their vision roamed out to the north, where the rolling hills melted away on the dim horizon.

As they stood silently gazing on the tranquil landscape, the bell in the latticed belfry of the Warlow homestead rang out in mellow clang, and Maud said :—

"Let's return, for it is the supper-bell. I do hope, though, that mother has prepared something more substantial for her guests than Clifford has done for us this afternoon."

"Why, have we not reveled in mystery?" cried Grace.

"And feasted on landscape?" said Miss Estill.

"And did he not hospitably entertain us with legend, mellow and old?" chimed Ralph.

"Sorry that I could not have treated you to fresher puns," retorted Clifford, laughingly.

On rowing down the tranquil stream, and coming once more into the shady yard of the Warlows, our young friends found the tea-table spread under the boughs of the ever-serviceable elm, and Rob and Scott busy assisting Mrs. Warlow with the evening meal.

As with deft fingers Maud culled choice bouquets from her garden, and decked the table, she felt a thrill of pardonable pride in the snowy damask, the crystal and silver that glittered with the polish of good housewifery, and the tempting, dainty dishes which her mother had, with true Western hospitality, prepared in honor of the guests.

Ah, hungry reader, I wish that you could have been there also; for my mouth vainly waters, even yet, at the remembrance of asparagus and green peas, spring-chicken smothered in cream (which I hasten to explain was not the fowl of boarding-house memory and tradition, with which the frosts of December had " monkeyed;" no barn-yard champion was it, with cotton-like breast and sinewy limb, but a tender daughter of the May-time, that had perished on the threshold of a bright young pullethood), and frosty lemon-pie, just tinged with bronze, flanked by the crimson moulds of . plum-jelly.

An hour later, in the gloomy twilight, as the guests were taking leave, Miss Estill said:—

"Your son has told me of the old tragedy that has saddened your life, Colonel; but it is very strange that I should resemble that ill-fated Mexican bride."

"Ah, Miss Estill, every hour you recall the memory of my lost friends; just such a daughter might have blessed them, *if they had lived*," he replied, with a sigh, as he searched the young face with his wistful blue eyes.

"It is only a chance resemblance, of course—a mere coincidence," she replied, in a tone of uneasiness. "My parents were living here at the time of the massacre; but I never have heard of the dreadful occurrence until to-day," she added.

"I would like very much to meet your father, and talk over the early history of this country," said the colonel, eagerly. "I sometimes find myself hoping that they might have escaped," he continued, in a half-musing tone, like one whose mind is wholly engrossed by an overmastering subject. She overlooked his incoherence, knowing well that he referred to Bruce and Ivarene. "Since I have been here on the scene of the tragedy, the thought often recurs that I took it for granted that they perished, and have trusted too readily to circumstantial evidence in confirmation of that belief."

"How strange it is that no trace of that enormous treasure of gold and gems was ever obtained!" she replied. "But, then, the horde of Cheyennes, which Hugh said to-day were reported as having been led by white men, found it an easy task enough, no doubt, to carry away even that great amount of coin after their murderous work."

"Ah! it is all a strange, dark mystery," he replied; "and to-day it is more impenetrable than ever. But if I could see your father he might remember."

Here the colonel paused abruptly, and threw up one hand with an involuntary start, and Miss Estill saw by the faint light that he was ashen pale. But as the others were now passing out through the gate, she reluctantly shook hands with the colonel, who, she saw, was trembling with repressed emotion; and then she took leave of the other members of the family, vaguely wondering why the courtly old gentleman should be so affected by events which had occurred more than a quarter of a century before.

When, an hour later, Clifford returned from Squire Moreland's, whither he had accompanied Miss Estill, he was accosted by Rob in the following vein:—

"What's up, Cliff?"

"Up where?" replied his brother, evasively.

"On the porch, if you have eyes for anything less attractive than a young lady with a mop of blue hair," said the indignant Rob.

"Oh—father and mother! Why, I can't see anything strange in our parents sitting on the porch," replied his brother, in a tone of feigned indifference.

"Well, but they have had their heads together and been plotting for an hour; but Maud keeps up such an everlasting racket with her singing and dish-clattering that I can't hear a word they say. That girl positively is noisier than a fire-engine. Now, just listen at that!" as Maud's voice sang in sweet crescendo:—

"Stars are shining, Mollie darling." (Crash, rattle.)

Mrs. Warlow.—"Do you think it possible that they were saved?"

Maud (diminuendo).—

"Through the mystic veil of night." (Rinkety-clink.)

Colonel.—"She may be their daughter, who survived." (Splatter.)

Maud (piano).—

"No one listens but the flowers,
  As they hang their heads in shame." (Klinkety-klink.)

Rob.—

  "Yes, Miss Maud, you noisy magpie.
    I hang ditto and the same."

Clifford.—"If you do n't keep quiet, I 'll—" (Klutter-terattle-tering.)

Coffee-mill, etc.—"Kr-rrrrr-r-rrr (Mollie) r-r-r (dar) rrrr-r-rrrr."

Colonel.—"She is the very image of Ivarene; and I am almost converted to Bruce's strange creed when I see them."

Maud (at the well).—"Ke-pump, ke-pump, ke-pump!"

Colonel.—"I saw them together to-day. I was perfectly bewildered; for they are the very picture of Bruce and Ivarene on their wedding-day."

Maud.—

  "Mollie, fairest, sweetest, dearest!
    Look up, darling, tell me this—"

Rob.—

  "Miss Maud Warlow, you 're a bull-frog,
    And I 'd like to have a hook in your nose."

But, as his rhyme ended with such an ignominious fizzle, he hurried away with a snort of disgust.

Clifford lingered a moment, hoping to hear more; but his parents rose soon after, and entered the house; so, in a thoughtful mood, he went about his farm duties.

Out in the wheat a quail called "Bob White," while down in the pasture a flock of prairie-chickens or grouse disturbed the twilight calm with their melancholy "ku-boom;" but, as the evening faded into night, the quiet of early slumber brooded over the Warlow household.

Chapter XII.

THE week which followed brought sad tidings to the Warlow family. A black-bordered letter came, bearing the post-mark of San Francisco; but before it was opened the family knew its import.

Mrs. Warlow's only brother, William, had been in the mines for several years, but since his health had failed he had been making the great coast city his home; and, although grieved at the announcement of his death, they were not unprepared for the sad news.

The lawyer wrote that he held a few thousand dollars of the deceased's money, which was left by the will to Mrs. Warlow, and they were also informed that the "Redwood" mine was left to Robbie, who was a great favorite with his uncle; but this latter property was as yet unproductive, though the attorney conveyed an intimation that it might some day prove very valuable, as there were mines of fabulous richness near by.

Soon the rumor went flying through the colony that the Warlows had fallen heirs to an immense estate, and as usual the report lost nothing by traveling; so our friends soon found themselves invested by the halo of riches without any of its substantial benefits.

Speculations and conjectures were rife among the

neighbors as to the " best manner of investing their friend Warlow's fortune ;" and, in fact, it became impossible for any member of the colonel's family to meet an acquaintance without being informed of some great opening for a judicious investment, that was only waiting capital and enterprise to develop the fact that there was " millions in it."

As Clifford paused one day to discuss the state of the weather in a neighborly way with a male member of this well-meaning but misguided class, he learned that all the vast tract of vacant land to the north, which still belonged to the government, had been condemned as being " unfit for agricultural purposes," and would be " offered " at public sale the following August at the local land-office.

When young Warlow parted with his informant the matter was dismissed ; but whenever he glanced away to the north or east at the billowy hills and level, rich dales, he would begin planning how he could secure a tract of the land before it passed into the hands of relentless speculators ; and one day he actually rode out over the fertile, picturesque country for miles, and with a blush found himself dreaming how that long, narrow valley should be sown to grain, and the galloping hills, clothed with rich grasses, could provide pasturage for his vast, imaginary flocks and herds.

Alas, that the lack of a few handfuls of " filthy lucre" only, stood between himself and the ownership of the broad acres on every hand ! With a dreary sigh he realized, for the first time in his life, how bitter is the lot of the poor but ambitious man,

13

who sees the avenues to wealth barred by his lack of capital.

As he stood on the spot where his father had lost his fortune so many years before, Clifford thought how many hundred thousand acres of that rolling, fertile country the lost wealth represented; and while his horse grazed quietly near, the youth threw himself down in the cool shadow of the ruined wall, dreaming and planning how he might recover the vast wealth that he had long suspected was buried here near the scene of the tragedy.

But when he calmly began to analyze the evidence on which his suspicions were based, he was disappointed to see how visionary it all seemed in the clear light of reason. But it was too dear and cherished a theory to be relinquished without a mental struggle; so again he began to persuade himself that those scheming white men, of whom young Estill had spoken—those inhuman villains—might have secreted the gold from the drunken Indians, and it might have been that the blood-stained, avaricious leaders had died a violent death in those turbulent days, and the great wealth was still sleeping, undisturbed, all these years, while his father was suffering under the heavy load of poverty and fallen fortune. As Clifford still mused, there flashed across his mind the lines of Rokeby:—

"Then dig and tomb your precious heap,
   And bid the dead your treasure keep."

Springing to his feet, young Warlow cried aloud in his excitement:—

"Ah! it is all clear now—the blood on the grass

and the newly made graves, of which Uncle Roger spoke! Yes, yes—they buried the dead and the gold in the same grave, and then decoyed the savages away! It may be that those bright doubloons, the red gold of the Walravens and my father, are buried but a few steps from where I stand."

Flinging aside doubt and uncertainty, he hurried down the hill to the spot where his father had said the treasure-laden vehicle had stood on that fatal night, and long and eagerly young Warlow searched for a trace of the graves. But it was all in vain; for the vast tide of travel that had flowed for a quarter of a century over the spot had not only obliterated all trace of those lowly mounds, but had also worn the mellow soil into deep gullies, down the sloping sides of which the knotted buffalo-grass crept like webs of pale-green lace.

In the old trail, where once the cannon of Phil Kearney had rumbled, as with his army he hurried forward to Santa Fe, and along where Coronado, Lee, Fremont, and Kit Carson had ridden, now the wild mignonette, in spikes of purple, fragrant blossoms, grew, loading the sultry air with their rich odors. The sensitive-rose, its fern-like foliage tufted with rosy balls of gold-flecked down, closed its leaves as Clifford hurriedly brushed by; but in the tangled thickets of wild indigo, now blooming in sprays of violet and creamy flowers, or among the tall, lush, blue stem-grass the young "fortune hunter" found no traces of the lost wealth—no sunken graves were visible to tell of that tragedy

of long ago; so it was with a slow step and feeling
of despondency that our friend sought the shelter
of his latticed porch.

While he sat, lost in speculation as to the best
method of prosecuting his search, which he was too
resolute to give up easily, his eyes rested on an im-
plement that at a glance showed its adaptability for
the very purpose. It was a long rod of iron, tipped
with twisted steel. ᐧ He remembered having had it
made the year before for the men who were searching
for a vein of water before sinking his wells. As he
seized it eagerly, and started once again down the
hill, he felt gratified and elated to perceive how
easily he could now test the earth to the depth of
five feet, and ascertain if there was any foreign sub-
stance in the mellow, loamy soil, which throughout
the valley was a bed of rich, black loam, entirely
free from stone or boulders.

He had but reached the spot near the river,
when he saw his father riding through the wheat-
field toward where our young schemer stood; and
hastily tossing the iron rod into a thicket, Clifford
met his father with an assumption of careless indifference; for all his allusions in the past to the
lost fortune had only met with the sarcastic disap-
proval of his parent, who, being an intensely practical man himself, could not tolerate any thing so
visionary as a search for the treasure seemed to be;
and young Warlow had decided to keep his investigations secret, thus avoiding the censure and ridicule of the colonel. After a brief discussion in

regard to the condition of the ripening grain, Clifford remarked: —

"It seems very strange, father, that no trace can be found of those graves which Uncle Roger mentioned having seen near the Old Corral, when he found you after the robbery and massacre."

"This is too busy a time for us to speculate on the past, my boy. The wheat has ripened splendidly—I never saw a field to equal that valley yonder—and we will have to start the header tomorrow; so if you will ride out on to the Flats and engage three more teams, I will go down to Squire Moreland's and tell them we shall begin early in the morning," said the colonel.

"But, father, first tell me as nearly as possible where those graves were located; for I have a strange curiosity regarding them of late. It must be near this very spot?"

"Yes, yes; near that old cottonwood-tree, or on the level space of sod just this side. But Clifford," continued he in a tone of suspicion quite foreign to the kindly colonel, "what nonsense are you meditating now? You are not still counting on that lost fortune?"

"Well, father, there has been a growing belief in my mind of late that the treasure is secreted near here. Think how impossible it would have been for a leader of such a band as those savages were, to divide the booty satisfactorily among the pack of drunken monsters. If the leader had the acumen that I believe he possessed, he, no doubt, buried the gold, at least, in one of those graves while the others were stupefied by the liquor; and there is a chance that he may never have returned, owing to the dangers to which such turbulent villains are always exposed. I have thought this over carefully, until at last I am convinced—"

"That your father has a damned fool for a son!" broke in the colonel hotly, as he rode away.

After supper Clifford said he would go up to his house and spend the night—an announcement which caused no surprise, as he frequently stayed there; but on this occasion Robbie remarked to Maud: —

"Cliff must be *schooling his courage* by staying of nights up at that old spook-ranch; but a fellow who can stand that, could pop the question to the witch of Macbeth without faltering."

"What do you mean by his popping the question, Rob?" said Maud, setting her pail of foamy milk down on the cellar-steps, while she regarded the handsome youth with a puzzled look from her round, blue eyes.

"Why just this," he replied, after "swigging" down a pint of fresh milk from his own pail, and deliberately wiping his lips with his shirt-sleeve; "Cliff has got more sand in his gizzard than most fellows; but I guess he feels too poor, or something, to talk *marry* to Mora Estill, so he goes mooning off up there to that old spectre's nest—just like fellows do in novels, you know," he added, lucidly.

But here the peremptory tones of his father called the young philosopher to take the colts down to the lower pasture.

When Clifford arrived at his dwelling he prepared several stakes, and fastened bits of white
paper to their tops ; then, securing the iron rod, he
placed it with the small sticks, which he had left
in the porch, and sought the dainty and comfortable bed which he owed to the thoughtful kindness
of Maud and his mother.

Sinking into a profound slumber, he was only
awakened by the alarm which sounded as the clock
struck one. As its chime died away, he arose and
stole forth into the tranquil night.

A waning moon had risen, and in its faint light
the water of the brook glimmered coldly as it wim-
pled over the stony ford. The fluttering leaves of
the old cottonwood flashed like silver, and the
hoary form of the great tree, every limb of which
seemed outlined in white, towered vague and
ghostly above the shadows cast by the more dense
foliage of ash and willows.

Clifford paused in the level glade where his
father had said the graves must have been when
Roger Coble passed the spot twenty-six years before. Thrusting the rod deep into the soft, loamy
soil, young Warlow threw his whole weight on the
instrument, which penetrated to the depth of several feet with little difficulty. On meeting with no
obstruction, he withdrew the rod; and after marking the spot with one of the stakes which he had
provided, he began again to prosecute the search
one step further south.

The precaution of marking the place where he
had sunk the rod was for the purpose of system-

atizing the search, thus avoiding confusion. In fact, these careful details were but an indication of the practical nature of the young Fortune Hunter, which, even on this weird night, strongly asserted its sway.

While the leaves murmured and whispered, as if striving to tell of the tragedies that had marred this spot—of the mystery that seemed to haunt the very air around—Clifford still pursued his investigations, patiently and in silence, only pausing to draw a deeper breath or a sigh of disappointment at each fruitless effort, as he toiled onward into the deep shadows near the bank of the stream.

At length, tired and weary, our young friend stood on the verge of the stream over the bank of which the dank grass trailed, and the rank vine of the wild-gourd, with its silvery leaves, rioted in wildest luxuriance and profusion.

Glancing up through the branches of the hoary old cottonwood, he could see the glittering constellation of Scorpio far out on the south-western horizon, the fiery star Antares, which forms its heart, glowing like a ruby in the blue vault of heaven.

For a moment Clifford rested on the handle of the deep-sunken instrument, and, lifting his heavy felt hat with its leathern band—a badge of the ranchman throughout all the West—he drew a deep breath of the cool air that swayed the wild hop-vines and pendulous branches of the willows to and fro in the moonlight.

Around, a thousand wild-flowers distilled their

odors. The sensitive-plant nodded softly in dew-drenched sprays, its rosy balls flecked with drops that glinted like gems, while all the air was heavy with its perfume of spices and honey.

The foamy elder-blooms exhaled an odor of entrancing sweetness, and over the senses stole the fragrance from pond-lilies and water-mint, wild-hyacinths and mignonette.

A large prairie-owl flitted by, lending a note of discord to the tranquillity which had reigned, with its dismal hoot, that mellowed away into a plaintive shriek as it lit in some far-off, sombre nook.

Then again silence brooded over the valley, broken only by the croak of frogs along the rush-lined shore, or the soft chirp of insects in the grass; but suddenly the jabbering wail of a lone wolf, distant yet distinct, pierced through the gloom, startling into silence all the minor voices of the night, and adding with its wild echoes a double sense of loneliness to the weird night.

Clifford turned to the iron rod, and with a few vigorous efforts sent it deep into the yielding earth; and as the quiet of nature once more reigned over the wild glade, he kept turning the handle mechanically, and listening to the gruesome sound of the answering wolves—faint cries that made him shudder—when, lo! the steel point grated harshly against some obstruction beneath his feet.

Quickly withdrawing the rod, he seized the sharp spade and began digging, throwing the black soil out of the pit with frantic haste as he sank rapidly down into the earth at each stroke. As he neared the goal he became dizzy and faint, his breath coming in quick gasps, and the blinding sweat streaming from his face, from which it fell in great drops like rain.

Pausing a moment, while the weird, horned moon peered through a rift in the boughs over-head, and gleamed coldly on his upturned, haggard face, he thought of the wealth that might lie be-low,—his father's lost fortune; the wealth of Mon-teluma; its gems and red gold, with all the power that great treasure represented; then, quivering with excitement, he dashed the spade into the earth, and in a moment more the head of a cask was dimly outlined at his feet.

Breathless and panting, he paused, leaning on his spade, while the hopes and fears, which so often, often, assail us on the threshold of some great enterprise, came thronging on with their mockery, causing him to stand irresolute, as if fearing to solve the mystery; but at length, after summoning all his strength, he struck the cask with his sharp spade, and the head fell in with a dull crash.

As he stooped to peer down into the gloom below, a pair of fiery eyes glared at him from the cavity, and, as he sprang back with a shudder, a sharp, whizzing rattle in the cask announced the presence of that dread reptile, the rattlesnake—a new and terrible danger, worse than the sting of poverty with all its terrors.

As Clifford stood frozen with horror, the slimy

monster rose from out the cask, still sounding its angry alarm. A moment more, enraged and writh- ing, it coiled at his feet, its head erected, slowly swaying to and fro—a gigantic, threatening monster.

Its eyes glowed like coals of fire, and in the bright light shed by the lantern Clifford could see it darting its tongue and glaring with a look of indescribable ferocity and malignant hatred, to which nothing else in the world can be compared. Those who have faced an angry rattlesnake, and who still turn pale at its remembrance, or start from sleep with a cry of fear at the returning vision of terrible danger, will recall the awful rage and menace that glared from the eye of the angry serpent—a glance that unnerves the bravest man in the world instantly. The reptile only seemed to await a motion on Clifford's part to strike like a flash of lightning. Then, with a clammy shudder, young Warlow thought of the agony and speedy death that was certain to follow. At the tremor which involuntarily shook his frame at the thought, the hideous serpent crested its head and paused in its vibrations. "Now all is over," our young friend thought, and breathlessly awaited the shock.

Instantly the face of Mora Estill rose before him, a fleeting vision of loveliness; and with it came a realization of the love for her that had rapidly grown into an all-absorbing passion in their short acquaintance. He knew at once what had sent him out on this midnight search, and why he had begun to wish for wealth so eagerly of late:—

It was because he craved fortune and a position which would equal that of the "Cattle King's" daughter. Yet even in this moment of deadliest peril he thought, with a grim smile, of the irony of fate—the reward of his first attempt at "fortune hunting."

While death stared at him from those glaring eyes, and the moments seemed to lengthen out to years, he thought of his friends at home, all unconscious of the dire fate that he was facing; then a wild longing for life seized him, and for the first time since the encounter he began to plan a way of escape.

The spade on which his hand rested was sharp and bright; but to raise it before the serpent could strike he knew was impossible; so he stood immovably eying the formidable reptile, which at length slowly uncoiled and glided away from his feet to an opposite corner of the pit. With a sigh of relief Clifford saw that the danger was lessened, yet he began to more fully realize the size of his deadly antagonist, which now reached twice across the yard-wide pit.

In moments of great danger we are apt to think with lightning-like rapidity, and quickly see any advantage that may arise. So it was with Clifford, who remembered that the rattlesnake always throws itself into a coil before striking; and as he saw it thus off its guard, with a quick movement he struck a violent blow at the snake's head and pinioned it to the earth—then throwing his full weight on the handle he felt the bones crunch beneath the sharp blade, while the reptile madly threshed its now headless body about and wrapped its jangling tail around his boot.

Springing out of the pit, with a desperate leap, young Warlow disengaged the writhing, heavy monster from his foot, and with the iron rod threw it away into the grass; then sinking down upon the ground, unnerved and exhausted, he lay, too weak to move for several minutes. But when he remembered the unexplored cask, he sprang to his feet again, and after listening cautiously a moment, and hearing no further evidence of danger, he dropped lightly down into the pit, carelessly tramping on the grim serpent-head that but a few moments before was so full of threatening danger.

Anxiously he thrust the long rod down into the cask. No rattle responded; but the despairing fact became apparent: the cask was empty!

With a sinking heart he groped about the bottom of the cask with the rod, and when its iron point struck against a round object that rolled over with a harsh sound on the bottom, he quickly thought of the casket of gems, and reaching down, with a thrill of excitement he clutched the mysterious, smooth object, and sprang out of the pit into the moonlight.

By the pale beams of the gibbous moon, now sinking low in the western sky, but throwing a path of shimmering silver on the bosom of the rippling brook, he saw—not the gems of Monteluma, but a human skull, that, with its wide, eyeless sockets, seemed to glare derisively, and with great white teeth laugh mockingly, at this ending of his "fortune hunting." With a cry of despair, the disheartened youth dashed the loathsome object to the earth; but, as if the sound of his voice had evoked its former spirit, there glided from out the wavering shadows a tall, gaunt form, gray-robed and silent, with tangled, flowing hair, and burning eyes, its lips drawn back from its snaggled fangs in a horrid look of hate and ferocity. With noiseless tread it seemed to float into the moonlit space; then snatching the skull from the ground and clasping it close to its breast, with an unearthly scream it faded away among the whispering willows.

Chapter XIII.

ON the morning following that Walpurga Night, Clifford came down to the Warlow breakfast-table with a weary, feverish air, that caused his father to say:—

"My boy, you are far from well, I fear! This first day of harvest will be quite hard on all of us; the day promises to be hot and sultry; so perhaps you had better rest in-doors. We might send Robbie over on the Flats, and secure you a substitute until you are stronger."

At this poor Rob mumbled something about "a sixteen-year-old boy having more legs than a centipede;" a remark which he was careful to address to his plate, however, while Clifford replied:—

"Oh no, father; a cup of Maud's coffee will set me all right, I am certain." Then, as he poured a quantity of yellow cream into the cup of fragrant Rio, he added: "I was wakeful and did not rest well last night;" all of which we know was correct, if somewhat evasive.

"Oh, Cliff! I had the most terrifying dreams last night, in which you were, some way, always mixed up," said Maud wearily; "and although I can't remember anything distinctly, I am so nervous that I shiver even yet."

"So, madam, you feed the hungry harvester on Cold Shudder, garnished with scrambled Night-

mare," said Rob, with a glance of contempt at the
bacon and early potatoes, of which even his rav-
enous appetite was now weary. Then, as he broke
an egg that was shockingly overdone, he added
spitefully: "Why did you *boil* your door-knobs?"

"I spent a weary, restless night, also," said Mrs.
Warlow, ignoring Robbie's sarcasm. "I was so
vaguely uneasy about you, Clifford, that I shall
object to your staying alone at the corral hereafter."

"Alone, nothing!" said Rob. "I guess, by the
way he goes fishing about of late, he will soon find
some one to keep him company," he added, with a
knowing giggle, at which Clifford tried to look un-
concerned, while Maud and her mother exchanged
pleased and amused glances.

After breakfast Clifford drove the header to the
wheat-field, which soon presented an animated and
busy scene. The great machine was pushed by
four horses, which were guided by young Warlow,
who stood behind on a small platform, and steered
the ponderous reaper with one hand, while with
the other he held the lines. The elevator carried
the heads of wheat into a large wagon, which ran,
barge-like, beside where a busy loader arranged
the load, until, towering like a hay-stack, the
wagon would hold no more. Then it was driven
away to the rick-yard by the careful driver, being
succeeded by another team with military precision.
The flapping of the canvas elevator, and the rolling waves of wheat, rippled and tossed by the
summer breeze, made a scene that recalled a sail on
the sea; all of which was as gratifying to Clifford's

sense of the picturesque as the prospect for gain was encouraging.

When the evening came twenty acres of the heavy grain was stacked in six trim ricks at the edge of the field. A square of golden straw remained standing, to be either burned at the end of harvest, or turned under by the plows to further enrich the soil. Ten more days of such labor would be necessary, however, to finish the Warlow harvest, and no doubt long before that time the picturesque side of the operation will be appreciated best by those who view it at a safe distance.

In the cool twilight Clifford and Rob were riding homeward, the former silent and abstracted, while the latter was calling "Bob White" to a badly-deceived quail, that answered back from the stubble-field. Finally, becoming tired of this, Rob turned a shrewd but freckled face to his brother, and said:—

"What was the matter up there last night, Cliff? You have been grim as an old mummy all day! I bet my boots *you* saw something *too*; so out with it."

"Why have you seen anything strange up there recently, Rob?" Clifford replied, evasively.

"Now, do n't give it away, Cliff, for the folks would raise an awful racket if they found it out; but last week I saw that old gray demon—of the camp-fire, you remember—by the corral. I was riding Pomp and driving the cows home through the dusk, when, as I came along by the old stone wall there, out popped that long-haired spook, and

glared at me like old Nick. Good Lord, Harry!
but I dug out of that, my hair bristling up mad-
dog style, and Pomp wringing his tail till it
cracked like a whip-lash," he concluded, with a
scared laugh.

".Well, I saw him, too, at the same place last
night," said Clifford, in a low tone as several
harvesters came up. "But let's keep the matter
secret, Rob; for it will never do to let the neighbors know it, and be ridiculed for our superstition.
Then it would only make mother and Maud uneasy. So let's watch and say nothing until we have
unraveled the mystery."

In the evening Clifford was starting up to his
dwelling, on the plea that the house at home was
crowded with the workmen; but Rob insisted on
going along and sharing the watch, which on this
and the succeeding evening was unsuccessful, for
no trace of the ghostly visitant was found. As
Clifford had quite enough of "fortune hunting"
the night of his first experience, he made no further
investigations for the recovery of the treasure.

The following Sabbath, which was the second
after the Estill visit, the younger members of the
Moreland and Warlow families drove down to the
Estill ranch. As they dashed up to the great pile
of creamy stone buildings, smothered in elms and
sheltered on the north by towering, tree-clad cliffs,
our young friends noticed with wonder the signs
of age which the vine-mantled and time-stained
building presented.

It was a well-dressed, animated group that

alighted from the handsome Warlow carriage,—
Maud in gray silk and dotted tulle; Grace in a
"Dolly Varden" costume, with her broad, white
hat wreathed by daisies; Ralph in superfine black,
with lawn tie and white vest, his handsome face
ruddy with health and happy contentment; Scott,
quiet and thoughtful, in Puritan-gray; while Rob
gloried in the splendor of spotless white, his small,
well-shaped boots glittering like jet. He had given
just enough cock to his jaunty straw hat to correspond well with the general air of pertness conveyed by a slightly freckled nose, dimpled cheeks,
dusky with tan, and a pair of round, hazel eyes, that
always danced with fun. But it was golden-haired,
pansy-eyed Clifford, with his Grecian face, smooth,
glossy cheeks, tinged with bronze, but fresh and
boyish still, who would rivet the gaze longest;
for there was a look of pride and strength about
him which caused one to forget the *boutonnière*
of fescue and lobelia, blue as his own eyes, and the
rich-textured suit of seal-brown, which he wore
with the easy grace of a planter's son.

The long frontage of the stately mansion was
broken by gables, balconies, and quaint dormer windows, and on the broad platform, or terrace, in front
of the building a fountain flashed in the sunlight.
The terrace was walled with creamy stone, and
railed about by a heavy balustrade of white magnesian limestone. In the angles and at the top of
the steps were great vases of the same alabaster-
like material, down the sculptured sides of which

trailed tangled masses of vines with their blossoms, scarlet, gold, and blue.

As our friends drove up, they saw Miss Estill sitting on the buffalo-grass which coated the lawn with its thick carpet of pale green. She appeared to be twining a garland of flowers about the neck of a pet antelope, as it stood with its head on her shoulder in an attitude of docile affection.

As the young lady arose to greet the guests, the graceful animal bounded away to the shrubbery, where, after peeping a moment with shy wonder at the new-comers, it skurried off to the top of the cliff behind the dwelling, snorting and stamping its foot angrily at the intrusion.

After greeting her friends cordially, Miss Estill led the way through a tessellated hall, where the walls were frescoed and hung with elegant paintings, past the winding stairs of dark, rich wood, and to a cool, long room to the east, the floor of which was covered with India matting, swept by the lace curtains that shaded the lofty windows from the fierce sunlight. An air of quiet refinement and simple luxury pervaded this apartment, which spoke volumes, in a mute way—all very favorable to the Estill family.

When Mrs. Estill came into the room, Mora presented her new friends, who were charmed by the elder lady's welcome; but when Clifford was introduced she gave him a swift, searching glance from her keen, blue eyes, that brought a flush to his face at her look of scrutiny and valuation. She must have read him aright, however, for she gave her hand to young Warlow in a very friendly way, and he thought he detected a subtone of graciousness in her welcome to himself a shade deeper than when she had addressed the others.

Mrs. Estill was a fair, dignified matron, whose flaxen hair was now slightly tinged with gray; but as Clifford contrasted the creole daughter with her, he failed to detect any resemblance between the two.

The elder lady must have divined his thoughts, or observed his look of wonder at the strange dissimilarity existing between herself and her only daughter, for she appeared to be embarrassed and constrained in her attempts at entertaining the guests; but Mora was so animated and vivacious that her mother's disquiet was unnoticed by all save Clifford, who vaguely wondered at this show of uneasiness over such a trifle; yet he had occasion before many weeks had elapsed to recall it all with a strange significance.

When Mr. Estill came in, and Mora had presented her new friends, the ruddy, genial old ranchman said with a smile:—

"Now this is something like civilized life once more! Why, it does my very soul good to see young company about the old ranch—a sight that is as rare as it is pleasant. I almost fancy myself back in the old home again."

The visitors were soon chatting gaily with the courtly and entertaining host, who proved to be a typical ranchman of the plains,—shrewd through long dealings with a business class noted for sagacity and wealth; urbane and refined in manner by hav-

ing been thrown among bankers and the leading
men of the city for many years; and lastly, hospitable, possibly owing to the fact that his hospitality
had never been overtaxed nor abused in that thinly
settled country.

"Where could this creole daughter have sprung
from? She looks as if she might have stepped out of
the Alhambra into this family of blonde Saxons," said
Clifford mentally, again contrasting Mora and her
parents; and while he noted the auburn hair, just
tinged with gray, of Mr. Estill, and the blue eyes
of that courtly old gentleman, the contrast with the
creole daughter became so apparent that Clifford
must have betrayed his surprise, for he was soon
aware that Mrs. Estill was regarding him with an
uneasy expression which only served to increase his
perplexity. "There is a skeleton in the domestic
closet at Estill's ranch," thought our young friend;
"but what can the mystery be?"

His speculations were cut short, however, by
Mr. Estill saying that all the cow-boys were away
with Hugh, shipping a "bunch of steers,"—omit-
ting the fact that the modest "bunch" consisted of
two long train-loads of sleek, fat beeves, and that
the duties of hostler devolved upon himself in their
absence.

The young men thereupon arose and left the
room with their host, who, after the manner of
Western people, believed in the maxim, "Love me,
love my dog," which finds expression in the care
lavished upon the horses of a welcome guest. This
spirit often leads to a foundered nag, however; but

it would be a very ungrateful man, indeed, who would grumble at such an evidence of esteem.

As they left the room to care for Clifford's team, Mora invited Maud and Grace up to her boudoir, which, she said, was so seldom visited that the spiders were more at home there than herself.

"You know about how much 'elegant leisure' falls to the lot of farmers and ranch people," she added.

"Yes, indeed," replied Maud, ruefully; "what with baking, scouring, and dairy-work, we have not much time for frivolous dissipation."

"Oh, what a lovely room!" screamed Grace in delight. "If I had such a sweet boudoir I'd steal an hour at least every day to play the heroine, even if the bread burned and the dishes went unwashed in consequence," she added, rapturously.

"When up here I often dream that I am a grand lady," said Mora, gaily; "but when I catch a glimpse in the mirror of a frumpy, frouzy creature with a towel over her head, then I awake to the sad reality that I am only the slave of circumstances."

Grace would have been perfectly justified, however, in indulging in day-dreams in such a place; for a more elegant apartment, or one where greater taste was evinced in every detail of adornment, was rarely to be seen in the West.

It was situated at the south end of the upper hall, and opened out upon the balcony by a door of plate glass, thick and beveled, through which could be seen the flashing fountain on the terrace below and a landscape of surpassing beauty. The wooded

stream wound away down the prairie valley, which
was dotted with innumerable ricks of wild-hay; the
white stone walls which fenced the ranch ran far
out onto the highlands, dimly defining the bound-
aries of the great estate.

The walls of the elegant apartment were draped
with and paneled by carmine and cream colored
silk, relieved by lines of white. A carpet of creamy
velvet was strewn with moss-roses of the same shade
of carmine, with all the furniture upholstered to
correspond. The walls were graced—not crowded—
by a tall beveled mirror of French plate and some
delicious paintings, framed in gilt. The low mantel
was of Italian marble, white, dappled and veined with
red shading to faintest rose. Vases of Sevres china,
statuettes of bronze, and elegantly bound volumes
were seen on every hand. There was a table of
mosaic, on which was a basket of fancy-work, that,
Miss Estill said, was destined never to be finished.
Through the draped door-way, on the east, could
be seen the snowy, lace-canopied bed of the mistress
of all this splendor. The sunlight, sifting through
the tops of the elms which grew below the terrace,
shone in fitful bars of amber on a picture which
was riveting the attention of Maud, who sprang up
from her velvet chair and cried with enthusiasm :—

"Oh Grace! it is ' Sunset on the Smoky Hill,'
do n't you see the Iron Mound looming up with
vague mystery? The serpentine river, fringed by
trees, is the Saline; and there, winding down from
the north, is the stately Solomon; while here at
our feet flows the Smoky Hill betweenit s timbered

banks. See that white blot, far out to the east, rising in the evening mirage,—it must be Fort Riley! There is Abilene; and all along the wide prairie valley, flanked by bold grassy headlands, are white villages and golden fields of wheat. Here, nestling down in the broad valley among the groves at the base of the Iron Mound, is Salina—which reminds me of Damascus, with its rivers of Abana and Pharpar. Out to the south-west see that long line of purple, jagged buttes, over which eternally hovers a smoky haze,—those are the Smoky Hills! Look at the twilight stealing down through their gorges. Oh, it is like a glimpse of heaven! Mora—Mora! who could have painted this?" she said, with tears of genuine emotion. Then seeing Miss Estill blushing hotly, she and Grace impulsively kissed the young artist—Maud saying with a little quaver of emotion:—

"Mora Estill, you dear, gifted creature—do you know that you are a genius?"

"I am not so certain of that, for I am often led to believe in Hugh's criticisms. He says that my best pictures are very similar in appearance to a newly flayed beef's-hide." Then, as the others gave vent to shrieks of feminine amazement, Miss Estill continued merrily: "I had a letter from him yesterday. He is at Kansas City, you know. Would you believe it?—he sent an order for me to paint the sign for a butcher's shop. The aggravating fellow charged me, carefully, to put a sufficient number of limbs on the figure of a cow that was to adorn the sign. Then he proceeded with a whole

15

page of caution, in which he charged me to avoid the fatal error of painting claws upon the animal's hoofs. There followed a long homily, showing the dire results of such a slight mistake—the innuendo and sarcasm, the cold suspicion and cruel neglect, that would alight upon the head of a butcher who was suspected of making beef of an animal that wore claws.

"This picture of Lake Inman," said Miss Estill, as the laughing group moved forward to where a beautiful painting hung, "Hugh persists in calling 'The Knot Hole;' and in his letter he said that as to the horns of the animal which was to adorn the sign, they were a matter of indifference to the public, and I could keep them for the trunks of the 'stately elms' in my next landscape, and I might transplant them with great success to the shores of Lake Inman, which you see is badly in need of shade."

"I 'd just like to teach him," said Grace, inadvertently; but seeing the amused look which Maud shot at Miss Estill she hesitated with a blush, while Mora quickly exclaimed: —

"Oh, I believe he is beginning to learn of late; but I hope you will give him a lesson in poetry, for I found an effusion among his papers, where he had evidently forgotten it, that will bear a *great deal of revision;*" and she took from a bronze cabinet a paper whereon was written, in lame and halting couplets, an apostrophe "To My Love."

But the author had failed so signally to secure either rhyme or measure, that the girls shrieked

aloud as Mora read long verses of the most trivial
nonsense and doggerel, where "golden tresses,"
"had went," and "blue eyes" were mingled with
loving ardor, but very bad grammar.

As the verses progressed, the sentiment became
more tender, but the diction and measure were perfectly appalling in their untutored originality. At
each new limp or poetical hobble, the girls would
laugh gaily; but when Mora looked at Grace with
a significant smile, the application of the following
lines was readily seen : —

> "My love she's golden hair and eyes
>   Of deepest, finest blue.
> I love her better than ['Gooseberry pies!' cried
>   Maud] any thing,
> My heart will always be true to you."

Although the author had promoted his lady love
from the obscure position of third person to the
station of second person in the space of a second,
yet even this was not enough to induce Grace to
remain longer; for she fled away with burning
blushes, while Mora still continued to read lines,
the syntax of which disclosed the revolting fact that
their author had throttled his own mother tongue,
had slain persons without regard to sex or condition,
and, like a vandal, had cut off the feet of his best
subject at some critical moment.

At the close Miss Estill folded the paper, and
as she placed it in a cabinet she said, it would yet
serve to pay off some old scores with Hugh. She
must have kept her word, for on his return he was
immeasurably shocked on opening his county paper

to see, staring at him from the first page: "A Poem
To My Love.   By H. E."

After Mr. Estill had praised the dappled Nor-
mans and cared for them in a very hospitable manner,
he led the young men out to a near-by pasture to
show them his Jersey cows.   While they were admiring the graceful animals, their host said: —

" For twenty-five years we had either depended
on Texan cows for milk, or had used the concentrated article without even once thinking of the
folly of such a course.   We had so long been accustomed to seeing the herders lasso the wild, infu-
riated creatures before milking them, that we had
actually forgotten there was any other way.   It may
have been owing to our trusting the operation
wholly to the cow-boys that no progress was made
in subduing the animals or reducing them to a
domestic state; but we never had thought it safe
to allow a woman inside of the corral since that
morning, a score of years ago, when my wife had
been kicked insensible by a beast that she had
attempted to milk.   One evening, after Mora had
returned from Cincinnati, she witnessed the usual
proceedings in the milk-yard,—two broad-hatted and
bespurred herders lassoing a cow.   Then, after tying
her head to one post and hind-foot to another, one
of the valiant milk-men stripped a few streams of
the precious fluid into a cup, while his partner stood
by, whip in hand, ready to punish any movement
on the part of the bellowing brute.   Only then did
she realize how infamously undairy-like the affair

really was. When I met her a few moments later, she said with a shade of contempt in her tone:—

"'Oh, why do you allow such barbarous work on the ranch?'

"'But, my dear,' I replied, 'there is no other way. Why, I would rather tackle a mountain lion than one of those fiery creatures while she is loose.'

"'Then, why not buy some Jerseys?' Mora said.

"Yes, indeed, why not? I thought, and so I lost no time over deliberations, but wrote at once to Major Kingsbury, who sent me these gentle creatures, which now we value above anything else on the ranch."

Nothing was said about the vast herds, the thousands of fat cattle grazing out over the great pastures around; but the visitors were impressed with the evidence of great wealth visible on every hand. The capacious corral and innumerable ricks of prairie-hay bore mute testimony to the thrift and opulence which reigned at the Estill ranch.

As Mr. Estill led the way back to the dwelling he said:—

"Hugh will be greatly disappointed when he learns that he has missed your visit. I have been away with him for the last fortnight, and only returned last evening, when I learned from my wife that—that—my children had a very pleasant day up at your place." Then in a constrained voice he added: "I would like to meet your father, Mr. Warlow; for there is a subject which I would like very much to discuss with him."

"My father expressed a wish to make your

acquaintance also ; for it appears that he is anxious to discuss the early history of this country with you," Clifford replied.

Mr. Estill seemed greatly agitated on hearing this ; but when about to reply, dinner was announced, and he arose and led the way into the long, walnut-paneled dining-room.   All this time Clifford was mutely wondering why the wealthy old ranchman should be so anxious to meet his father.

"Can it be that the cattle-king is opposed to the intimacy growing up between myself and his daughter?" young Warlow asked himself.   Then he thought of the friendly manner of his host, and rejected the idea at once.

They were soon gaily chatting over the soup ; but as Clifford's eye glanced along the wall his attention was attracted by a painting, which hung where the light fell upon it in such a way as to bring out every detail with perfect clearness.   In its foreground was a mammoth tree, shading the gables of a stone cottage ; a ruined wall, half smothered by vines.   Across the stream, which had half encircled the knoll where the building stood, were fields of ripening grain, that rippled in the billowy waves, stirred and tossed by the summer breeze, wheat of coppery red or palest gold, the silvery sheen of rye and oats contrasting with the tawny prairie and dark, green groves, through which shimmered the brook and pools that he recognized as old friends.

As his eye sought the author of this delicate compliment, which was a truthful picture of his place—the Old Corral—he caught Miss Estill's amused look; for she had been watching the pleased surprise which had grown upon his face as he realized what the picture really was. His glance must have been very expressive in reply; for a blush swept over her face, usually serene in its quiet dignity, or vicacious with blithesome wit, and her blue eyes retreated behind their long lashes—a guilty admission that she was the artist who had painted the scene.

This silent by-play was not unnoticed, quiet as it all seemed; for as Clifford turned to take the plate of rare good things which the host passed to him, he encountered the eyes of Mrs. Estill fixed upon him; but the lady smiled with a look of such evident enjoyment of the situation that he half forgot that Mr. Estill still held the plate, which young Warlow seized with an air which was neither as graceful nor self-possessed as a hero should have worn.

With ready tact Mrs. Estill came to the rescue by saying:—

"It all looks strange, no doubt, that I treat you to a ranch fare of canned beef from St. Louis, and vegetables from Baltimore and Rochester, but if it were not for our Jerseys we should have been compelled to call on Chicago for condensed milk also. I never realized the absurdity of this course until Mora told me of the luxuriant gardens and fields of grain which you are raising in the upper valley. Why, Hugh says it is a marvel how prosperous everything appears up there."

" We never before have regarded this as a farming country; it has remained for your brave colony to explode that fallacy; and I hope your prosperity may be as lasting as it is merited," said Mr. Estill.

An hour was spent in the parlor after dinner; then a long stroll followed out among the cedars to the north of the dwelling. Here Mora and Clifford soon found themselves deserted by their companions, and were left to their own' resources for entertainment.

They had been longing, no doubt, for this moment to arrive; so we will not intrude—a proceeding that would be alike odious to the couple and cruel to the reader; but when they emerged an hour later from the jungle of evergreens, Mora was heard to say :—

" I can not imagine why mamma was so agitated when I told her. She never was affected by anything before. But she positively forbade my mentioning the subject again in her presence. When I begged her to tell why she talked so strangely, she replied that the story of the old tragedy had completely unnerved her; and then she again questioned me as to every detail of that terrible affair."

" No doubt the remembrance of those early days, their danger and trials, all recurred with painful minuteness as you related the story, Miss Estill, for your parents were residing here at the time of that sorrowful event," Clifford replied.

" No; I fear that there is some deeper reason yet; for when papa returned from Abilene—whither he had been with Hugh shipping cattle—mother sought

an interview alone with him, and when I came into
the room he said that I must be very careful to
avoid the subject in the future. My parents never
could be taxed with being sentimental—of that I
am certain. But what the mystery can be—for a
mystery it certainly is—I am at a loss to conjecture."

"The air seems full of mystery since you and
my father met," replied Clifford; "but I hope it will
soon be all explained, Miss Estill."

"I was very glad to see you come to-day; for
although papa only arrived last night, he had concluded to go up to see Colonel Warlow at once.

"I can't guess why he seems so anxious about
meeting him. I tried bribery with a kiss; but he
would not tell me why he was going—would always
evade my question by replying that it was business,
only, that prompted the visit."

"He must be very obdurate, indeed, not to yield
on such terms," Clifford replied, with a look which
betrayed how willingly he would surrender at such
a proposition.

You have discovered, no doubt, that although
our friend Warlow often spoke with his eyes, yet he
allowed the lady to do three-fourths of the talking.
This is a very dangerous experiment for an un-
fettered youth to indulge in; for I have always observed that when a fluent, silvery-tongued woman
finds a ready listener, provided the victim be young,
handsome, and manly, she first becomes more fluent,
then, when answered in monosyllables, she shows
her admiration of his "great conversational powers,"

16

and proceeds to make herself irresistible and capti-
vating at once—all of which ends in chains and
slavery for the brilliant listener.

After a moment's silence, Miss Estill said :—

" I notice a strange change has come over you
since we last met, Mr. Warlow. Is it possible that
you, also, have been seized by that strange infection
of mystery which seems to possess all my friends in
the last few weeks?"

"Why, Miss Estill, do you really think me
changed?" Clifford replied, with due regard to the
three-fourths rule.

At that moment the other members of the party
came up and proposed returning, thus precluding
Miss Estill's answer.

As the guests were taking their leave, Mr. Estill
said, in reply to their cordial invitations to visit.
them, that he would drive up the next day in company
with his wife, that he had business with Colonel
Warlow, and that himself and wife would call upon
the Moreland family, if it would be agreeable to
that family to receive them.

On hearing nothing but great pleasure expressed
at this announcement, the matter was settled defi-
nitely in that way; then the guests took their leave,
and drove home through the cool twilight, vaguely
wondering what business Mr. Estill could have to
transact with Colonel Warlow.

Chapter XIV.

EARLY next morning Clifford rode away, on the pretext that he was going to buy cattle of a ranchman in the next county; but his absence was mainly owing to the fact that he suspected the Estill visit was in some way connected with his intimacy with Mora; so he had decided that he would take himself off, and thereby avoid a disagreeable scene.

The cattle-king and his wife arrived at an early hour, although they had called a moment at the Moreland homestead and given a promise that they would stop for an early tea on their return homeward from the Warlows. When they had been introduced by Maud, the colonel and Mr. Estill went to the stable to care for the team, and when that important rite of hospitality had been duly observed the gentlemen rejoined their wives in the Warlow parlor.

Robbie was away in the fields with the farm men; Maud was busy with household cares, on the plea of which she had absented herself from the parlor. The kitchen, which was the scene of her culinary operations, was situated in an ell of the building, and as she stood by a window that looked directly through into one in the parlor, she could see and hear a great deal that was transpiring therein.

An hour after the arrival of the guests she was standing by this open window, putting the last touches of frosting on a cooca-nut cake, and so deeply, indeed, was she engrossed with her labors that she had failed to observe what the situation really was in the parlor, until she heard a hoarse cry :—

"Oh God! it is Bruce and Ivarene!" and as she glanced hastily into the room she beheld a sight that perplexed and mystified her for long days thereafter. Her father stood by the window holding a jeweled locket in his hand; but at that moment he lowered the window-curtain, thus shutting off all view of the parlor.

When, an hour later, Mrs. Warlow came into the kitchen, traces of tears were visible on her usually placid face; and when Maud, unable any longer to restrain her curiosity, eagerly asked the meaning of the mysterious conclave in the parlor, her mother evaded answering; so Maud wisely concluded to await her parents' confidence, which she felt certain of sharing at the proper time.

At dinner Colonel Warlow ate but little of the tempting food; and the guests, although they praised the roast-chicken with its savory dressing, the delicate float and frosted cake, left their plates almost untouched.

When the constrained and quiet meal was finished, and all had returned to the parlor but Maud, Rob came back again to the table, and as that youth, with an unappeasable appetite, helped himself to a plateful of "stuffing" and gravy, he turned to his sister and said:—

"What's the matter now, Maud? The colonel seems to be all broke up; and that old Lady Estill—by grab!—*she* looked like death on a—a—white pony! Mother, too, appeared as if she might have been sniffling; but that's nothing but a common pastime with her. You know that all women, more or less—yourself included, madam—are very much given to the chicken-hearted habit of dribbling at the nose."

"Chicken-hearted, indeed! It is a great wonder, then, that you did not devour us long ago, sir!" said Maud, with a great show of asperity, but very glad to lead the subject into other channels and elude further questioning; for she saw by her mother's manner that there was something about the Estill visit which they wished, for unknown reasons, to keep secret, and it was a matter of honor with the noble-hearted girl to help them conceal what she herself was longing to know.

"Well, big guns of the Estill calibre don't *go off* on slight occasions," persisted Rob, with his mouth half-full of the adored "stuffing," and as he reached for a tall glass of ruby-colored plum-jelly, Maud quickly said:—

"Won't you have a bit of the cake, Rob?"

"Thanks—yes," said he, as he helped himself to the last solitary quarter of that frosted dainty; "and I would be pleased to taste a morsel of that chicken also," he mumbled.

"What choice, sir?" she asked sarcastically.

"The running-gears, if you please," he replied with polite gravity.

With a gesture of scorn and disgust, Maud passed him the carcass of the fowl; then, after filling a large platter with crusts, bones, and egg-shells, she placed them before him with the injunction to help himself. Retiring to the window, she watched him devour cake, chicken, jam, and potatoes with an appetite that knew no discrimination.

"I am afraid you have not done justice to my dishes," she said, as Rob at length arose from the table.

"Oh, now don't give us any more sarcasm," said he, while picking his teeth with a broom-split. "It is so long from breakfast to noon, Maud, that I just get faint waiting on that slow old dinner-bell."

"No doubt; but you remember how ravenously hungry you were last week, when the pup got the bell-rope in his mouth and summoned you in form the field at nine in the morning," she retorted, laughingly.

"Well, that was a cloudy day," he said, good-naturedly; then, taking his straw hat from its hook on the porch, he hurried away to the field.

After finishing her domestic duties, Maud joined the guests in the parlor, with a faint hope of learning something further of the mystery which seemed to enshroud their visit, of which she had got such a tantalizing glimpse an hour before; but her expectations were, however, sadly doomed to disappointment, for nothing was said that would throw any light on the subject; and, after spending a while at the piano, she invited the guests out to look at her flowers.

The party thereupon adjourned to the garden; and when they had admired the flowers and shrubs, they sauntered on to the barn-yard, to look at the peacocks and other fowls, of which Mrs. Warlow was justly proud.

"I should like to take a nearer view of your crops, Colonel. It has been so long since I saw a well-conducted farm, that it appears quite a novelty to me," said Mr. Estill, with evident interest.

In a few moments they all embarked in the boat, and were rowed up to Clifford's dwelling; for if there was one thing of which the colonel was vain it was his son's farming.

As they stood in the level valley south of the river, a scene of perfect rural beauty was visible. On the north was Clifford's gothic cottage, half hidden by the drooping elm; to the east, the chimneys and gables of the Warlow homestead peeped above the trees; while out to the south, on a green knoll, stood the stone school-house, with its tower and rose-window.

The yellow wheat-stubble shone like gold beside the silvery oats, fast ripening for the harvest; the rank corn stood in clean, dark rows—great squares of waving green; scores of ricks were standing along the valley; while the clank of the header and shouts of the workmen were borne on the breeze from the neighboring field.

"Ah! this is a very home-like scene, indeed— a great contrast to the one presented here just two

years ago when last I visited this spot," said Mr.
Estill. "My ranch, ten miles below here, was then
the last settlement on the frontier. There was not
a human habitation in sight—only antelope and
buffalo to vary the monotony of perfect solitude.
In fact, there had never been an owner for the land
nor a furrow turned here since the dawn of creation.
Marvelous change!" he added.

After crossing the stream on a foot-log, which
here formed a rustic bridge, they all walked up to
Clifford's dwelling, and while standing by the vine-
mantled wall of the Old Corral, the colonel said
in a musing tone:—

"If this inanimate ruin could but speak, we
might learn the sequel to that tragedy which has
risen again, as it were, from the grave of the past.
The robbers were led by white men, who no doubt
divided the treasure among themselves while the
savages were stupefied with liquor."

He was interrupted by a cry of wonder from
Maud, who could not repress her astonishment at
his assertion that white men had led the Indians—
a fact which Hugh Estill seemed to have been aware
of also, and which, taken in connection with the
incident of the miniature, led her to believe that
the Estills were in some way connected with the
massacre.

"Maud, dear, will you go and see how Clifford's
young catalpa-trees, down the drive, are growing?
and if they need cultivating again, we will send one
of the boys over with a plow soon," said Mrs. Warlow, with a warning glance; and Miss Maud moved

quickly away, somewhat chagrined at her summary dismissal.

As she passed along, she was pondering over the strange fact that her father had at last obtained a clue to the perpetrators of the outrage at the corral; and she became so deeply engrossed with the thought that she was quite unmindful which way her steps led, until her eye was attracted to a place where the earth appeared to have been recently disturbed, and she paused a moment, vaguely wondering what could have been buried there.

The tall blue stem-grass was tangled and dead, while the square outlines of a cavity showed through the mass of dead vines and leaves, which had been suspiciously strewn over the place, with a view, it seemed, of concealing all trace of the disturbance. She became also aware of a most disgusting odor near the old cottonwood-tree; but, unmindful of this, she raked away the grass and litter to examine more closely the cavity in which the soil had been firmly trampled, but her curiosity was in no wise abated when she discovered that it was Clifford's boot-tracks that were visible in the soft, yielding earth.

"What has he buried here, that he seems so anxious to conceal?" she was asking herself, when a puff of wind brought the odor with such added strength that she nearly fainted, and was hastily retreating from the proximity of that mysterious place, where she feared some strange, dead thing was buried, when she saw the bloated and mottled form of that hideous reptile which the reader may remember as having greeted a "Young Fortune Hunter" one weird and murky night the week before.

With a stifled shriek, Maud fled by the vile-smelling and repulsive object, which she saw at a glance was mangled and dead; then, as she slowly returned and walked south of the reptile, she surveyed it carefully, and saw, with a shudder, that it was a hideous rattlesnake, with its head severed from the body. Appalled at the thought that it was her brother who had slain this formidable monster, the bite of which, while living, she knew meant certain death, she was retreating again from the place, pale and trembling, but paused at the excavation, to wonder, even then, what it meant, when her eye, which was scanning the ground carefully, caught sight of a curious, small object lying at her feet.

Stooping and picking it up, she was disgusted and surprised to see that it was a human tooth. She was about to dash it down again, when a thought seemed to occur that caused her to look carefully about for some minutes; then, as nothing else was found, she stripped some leaves from a grape-vine near, and, after wrapping them about the tooth, she put it carefully away in her purse, and then returned to where her parents and guests were embarking for home. As they rowed down the willow-fringed stream, nothing was said concerning the strange discoveries that had been made that day, and on arriving at the house, the visitors prepared to take an early departure. As Mrs. Estill stepped into the carriage, Mrs. Warlow gave a promise that she would drive down to the Estill ranch one day that week.

Clifford returned late that evening with some animals which he had bought; and, as all was hurry and bustle, and several laborers remained over night, there was no chance for confidential conversation among the younger members of the Warlow family. But the next morning broke with a lowering sky, and the misty rain which followed precluded any effort at farm-work; so the laborers went to their respective homes, leaving the house to its customary quiet.

As Rob was plodding about in the rain and whistling shrill as a locust, he was signaled by Maud, who stood out by the gate, and when the youth joined her they held a low, hurried conversation for a few minutes; then Rob darted down to the boat, and rowed rapidly up the stream.

He was gone but a few minutes, however, when he returned flushed and excited, and placed something, which was wrapped in leaves, into Maud's outstretched hand.

"How did you manage it?" she said in a low tone, as they paused under an ash-tree near the river.

"Why, that was easy enough—I just put my boot on his snakeship's tail, then taking hold of the rattles with a handful of leaves—and—here they are. But—oh fury!—how it did smell, though!" he added in disgust. "Fourteen rattles and a button! Don't that beat the snake-tale of the oldest inhabitant, Maud?"

Then, without awaiting a reply, he added, out of breath with excitement:—

"Cliff had a shocking time of it up there last Friday night, for this is only a small part of his experience."

"Rob—what—oh, what can you mean?" cried Maud, in wildest excitement.

"Well, I do n't know much; but this much I did learn by guessing at it first, then making him own up; for Cliff is as close-mouthed as an oyster. From what I could learn, it appears that, while prowling about that night like a vagrant tom-cat, our good-looking brother ran into that old spectre which shrieked so like a demon that night by the camp-fire. This time, of course, it gave him the slip, as it always does," he answered.

"You do not mean to say that horrible sight has been seen again, Rob?"

After cautioning her not to raise such a racket, Rob proceeded to tell of his encounter, and also what he had learned of Clifford's experience likewise.

"Oh, Rob—what a horribly unreal thing it all seems! But everywhere there is so much of mystery that I am almost wild," she cried, with a good deal of incoherence.

"Why was Clifford digging about the old cottonwood that night, Rob?" she added, after a moment's pause; but, as her brother only expressed both surprise and ignorance, she continued: "But this is not all, Robbie; for I made a most startling discovery to-day—one which throws a gloomy light on the old tragedy of Bruce and his wife."

"Why, thicker and thicker!" cried Rob. "But what kind of a mare's-nest did you run into this time, Maud?" he added.

In reply, Maud told of seeing the locket, and of hearing her father exclaim that it contained the pictures of Bruce and his wife, and the strange assertion which he had made while the Estills were standing by the ruined wall.

"But how did the locket ever get into the Estills' hands?" Rob said, with a perplexed look; then, after a moment, he added, excitedly :—

"Oh, now I know what father and Mr. Estill were talking about in the barn. I had just stepped into the upper hall-way to lay a fork on the rack— you know how strict father always was about our putting everything in its proper place—so, to save myself a blowing up, I went out of my way and had left the fork there, and was about to hurry on to the well for a jug of water, when I heard Mr. Estill say :—

"'This must be a matter of sacred confidence between us, Colonel; for if it were known that any one of my people had participated in that affair, or had been engaged in the murder, there are people who are malicious enough, no doubt, to connect myself and wife with the crime; and for that reason alone I have always kept the matter a profound secret, even from Hugh and Mora. The locket was set with rubies and engraved with the name which, you see, we have used, and have only shortened; but she has never learned its origin, nor anything of the tragedy.'

"Then, after a moment, he continued, after father had said something which I could not quite catch :—

"'If Olin Estill had only lived, the mystery might have been explained; but I found him dead and mangled beyond all resemblance to a human— nothing to identify his remains but the tattered clothing, which I recognized; for the wolves had torn his limbs away, and left his skeleton bleaching out on the prairie. Yet the strangest part of it all is the mysterious resemblance of the faces in that miniature to Mora and your son. Why, my wife was terribly agitated when she first met that boy of yours; for he is the perfect counterpart of the picture of your friend, who must have died years before either of those children were born. Mora's resemblance to Ivarene—'

"About that time I grew weary of such rot, and did not pay any further attention to what they said. How much more I might have heard I can't guess; for I hurried away to the well, as I was mortal thirsty and tired. I am sorry now that I did n't stay and hear it out, for there certainly is something up."

While talking thus they had sauntered on into the house; and while they stood by the parlor door Rob had made the concluding remark, which Clifford chanced to overhear, as he came upon them silently through the carpeted hall.

"Here, you young conspirators—out with it, and confess at once 'what's up,' as this bold robber says with such an air of deep mystery," Clifford said, with a smile of curiosity.

Maud looked up with a flash of resentment in her honest Warlow eyes; for she did not half like the idea of this Adonis-like brother keeping anything from her. Thrusting her hand into her pocket, she drew out her *porte-monnaie*, as he continued:—

"Well, Maud, did you learn anything yesterday?" while an anxious look crept into his face.

"Yes, I learned this!" she replied, while holding out her hand, in which, resting on a piece of muslin, was a human tooth, and that long, reticulated tissue, which he saw at a glance was the rattles of the enormous reptile he had encountered while digging for the treasure.

He looked at them in a startled, wondering way for a moment; then, as if comprehending it all, he said:—

"Ah, yes—the rattles! But the tooth—that is the hardest part of all."

Maud and Rob could not restrain a smile at the ghastly pun; but the former replied:—

"I found them where you had been digging, near the old cottonwood-tree. We know about the rattlesnake and that gray-robed figure, which was the same one that startled us by the camp-fire, I really believe. But that human tooth?—I shall certainly go raving mad if you keep anything further from me."

Clifford glanced from her pale face to that of Rob, which wore a look of startled perplexity.

"I find it impossible to keep anything from your sharp eyes. So it is myself, after all, who has to confess!" he said, seating himself on the divan.

Then, while the rain lashed the windows and the chill wind wailed through the tree-tops without, he told that story of midnight horror. When he finished, Maud was pale and tearful, and Rob's hazel eyes were round with mute astonishment.

"But Maud, did you learn the reason of Mr. Ess—that is Mora's folks—well—why they came up yesterday?" Clifford managed at length to say in a confused manner, that revealed a great deal of uneasiness on his part, which was not at all lost on the sharp-eyed couple beside him.

Then, drying her tears, Maud told of the strange revelations which the visit of the Estills had disclosed; and when she repeated the singular conversation which Robbie had overheard in the barn, Clifford cried out excitedly :—

"Ah! that was the mysterious kinsman who Mora said was buried on the hill-top at Estill Ranch. He was one of the robbers who perpetrated the outrage at the corral years ago. *A bandit and murderer!* 'T is no wonder that nothing but nettles ever grow on that grave. It was through him, Maud, that they obtained the locket, with its picture of Bruce and Ivarene. But it can not be that Mr. Estill derived his great wealth from the same source! If so, he never would have betrayed himself by showing the pictures of the people that were murdered by his own kinsman. What, then, became of the great treasure?" he sadly asked. But no one seemed able to answer his question; for the whole affair had now assumed a tone of mystery such as it had never worn before.

17

Chapter XV.

"WHY should they have given 'her' the name which was on the locket? and who was the mysterious female that never had learned of the tragical circumstance?" said Maud, with a puzzled face.

"I am unable to answer your question, Maud," Clifford replied; but there was something in his manner that led the sharp-eyed couple before him to suspect he had detected some clue which had eluded them in their investigations of the mystery.

"Cliff, what the deuce was that old skull doing in the cask?" said Rob, innocently; but, seeing the look of amusement on his brother's face, he added: "Or I mean to ask, how came it there?"

"To answer your first question I shall have to remind you that a dead man's skull has a very limited field of action, confined principally to the pastime of rolling over and rattling its teeth when touched; but how or why it was there, seems only known to the ill-natured ophidian which kept it such close company," Clifford replied, with his usual strain of jocular sarcasm.

"Oh dear!" said Maud, drearily, while drumming on the misty window-pane. "It is very exasperating to be shut up in a house on such a day, where every closet is full of skeletons, and not dare to peep into one of them," she added.

"But Cliff has been peeping, and with wonderful luck, too," Rob observed, dryly.

"Oh, I am not the first fortune hunter who has found a skull or serpent where he had hoped to find gold!" Clifford replied, with perfect good nature.

"Oh, Clifford, I shudder to think of the danger you passed through on that terrible night—all alone in that dismal place, fighting that venomous monster, with death in its fangs, while the gray-robed demon hovered near with its fiery eyes and blood-chilling scream," said Maud, tearfully, while winding her arm about her brother's neck.

"Now, dear, soft-hearted Maud, you must remember that the path of those who strive for pelf is thickly beset by demons and serpents, although they may wear the human guise and lurk in the shadow of friendship. Many, many are the skeletons of dead hopes and buried dreams that start up as the graves of the past are disturbed," Clifford replied.

"But you shall never spend another night alone up at that ill-omened dwelling, Clifford; for Rob shall go with you hereafter," she said, while drying her tears.

"Well, but suppose I might choose some fair lady to grace my spectre-haunted home—that would answer as well?" he replied, gaily.

"Oh! that would be a capital plan indeed; but I shall insist on the right to choose her," his sister cried, with returning animation.

"Oh! you are growing very liberal, to say the

least, Miss Maud. I guess you will have to be satisfied with second choice," said Cliff.

After talking awhile over the mystery which had woven such a tangled web about their home in the last few days, Maud exclaimed :—

"Robbie, dear, won't you go and ask father what name was engraved on the locket? Also learn all that is possible, for I am just dying of anxiety ;" but as he began to smile with derision, she added, coaxingly: "Now do go, Rob, please; that's a man ; father never refuses you anything."

" Catch me at it !" cried Rob, with a shrug. " I do n't hanker much after the dry job of pumping the colonel," he added, winking at Clifford significantly.

" No, no, Maud, that would never do. Let us await the confidence of our parents, and try, in the meantime, to pick up what facts we can. Who knows," he added, " but we may stumble on to some great discovery ?"

Little, indeed, did he suspect the great revelations which the day held in store for them, and that events were about to transpire which would change the tenor of their whole lives.

At Mrs. Warlow's entrance the conversation took on a less sombre hue, and when she told of the news confirming the great land-sale which was soon to be held at the land office—a fact which she had learned from the Estills—it was proposed to take a drive out over the country north-east, and find a section for Maud and Rob, which the colonel would buy for their benefit at the sale.

Accordingly, after dinner, as the weather had cleared, the Warlow family drove out and viewed a well-watered, rolling tract, equal in extent to the farms of the colonel and Clifford. After an hour spent thus, it was thought advisable to drive on westward and examine a country which, in their busy farm-life, had never been viewed, save at a distance.

On arriving at a point about three miles west of their home, they drove down into a narrow valley or glen, clothed with tall blue-stem and rank sunflowers, now beginning to unfold their golden blossoms. This jungle of vegetation was woven together by the slender, leafless tendrils of the love-vine, which threw a veil of coppery red over the brilliant green of the other vegetation.

While driving slowly through this almost impervious mass of vegetation, they discovered a winding but well-beaten trail or pathway, leading on down the valley, and which, out of pure curiosity, they followed until it disappeared in a thicket of plum-trees at the base of a low cliff of magnesian limestone.

As they paused at the scrubby grove, wondering what could have made the path, Clifford sprang out of the carriage, saying he would like to investigate the matter, and disappeared among the trees. He was gone so long that, after they had called him repeatedly, Rob was on the point of starting in search, when Clifford reappeared. As he sprang into the carriage their questioning was forestalled by his saying that the path was possibly made by

wolves, and that he had been examining the cliff,
but had not succeeded in finding their den.

He appeared so pale and agitated, however, that
Maud regarded him suspiciously; and when the
horses flew up the glen along the winding pathway
and through tangled thickets of blue-stem and sunflowers, she managed to ask in a whisper: —

"What have you discovered, Cliff?"

"A clue to the old mystery—but wait," he
whispered in reply; and in silence they drove
rapidly back to the Warlow homestead.

As the boys were leading the horses into the
barn, Maud called for them to assist her in nailing
up some of the lattice which the wind had shaken
down in her arbor; and when they joined her a few
minutes later in the vine-clad bower, she cried in a
low, eager tone: —

"Clifford—Clifford! what did you see in that
thicket?"

"Yes, out with it—quick!" said Rob; "for I
know by your looks that you saw something queer
up there."

"The pathway," said Clifford, hurriedly,
"plunged into the thicket of plums; then, after
winding about in a mazy labyrinth, it led up to the
base of a low cliff of limestone, and there ended so
abruptly that I was puzzled to know what to make
of it, but noticing that the heavy festoon of grape-
vines that hung down from the soil above, looked
as if they had been disturbed, I hastily drew them
aside. Imagine my surprise when a rough door was
revealed, hung in the face of the cliff. Drawing it

open, there was disclosed a low cell or cavern, which had been partly carved out of the soft magnesian limestone. Peering into the room, I became satisfied that it was empty of human occupants.

"The room was not more than a dozen feet square, the little furniture which it contained being dilapidated beyond description. As I stepped into the room to examine things more closely, the fact became very plain that some one had occupied it recently, for the mouldy couch still showed the imprint of a human form.

"Some broken utensils stood about on the hearth, where a fire-place had been hewn out of the soft rock. The ashes and charred wood, the bones of fish and birds, scattered about on the floor, confirmed the fact that it was used, in a desultory manner, as a habitation.

"I was turning to leave, thinking perhaps that I had invaded the private dwelling of some squatter, when my attention was arrested by seeing a vial half concealed in a cleft in the rocky wall. Inly wondering why any one should wish to conceal such a trifle, I drew it forth, rubbing the grime and dust from it as I did so.

"What was my surprise to see that there was a paper within. In eager haste I uncorked the bottle and drew out this document," said he, holding up with trembling hands a sheet that was discolored with age and blotted with mildew, but covered closely with writing, still faintly legible. "I had only time to glance at the startling title when I heard your voices calling, so I closed the door, drew the vines carefully over the entrance, and joined you, feeling like one in a dream.

"Now let's hasten," he said, "and read this document, which will, I believe, unveil the mystery of Bruce and Ivarene." Then, unrolling the time-worn paper again, with bated breath and loudly beating heart, he read aloud as follows: —

SEPTEMBER 14, 1849, }
"NEAR THE STONE CORRAL, ON THE SANTA FE TRAIL. }

"This is written by Ivarene Walraven, late of the City of Mexico, who offers prayers that it may fall into hands of kindness, who will convey to my kinsman, Herr Von Brunn, of Vera Cruz—to him this missive, full of grief and misfortune.

"We were attacked by savages on the night of August 22d, our servants slain, our wealth all gone, and our kind and tender friend, Senor Warlow, murdered. Bruce, my noble husband, he did me wrap within the folds of a serape, and dashed away out on the dark prairie with me in his arms, far, far away from the noise of murder and savagery. He watched by my side in the tall grass all that day next come; for I was ill to death's gate.

"Then, near eventide, there came to us a hunter strange, who said he slay the bison-flesh for trailers by, and beg we go to his hidden cell in a cliffy rock. His evil eyes I much mistrust; but he seem friendly be, and food prepare for us when there we go. On morning rise my babe is born—a daughter sweet—and darling Bruce he tenderly nurses me while the hunter watches near the trail for wagons go by; but day by day nothing sees he;

then Bruce he say, 'I shall go myself to-morrow day.' The hunter frown when this he say. That morning, as the hunter go, he say, with cunning smile : 'A flask of wine for senora and senor.' Then leaves he it and go away as at all time. When him had disappeared, I scent a strangeness in the flask, and Bruce poured out a larger part; then broke he the glassen flask upon the floor. When a cup he bring, and say : ' What is the scent of this wine he gave?' I perceive the deadly loco's odor there, and say it poison is; it drives them mad for evermore. Bruce he frown, and meat and drink prepare ; and when the hunter he return he say : 'The flask is broken all! give us wine some more.' But the hunter rudely began the meat to eat, waiting not at all. After him did partake in his rude way of the food he threw his coat by; then sat he strangely still awhile. Sprang he at length to his feet with loud shriek and cry, then rushed away into the night. 'Ah! the wine I put into his food is poison be,' Bruce he say while bar the door. In the hunter's coat we find a little book for writing some, and one leaf did have these letter writ:—

" ' EAGLE BEAK,—Take all the braves to Pawnee Rock, and there I will go soon. Several jugs of wine are ready for you to take along; but do not let them taste until there ; I have put deadly loco in the wine, which will kill them all, or drive them mad; so there will be the less to share the cask of gold—'

" Then it was left unfinished, and another leaf had been torn—some out.

18

"I shall write it more for Bruce; he go to the trail to watch for travelers go. I am all by me, and my blue-eyed, dark-haired daughter here, with barred door I am much secured; but lonely so for darling Bruce.

"I try so hard to plainly use this English tongue, but strange it seems. My baby dear I deck with my mother's locket, where is the picture of dear Bruce and me—my dear mother's name on it: Morelia. Oh, time is lonely now while Bruce away. I will lay this aside, its vial in, and will write it again after I unbar the door and watch for him."

Chapter XVI.

"OH! they were murdered by the wild hunter,—
and this is all that remains to tell the fate of
our father's friends," cried Maud, tearfully. "But
do you think, Clifford—" She paused a moment,
leaving her question unfinished; then, springing to
her feet in wildest excitement, she exclaimed:—

"We have been blind—blind! but it is all clear
now!" and as Rob stood by, dumb with astonishment, she said, in a hoarse whisper, while she
wrung her hands in the intensity of her great
emotion: "Bruce's daughter—Morelia—Mora!"

"Yes, yes! I have suspected it since the day
father called her Ivarene. I always felt, from the
moment that we met, as though I had known her
all my life. There seemed to be a look of recognition beaming from the eyes of Mora Estill that has
haunted me for months. My God! is it possible I
have only known her three short weeks? it seems
like an eternity," said Clifford, in a musing tone,
while Rob exclaimed, hurriedly:—

"That mad hunter was Olin Estill; and it was
he who must have stolen Mora at the cavern from
Ivarene, and left her at the Estill Ranch before he
met his tragic fate. His is the haunted, lonesome
grave on the hill-top, of which Mora spoke."

"But, oh, what a terrible retribution!—his

limbs torn away by wrangling wolves, and his grinning skull left bleaching on the wild prairie," said Maud, tearfully. "Dear Bruce and Ivarene," she continued, with a sob—"must their history end in silence and oblivion?"

"Do you think, Maud, that the hunter, with all the devilish cunning of madness, could have crept back and poisoned them, and then stolen the child?"

"Ah! it is too sad to contemplate," she replied. "Their fate would have been worse than death; for I now remember having read how ill-starred Carlotta, Maximilian's unhappy empress, was poisoned by some terrible Mexican drug, and all the world knows of her hopeless madness, which will last until death."

"I shudder to think who that gray-robed, ghastly creature, with its tangled locks and glassy eyes, may be," said Clifford, hoarse with emotion.

"Not Bruce! Oh no, no! it can not be! Oh God! what a fate!" cried Maud, with another flood of tears, as she thought of the hideous contrast with the smiling, handsome lover in the flower-entwined balcony of Monteluma.

"I will go and take a more extended search up at that cavern," said Clifford. "It may be possible to make some more discoveries. But let us keep this matter secret, and when our parents are willing to give us their confidence, then we will divulge it, but not before," to which the others agreed; and while Maud was still cautioning him to be very careful of danger, our young hero rode up by his dwelling, then galloped rapidly along the winding pathway to the cliff where the cavern was concealed.

Alighting, and securing his horse to a low plum-tree in the thicket, he went to the door of the cell, and, finding all as he had left it, began searching the room critically.

He was reasoning in his mind the probabilities of finding the treasure, which the letter of the hunter led him to suspect was hidden near; for he had got a very clear glimpse of that villain's nature, when he read the part that was crossed out after he had written: "The fewer to share, the greater the gain."

Clifford felt certain that Olin Estill had remained with the treasure after he had induced his confederate in crime, Eagle Beak (who was, no doubt, an Indian chief), to decoy the Indians away to Pawnee Rock. The wretch must have decided to poison Eagle Beak when he marked the letter over, and no doubt he had suppressed the fact of the wine being drugged, so that his confederate would also drink of the liquor.

"Eagle Beak must have been a white man, disguised as an Indian, or he would never have been able to read," thought Clifford; but as he knew a great many half-breeds had become prominent Indian chiefs, he reconciled this fact with the position which that marauder held. Allowing such to have been the case, young Warlow knew that he could have been no match in cunning deviltry for the educated scoundrel, Estill; so he must certainly have fallen into the diabolical trap which the latter villain had laid for him, and, with all his Indians, he had drunk himself to madness and death from the flasks and jugs of drugged and poisoned liquor. They had all shared a common fate long before reaching that towering and legendary land-mark of Pawnee Rock. All the actors in that dire trag-edy had met with such swift retribution that no one was left, in a few days after the robbery, to care for the great treasure.

"Yes; the mighty fortune of Monteluma, its red gold and gleaming gems, is hidden away near by, only waiting to be restored to their rightful heir, Mora Estill," said Clifford aloud, as he clenched his hand, and the blood surged to his face in a crim-son glow.

The gold, he believed, had been hastily buried near the Stone Corral by the leaders while the savages were stupefied with liquor; but the casket of gems, our hero believed, was concealed in the cavern; so it was with a wildly beating heart that our young friend began searching the mouldy pallet of straw, but nothing rewarded his scrutiny.

He had provided himself with a large dirk-knife, which his father had carried in the turbulent mining days, and with the heavy metal handle of the weapon Clifford proceeded to sound the walls of the cavern; but no hollow echo replied, to betray the cavity which he hoped to discover. The fire-place, chim-ney, and the ceiling, also were subjected to the same scrutiny, but with no better result. Then he began near the door, and sounded the solid floor until he arrived at the old couch; but the stone seemed to be a solid sheet of limestone, on which the hilt of the weapon rang with a clear, metallic clang, resonant but disheartening.

Hastily removing the old mattress, young Warlow resumed his explorations; and as he vainly searched the floor his heart sank like lead, and he paused to wipe the cold sweat from his face before finishing the last remaining spot in one corner. A feeling of dread and apprehension overcame him, and he shrank from the ordeal. Hope deferred began to dampen the enthusiasm of our young "Fortune Hunter," and he could scarcely summon his courage to the final test of searching that one remaining spot; but, drawing a long sigh, he resumed the operation, and the very first blow caused his brain to reel and the blood to bound madly in his veins; for the hollow sound which the blow elicited proved that the hidden cavity was reached at last.

The bottom of the cavern was thickly incrusted with filth and damp earth at that place; but he dug with frantic energy, and soon the dim outline of a square flag-stone was visible. Breathless and panting, young Warlow pried at the stone, and as it slowly arose he closed his eyes, as if fearing to glance down into the cavity below.

"Ah, if this is the casket of gems, Mora will be the greatest heiress in all the land, and the gulf which the riches of the cattle-king made between myself and her will only be widened by this great wealth," Clifford thought; and he now, for the first time, regretted having come out on a search which might lead to his life-long misery.

For one moment the tempter whispered in his ear; but quickly the Warlow honor triumphed, and he looked down resolutely into the cavity.

Yes! there was the casket, and beside it a roll of papers.

Fate had been fickle and cold so long; but now, when her smile was worse than a frown, she could easily relent.

Catching up the papers and casket, he sprang across the room to the door with a hoarse cry of delight. Upon the decayed old parchment he could only discern one faint word, Monteluma; then the casket dropped from his nerveless grasp and fell to the stone floor with a crash.

An exclamation of delight escaped him as the gems which had fallen upon the floor, flashed back the sun-rays in scintillating splendor, and the low, dull room was lit by a glare like the lightning-riven storm-cloud.

It was a scene of bewildering beauty—of fascinating splendor—that met his gaze:—great diamonds, that shot broad flashes of rainbow light; strands of pale pearls, glinting in fitful splendor; burning rubies, that poured forth flames of crimson, which mingled with the rays shed by the amethysts of rose, purple, and lilac; while the lurid, baleful fire of opals and emeralds flickered and glimmered in the sunlight.

Stooping down, young Warlow gathered up the priceless gems, trembling meanwhile at the strange, unreal event, and after securely placing them again within the casket, and rearranging the room, he mounted his horse and galloped back over the swelling hills. ·

As the hoofs of his gray Norman tore through the thickets of rank grass, tangled and woven in a maze of golden, leafless tendrils by the slender love-vine, or bruised the mignonette until all the moist, sultry air was rich with its pungent fragrance, Clifford was revolving in his mind several plans for concealing the mighty treasure of which he had just become the guardian. He concluded that he must find a secure hiding-place at his dwelling, where the casket might remain until the proper moment should arrive when he could reveal the discovery, and restore the property to its rightful owner.

On arriving at his dwelling, Clifford tied his horse in the stable, then entered the house, locking the door and drawing the blinds, so as to be safe from intrusion while he pondered over the situation. ·

The room was a tastefully-furnished apartment, carpeted with a rich, dark carpet, a remnant of luxury that had once adorned the old plantation home, and supplied with easy chairs, a book-case, well filled, and some good paintings, which were gifts from his early friends.

This room was the gathering-place for the men and boys of Clifford's neighborhood on rainy days and lonesome Sundays, and here it was that he spent most of his leisure time in reading or study.

At length he arose and went to the attic, from which place he soon returned with a case of tools.

Then, taking up the carpet in the corner of the room, he sawed out a place in the floor large enough to admit the strong, iron-bound chest, which he had dragged out from the adjoining room.

After hastily tacking some cleats on the boards, which he had sawed out of the floor, thus providing a lid for the cavity, he placed the chest within the aperture. The bottom of the strong box rested on the earth below, and its top came nearly even with the floor. In a small compartment of this chest young Warlow placed the jewels; then he paused awhile to look at the roll of parchments.

These documents proved to be the patents to the estate of Monteluma, and Clifford could dimly see the signatures of Charles V and Philip II, with the broad seal of the Spanish crown on the mildewed, discolored, yet precious parchments.

There was, in addition, a large envelope, heavily sealed, on which the superscription was quite dim. In the waning light young Warlow failed to decipher it; but promising himself that he would soon examine this mystery-hinting missive at greater leisure, he placed all the papers in the chest, which he securely locked, closed the trap-door, and tacked down the carpet; then, fastening up the house with great care, he hurried down to his father's dwelling.

Chapter XVII.

MAUD and Rob met Clifford at the gate, and as he passed under the latticed arch where the trumpet-vine clambered with succulent ambition, its sprays of flame-red bugles mottled with spots of velvety black, Maud said eagerly:—

"I was growing uneasy about you, Cliff. Did you see nothing of that strange, gray-robed creature up at the cell?"

"Nothing whatever; but I am led to believe that mysterious being often stays there. We must keep a sharp watch on the place hereafter, and perhaps we may unravel the mystery," he replied, anxious to lead the subject away from his recent search.

As he stood, dreading further questioning, the supper-bell sounded, and he quickly moved on into the house, determined that he would conceal his discovery until he had made a search for the gold also.

The Warlow family retired early that night; but as the clock struck two Clifford arose, and listening to be certain that Rob was safe in the arms of Morpheus, he then stepped lightly out on to the veranda, and, after pausing a moment at the foot of the steps to draw on his boots, hurried down to the barn.

After saddling one of his Norman horses, he rode up to his dwelling, where he secured the iron rod and spade with which he had prosecuted his former search, and then galloped on down to the old cottonwood-tree.

Tying his horse to an ash-tree on the river bank, he began digging on the very spot where he had unearthed the cask with all its attending horrors. While throwing the soil out of the pit, he soon forgot the dangers and disappointment which had attended that adventure, and in his eagerness to reach the shattered cask, still remaining below him, he labored with such energy that he soon reached the object of his search.

As he began to clear the dirt from the shattered cask, he often listened to hear the warning rattle that would announce the presence of the mate to that venomous reptile which he had slain here · a few weeks previous; but no trace of the serpent was found. While removing the last spadeful of earth, the thought came to him like a flash of sunlight that the snake had been placed within the cask for the very purpose of terrifying and discouraging any one from searching deeper after he had unearthed it.

He remembered having read of circumstances where reptiles had been found imprisoned in rock, where they had survived the confinement of an era of time to which twenty-seven years was a short period in comparison; so it appeared that the snake might have been placed there when the cask was buried, and had lived and developed into the enormous reptile which had served to unnerve him and arrest his search on the first occasion.

It had occurred to him, before digging, that the

cask had been buried by the wretches who were engaged in the massacre at the corral, and that the treasure was secreted just below the cask. This belief had resulted from his successful search at the cavern, and had ripened now into almost conviction; so he had resolved to search deeper on the same spot where he had met with his first signal failure.

"How true it is that we should always look below the surface of treachery, enmity, and failure for the true gold of success!" said young Warlow, meanwhile removing the last stave of the old cask, and boring down with the iron rod into the bottom of the pit.

As the instrument struck hard against some resisting object, but two feet below, he felt the shock of a hot thrill of excitement; then grasping his spade with trembling hands, he soon reached the goal of his labors.

Another cask was revealed!

Yes; there was the treasure, he felt with all the conviction of certainty, that he had so long vainly hoped to recover. He struck the head of the cask several blows with his spade, and as the wood crushed in, he paused with the same old feeling of vacillation and dread that had seized him when the precious casket lay unopened before him at the secret cavern,—the irresolute, wavering sensation, the fear of disappointment, which so often assails us when fortune's phantom stands dimly near, and we hesitate to grasp her beckoning hand, fearing vaguely that a buffet may await us. It was in such a mood young War-

low stood, while the hopes and fears coursed
dreamily through his soul.   The sweat-drops rained
from his brow, and fell trickling down through the
pale moonlight.   At last, with shaking hand, he lit
his lantern and peered down into the cask below;
and as he slowly cleared out the fragments of the
shattered head, he saw that there was a mass of
fleecy wool filling the cask completely.   Tearing
this aside with nerveless fingers and panting haste,
there was revealed row after row of deer-skin bags,
with the words,

"GEORGE WARLOW, 1849,"

plainly lettered upon their sides.   With his knife he
quickly severed the thong that bound one of them,
and the dull, red gold gleamed back in the flickering light!

"Oh God! at last—at last!" cried our hero
(who certainly has earned his title), as broken sobs
shook his frame, and he leaned faint and dizzy
against the side of the pit.   But while he stood,
weak and panting, a wild, frightened snort from his
horse caused him to bound out of the pit, and
hurry forward to where he had fastened the animal.
When he reached the tree the usually quiet creature
was found to be trembling with fear or excitement.
After caressing the sleek Norman for a moment,
and speaking in a soothing tone to quiet the creature, Clifford walked back toward the pit; but as
he came into the moonlight, he paused a moment
to take a full breath of the light breeze, which was
rippling the water and whispering among the trees.

Far down the valley he could trace the silvery veil of vapor, revealing the course of the narrow stream, and among the dense shadows of willow and vines the fire-flies wove their webs of glimmering light. The midsummer night was still and tranquil, the silence only broken by the moan of the brook and the chirp of insects; the heavy dewdrops on tree and shrub glinted and flashed in the moonbeams that sifted through the willows in a sheen of wavering silver.

The quavering scream of a wolf on some dismal hill-top—a sound heard nightly all over the Western prairies, but one that never fails to send a cold thrill of horror through the lone traveler—startled Clifford from the momentary reverie into which he had fallen, and brought back vividly the remembrance of that night of terror and danger, which now seemed so long ago; and, as if the very thought had conjured up the spirits of the past, that well-remembered spectre, gray-robed, with snaky locks and glaring eyes, darted from among the shadows and with its bony, talon-like fingers clutched at young Warlow's throat.

Not a sound came from the lips that were drawn back from its snaggled fangs, but with its loathsome, grave-like breath full on his cheek, it closed in a death grapple with the startled and horrified youth. A wild struggle ensued; the rank vines and slender willows were trampled to the earth; and soon the combatants stood on the banks of the stream, by a deep, dark pool, and the fierce, unearthly creature, tried to force Clifford's head beneath the water.

As the fiendish, murderous intention of his assailant became apparent, young Warlow sprang back from the danger that yawned before him, and tore loose from the fury-blinded wretch, which again darted at Clifford, grappling with him in all the frenzy and desperation of a maniac.

The failing strength of the strange creature became more apparent every moment; so Clifford determined to first exhaust it by a violent struggle, then bind it with the lariat which hung at his saddle; and soon it was an easy matter for our athletic and vigorous young hero to drag the panting wretch to where his horse stood trembling with terror and wild with fright. Clifford spoke in a soothing tone, and when the horse became once more quiet, he reached for the lariat, while holding the maniac with one hand; but with a desperate wrench the spectral being tore loose from his grasp, and bounded away with a loud yell. Then, as it fled swiftly away over the prairie, at every step it would shriek like a mangled hound—the soundg rowing fainter, until at length it died out in silence on the grassy hills.

With a prolonged shiver, Clifford started like one awakened from a terrible night-mare; then remembering the new-found treasure, he hurried back to the pit, and peered down—as though fearful that he should find it all a dream.

But no—there was the red gold, resting where it had lain so long.

Clifford paused a moment, irresolute and uncertain what course to pursue. How should he remove this vast treasure to a place of security? he was asking himself, when there recurred to his mind the fact that there was harness in his stable, and an old, stout sled there also. The latter had been used in transporting stone from the old wall to build his dwelling, and was admirably adapted to just such a purpose as bearing up the heavy sacks of coin. So young Warlow lost no time in hurrying down to the stable.

As he nervously harnessed the horse by the dim light of the lantern, he was devoured with anxiety, lest something should occur that would yet rob him of the fruits of his great discovery. " What if that uncanny demon should return, and undo all his labor by some diabolical plan or act?" he found himself saying in a half-audible tone, as with trembling haste he hurried back to the treasure—and found all his fears were groundless, for every thing remained as he had left it.

When he attempted to lift the sacks of coin he found that it was no light task, for each one of the stout bags weighed fully forty pounds; but with great difficulty he loaded ten of them on to the low vehicle, then led the horse up to the dwelling, close to the door, where, unhitching the animal and securing him to the stone post near by, he proceeded to carry the sacks into the dwelling.

Five of the first were lettered with the name of his father. These he placed by themselves. Then, taking up the carpet and the floor where he had concealed the chest, he untied the remaining five sacks, and emptied their glittering contents into the iron-bound box. When all this was completed, he

19

returned for another load, but not without again entertaining grave fears for the safety of the precious
cask, which he found still undisturbed.

Four more loads of the coin emptied the cask.
Then came the work of refilling the pit, and obliter-
ating all trace of the search. Then, after returning
the sled and harness to their accustomed places,
Clifford sat down, faint and weary, to feast his eyes
on the grand sight, the enormous wealth that was
displayed by the lamp-light.

More than four hundred thousand dollars in
gold lay in a glittering, red mass before him! The
coin almost filled the chest, while in the shallow
compartment were the gems, which he had taken
from their casket, that he might once more admire
them and feast his eyes on their splendor.

The gems—he remembered having heard his
father say—represented more than half a million
dollars; and he tried to realize what this vast aggre-
gation of wealth meant—this million of treasure that
he had restored to the light since the last sunrise;
but only faintly could the young " Fortune Hunter "
comprehend the power and grandeur of the treasure
before him.

Out among the mass of red and yellow gold
trailed a strand of frosty, glimmering pearls. The
great diamonds, that flashed their rivers of light;
and rubies, that mingled their rays of rose and
crimson with the green glint of emeralds; lurid
opals, sapphires of sparkling blue or violet red;
amethysts of pink, purple, and lilac,—all spoke in
proudest tones of the wealth of Monteluma; and,

with a weary sigh, Clifford thought of the wide social gulf which now yawned between himself and the heiress of all this splendor.

After securing all the treasure in the chest, and locking the door securely behind, young Warlow rode stealthily homeward as the first blush of crimson was mantling the eastern sky, and the great planets were growing pale.

Chapter XVIII.

IN the cool of the following evening we find Clifford swinging dreamily in a hammock on the porch, while near by is ever-busy Maud, preparing a basket of martynias for the pickle-jar. As she deftly snipped off the curling ends of the green pods, locally known as "Devil Claws"—a very appropriate name indeed, when applied to the mature fruit—she cast a glance of suspicion toward her brother, and said:—

"I never like to see you so quiet, Clifford. I have always noticed that silent people need watching. Now, here is Rob, for instance:—Just so long as we can hear him whistling or singing, we rest contentedly; but the very moment he becomes quiet—ah! look out! There is mischief on hand every time; and we are likely to miss pie from the pantry soon, or find that the rogue has filched a bowl of cream down cellar. No, sir; you have been so suspiciously reticent to-day that I am led to think you have learned something since we had our talk yesterday."

"I always endeavor to store up some treasure of wisdom daily, my sister," Clifford replied, with lazy evasion, as he swung a polished boot to and fro over the hammock's side, and turned a feverish face toward Maud. Then, while a look of sarcasm gleamed in his half-closed eyes, he added, as she continued to glance askance: "Who was the philosopher, sage, or poet that said—or should have said, at least—something about the moral obloquy of groping through life with a cross eye?"

"Whoever that fellow was who strangled on such a proverb, I'll bet my boots he never clanked round of nights, like a loose horse, all the while fancying himself sly," said Rob, with a knowing chuckle, as he cocked his head on one side to view the horse-hair bridle-rein which he was braiding while seated on the edge of the porch.

A loud-mouthed clamor from the dogs precluded an answer to this thrust, and as the group on the porch looked toward the gate, Grace, Ralph, and Scott Moreland came into the yard, and they were all soon eagerly discussing the plan of holding a picnic in the Warlow pasture, on the opposite side of the river from the colonel's dwelling.

Before their neighbors left it was decided that the event should take place the last of the following week; but in the excitement of agreeing on a programme, and the wordy debate as to the propriety of including dancing in the list of amusements, all the leisure time of the next two days was consumed; so nothing more was said regarding the great discoveries which the week had revealed.

Verbal and written invitations were sown broadcast throughout the colony, bidding their friends to the picnic; and not many days had elapsed before Clifford had ridden down to the Estill Ranch to deliver the compliment in person to the members of that aristocratic household.

At the door he met Hugh, who was as cordial and genial as ever, and entered into the scheme of the picnic with his customary zest of pleasure, sharpened now, no doubt, with the desire to meet the fascinating Grace once again.

The call lengthened out astonishingly, as Clifford strolled back and forth on the star-lit terrace with the vivacious heiress of Monteluma and Estill Ranch, who promised to come up with Hugh the next day, to practice, with a dozen others, who were to meet at Moreland's, and agree on the music for the entertainment.

"What a delightful evening this has been!" said Clifford at a very late hour, as they walked down to the steps, at the base of which his horse was tied.

"Oh, charming indeed! And do n't you think that we are progressing well with our "practicing," for here we have had all the elements of a flirtation without the aid of either a moon or a gate," she said gaily, as he unfastened the chain at the steps, which served to bar the way at the top of the stairs, which led down from the terrace.

A cool "Good evening, Miss Estill," was all the answer this sally elicited from young Warlow, as he rode away, thinking gloomily that the proud heiress meant to show him, under the cover of her levity, that she was only amusing herself or "practicing" the arts of "flirtation" at his expense; and he determined that when they met again he would show her that he understood the hint, and would give her no further opportunity to repulse his advances.

So, accordingly, it was with a great deal of hauteur he met Miss Estill the following afternoon at Morelands'; but either that young lady was too indifferent to notice his behavior or had been gratified at the result of her light remark, for she was as gay and unchanged as ever.

All of our hero's stern resolves dissolved into smiles and admiration while he stood talking with the charming young lady; but when the wealthy, dissolute aristocrat, Major Stork, of Devondale, came up, and proceeded to monopolize Miss Estill, Clifford froze up completely, and became so polite and attentive to Grace that she at length declared she would box his ears if he did not quit persecuting her so; which persecutions consisted merely in keeping Hugh Estill away from her side—a crime which Clifford told her, hotly, was worse than murder in her eyes.

"Cliff Warlow, you are a booby!" said Miss Grace, with astonishing candor; "and you need n't come round me with any of your second-hand attentions; for I've got a pair of eyes in my head, and know how to use them too. The idea of your being jealous of that hawk-billed old reprobate. Why, it's perfectly absurd," she continued, casting a glance of scorn toward the spot where the stately major and Miss Estill were talking. "Oh, you should remember, Cliff, that a girl who is worth having is not going to fall into a fellow's mouth like a ripe persimmon whenever he shakes the tree."

Then in a tone of confidence she continued, with a look of wisdom, which Clifford thought, with an ill-concealed smile, resembled that of a prairie-owl: "Girls are very apt to pretend a great coldness toward a fellow that they want to catch; that is, after they see they have made a safe impression on him; and to see such a girl begin manœuvring around another fellow, one too that you know she can't care a straw for, why, it always shows plain enough that it is only to decoy fellow number one."

"There you are now far beyond my comprehension," Clifford interrupted, with returning good humor; and as Hugh Estill joined them he added: "I will now retire in favor of number one."

Emboldened by Grace's homily, young Warlow sought Miss Estill's side, and in her vivacious friendliness he soon found the happiness that had taken flight on the appearance of the major; but the returning bud of confidence, which her smiles had called forth, was nipped by a most untimely frost in the appearance of a new rival—John Downels, of Diamond Springs.

Mr. Downels was a *debonair*, graceful specimen of the gilded youth of New York, from whose make-up the last remaining trace of effeminacy had been eliminated by a stern course of ranch-life in the West. He appeared to be an old friend of Miss Estill, who presented him to Clifford; but after a moment's civility, young Warlow took his leave and retired, while the late comer devoted himself to the heiress.

While pretending to discuss music with Mrs. Warfield, Clifford watched the pair furtively. He began to realize that now he had just cause for uneasiness; for there was an air of culture and polished ease about the blonde-haired young ranchman which made him very attractive, and young Warlow became so absorbed and miserable that he only half realized what he was saying.

"Do you think we shall have time at the picnic to sing all the songs on the programme before dinner?" Mrs. Warfield inquired.

"Why, no; I believe it would be a better plan to dish it out by the quart to the individual tables," he replied, absently; then seeing a puzzled look sweep over her face, he hastened to add: "You know it would be more liable to melt if it was in such small quantities."

The situation flashed at once upon the keen-eyed lady, and although flirtation, jealousy, music, and ice-cream was a combination sufficient to upset the gravity of a sexton, yet she replied in a tone of perfect suavity while toying with her bracelet of jet and gold:

"A very good plan indeed, Mr. Warlow."

When evening came, and with its brooding shadows the company dispersed, our hero returned home with a heavy heart. As he pondered over each word and action of Miss Estill, he had to confess that there was nothing in her demeanor towards him but friendly courtesy at all times. The only way that he could interpret her remark on the terrace, regarding their "flirtation" and "practicing," was that she had seen his growing attachment for herself, and she had in that way shown him that it was only a flirtation, and that his case

20

was hopeless. "Yes; she was too genuinely a lady
to encourage his suit, then discard him at the last
moment," he concluded, despondently.

A miserable day followed a sleepless night, and
Clifford busied himself with the farm duties, trying
vainly to forget the bewitching voice that was ever
haunting him, and which, as he drove the reaper
over the wild meadow, seemed to be singing above
the clang and ring of the sickle the sweet refrain,—

> "There blooms no rose upon the plain
>   But costs the night a thousand tears,"—

in the tones of luscious melody that he never—no,
never—could forget.

As he swung in the hammock again that evening, while Maud's guitar and the sweet strains of
"Silver Threads" lulled him into a drowsy reverie, he remembered suddenly the incident of the
"Moated Grange" which, Mora laughingly said,
had secured her such "a round scolding" because
she had neglected her household duties through
too much reading of that affecting poem. Why
should she have felt such sympathy for the forlorn
Mariana, unless the pathetic cry,

> "'He cometh not—he cometh not,' she said,"

had found an echo in her heart also?

"Yes; she was heart-free, and waiting for
some one to come and fill its empty chambers with
the treasures of his love," mentally concluded our
hero in a flash of joyful conviction. But again the
doubt and despondency prevailed; and in no very
enviable mood he rode down to Estill's ranch alone

the next day, to join the company that were to meet and practice for the coming musical festival, which now was the all-absorbing theme of the colony.

As he rode slowly along, Maud and Ralph passed him in a gallop, flinging back some gay badinage—something about "a laggard in love"—which he affected not to understand; then, as he saw Hugh and Grace cantering up the road behind, he put spurs to his horse, and arrived at the imposing mansion just in time to see young Downels and the military Stork alight from the latter's carriage, and, in the most amicable manner imaginable, both seek the young hostess and rain a shower of compliments upon her gracious head.

While these two devoted cavaliers, or rather charioteers—for they had ridden over in the barouche of Devondale, a vehicle sumptuous and costly—were engaged in a graceful skirmish of wit and verbiage with Miss Estill, our hero, after bowing coldly, passed on to the piano, where Mrs. Estill was chatting in a good-natured strain with a group of friends.

"You are late, Mr. Warlow, and we have been waiting for some one to 'break the ice' at the piano," she said, with her pleasing smile, as she shook hands with Clifford. "Let's see," she continued, "the quartette, 'My Native Hills,' is the first on the programme. I am very eager to hear your tenor since Mrs. Warfield said you made her home-sick when you sang it at the Moreland rehearsal," concluded the hostess, innocently.

"It would require a large bump of self-esteem

to construe that into a compliment," thought
Clifford; but meeting Mrs. Warfield's amused look,
he said, with a smile:—

"I hope her longing for home was not of the
same nature as that which a hand-organ inspires,
Mrs. Estill."

"No, indeed, Mr. Warlow; but you will excuse
my faulty compliment, and only remember that
I've been totally isolated from society for a quarter
of a century, and am apt to say the wrong thing in
the right place."

"There she goes again!" the face of Mrs. Warfield seemed to say; but Clifford only answered
with polite gravity:—

"Thank you, Mrs. Estill. I shall never forget
that you are very kind; and if Mrs. Warfield
will promise not to leave at once we will proceed
with the singing," he added, with a twinkle of
humor in his blue eyes.

"I will promise to stay as long as you are singing a tenor like an alpine horn," replied Mrs. Warfield, graciously.

"Well! good-bye, then?" said Clifford, as he
joined the singers; and soon his voice was heard,
clear and ringing, like the soft tones of a church-
bell in some quiet mountain valley—pealing out
with soaring, crystal notes, or floating down the
wind with a vibrant, thrilling sweetness, that
caused even the garrulous major to pause and say
at the end:—

"Why, pon honah, Miss Estill, this young Warlow is a wonderful singah; indeed he quite reminds

me of Mario, the enchanting, velvet-toned tennah, you know, whom I often have heard at the grand opera—aw—in delightful Paree. What a pity that he is—aw—only a pooah homesteadah, or was until of late, I heah."

"I am certain he is an earnest, industrious gentleman at all times, Major," said Miss Estill, with just enough reproof in her tone to cause the dissolute aristocrat to wince; then, pausing, only to see that her arrow had hit the mark, she continued :—

"His father was a wealthy planter who was ruined financially by the war; but we certainly respect the energy that has enabled him to repair his fortunes and found such a delightful home, as you will find the Warlow homestead to be. His example should encourage others to a similar course, instead of remaining in the overcrowded East or South to struggle along, hopelessly, amid the scenes of their misfortune."

"Ah! indeed—a plantah before the wah? Why, really, that is another mattah, Miss Estill. My fathah was also a plantah; but when the wah began he sold his niggahs and left Kentuckah, but finally returned and located thah again."

"You appear so sad, Mr. Downels, that I fear you are not enjoying our rehearsal," said Mora, ignoring the transaction in "niggahs," and turning with a questioning look to young Downels, who stood by her side yet, but seemingly lost in reverie since the music had ceased.

"Pardon the ungallantry, Miss Estill; but that

song carried me back to the Hudson, and I almost
fancied myself rambling over the hills and dales of
my boyhood's home once again." But his sadness
was seen to melt into an amused smile as Grace
sang in a rich brogue :—

> "Ould bachelor's hall—what a quare luking place it is!
>   Kape me from sich all the days of me loife ;
> Och ! sure an' methinks what a burnin' disgrace it is,
>   Niver at all to be takin a woife.
>
> Pots, dishes, and pans, and sich greasy commodities—
>   Ashes and tater-skins kiver the floor ;
> His cupboard 's a store-house of comical oddities—
>   Things that were niver heard tell of before !"

Several glees followed; then Miss Estill took
her place at the rich-toned piano, which was banked
in a bed of wild-flowers, where the flame-colored
blossoms of the desert-sage and the golden sunflowers were relieved by sprays of snow-powdered
lace-plant and rose-colored convolvuli, mingled
with tufts of white and purple mignonette, which
grew in fragrant profusion over all the surrounding hills. As the grand strains of Schubert's "Ser-
enade" floated out through the open windows, or
reverberated along the arched and frescoed ceiling
of the elegant apartment, the listeners preserved an
appreciative silence,—all the more flattering when
we remember that not a baker's dozen of the audience understood a word of German.

"It was all very fine and grand, no doubt, but
still perfect Greek, or Dutch—which is about the
same—to my poor, untutored ears," said Grace at
the close of the celebrated song, as she turned to
Rob and spoke in an undertone.

"Well, it was not all quite plain," returned that youth, with a droll grimace; "but it was certainly p-r-r-r-r-rrretty." Then, as Grace strangled and recovered from an effort at swallowing her own chin, he added facetiously: "Did n't you recognize the place where the old fellow shuffled out in his wooden shoes, and, after threatening the serenader with 'a schlock on the coop,' finally turned the bull-dog loose?"

"No, I just did nothing of the kind; and I do n't believe you understood one word of that heathen gibberish either," said Grace, with a sniff of suspicion.

"Oh, that only shows you can't interpret operatic music," Rob replied, with a derisive grin.

"Rob Warlow, you horrible creature! I never know when you are in earnest," she retorted, with a puzzled look, as she smoothed down the fluffy ruffles of her white muslin gown.

"Why, no—honest injun!—any one can learn to understand this classic music. It only requires a sufficient stretch of imagination, and then all is clear as—mud. Now, when Maud is playing Mendelssohn's 'Wedding March,' I can hear the cat squall like a panther when the baby pulls its tail; and she—that is Mrs. 'Sohn—takes an awful tantrum when 'Sohn wants her to get up of a cold morning and make a fire; and the way they shout and gabble—all in Dutch—would scare a kroutbarrel," said Rob, with perfect gravity.

"Oh, humbug!" she replied with a shrug, as she flounced away to where Maud stood examining a book of engravings.

"Cliff and Mora are acting like a couple of idiots, Maud," whispered Grace, as she surveyed the elegant and finished picture, "The Carnival in Venice," with a critical glance that reminded one of a wren; but as Maud failed to reply to this personal comment, she continued in an undaunted undertone :—

"I don't pretend to understand flirtations, but if I did, I'd say that Mora Estill was a pronounced coquette. She bears all the ear-marks of a born flirt, and the way she throws herself at the head of young Downels—the sophisticated creature!—is just shameful. But still my fingers itch none the less to pull Cliff's ears; for there he goes, with his lip hanging so low you could step on it—and all on her account, too."

"Well, Grace, let's reserve our sympathy and censure for the future," said Maud, in a tone meant to discourage any further discussion of the subject; and as the supper-bell announced the unfashionable hour of six, and the guests were preparing to follow Mrs. Estill and Major Stork into the long, fresco-paneled dining-room, Grace ceased her comments, and soon forgot all about her friends while leaning on the arm of Hugh Estill and hurrying into the damask-draped and luxury-laden table.

However, she noticed that Clifford and Mrs. Warfield sat next to Mora and young Downels when they were, at length, all seated, and that while the latter couple were silent, the former kept up a semi-animated, constrained run of small talk during the meal; but she soon became so engrossed while

listening to Hugh's not over-brilliant wit that all
else was devoid of interest.

When the many luxuries had been discussed, and
the guests were loitering in the parlor or sauntering
out upon the terrace in groups of twos and—well,
twos also, I believe—Clifford walked out alone to the
fountain, and sat down on a stone seat near the basin,
which was brimming with water. Here the broad-
leaved lilies floated, with their blossoms of pale
rose and cream, distilling an odor of entrancing
sweetness for yards around the cool, moss-set brim.
As he sat lost in bitter meditations, the twilight began to deepen, the cicadas tuned their shrill pipes,
and Venus shone out with unclouded splendor over
the tree-tops of the valley below, followed, as she
has ever been, by an ardent host of glittering stars
and planets. That great midsummer constellation,
the Scorpion, seemed stinging the "milky way"
with its venomous tail, while the jeweled Sickle
sank in the west—an omen that the harvest-days
were nearly ended. A shrill katydid, overhead in
the branches, heralded the coming frost, while a low
ripple of voices mingled with the faint notes of the
piano and snatches of song from within the house.

As Clifford sat, trailing a lily through the water,
thinking, alas! of the time when he had strolled
here with Mora, only two short weeks before, and
how trustfully she had told him of "the mystery
that seemed haunting the very air of late," he found
it hard to realize that another had supplanted him,
and that henceforth they were to be as strangers.
But slowly it began to dawn upon him that their

paths had diverged since that fatal night upon the starlit terrace, when she so lightly remarked upon their "practicing" and "flirtation," until now he felt they were rapidly and surely becoming totally estranged.

"It is better that I should never, never look upon her fair, proud face again; for when I meet her eyes—ah! 'what can it mean?—there seems such a look of pleading, mingled with pride and—something that I can never understand—that it totally unmans me, and I can not trust my lips to speak a word for fear of betraying the secret of my love. No; she will find that the Warlow pride will be a match for her own; for I would rather tear my heart out and fling it at her feet, than have her spurn my love, as only a proud creature like her can.

"To know that she looks upon me as a fortune hunter, and scans me with those haughty — oh, lovely — violet eyes, classing me as 'poor and proud,' but far beneath her caste,—oh, Heaven! it is more than I can or will bear!" mentally exclaimed fiery young Warlow with a flash of hot wrath,—which is about the best remedy known for a sore heart, I really believe.

"A fortune hunter? Well, can't a fellow who has yearned all his life to meet a high-bred, dainty, and elegant woman, dare to love her when he does meet such an ideal, for fear of being called by that contemptible name?" continued our hero, impatiently plucking another water-lily, and beginning to pace up and down the path in nervous haste, and resuming his meditations, saying, half audibly : —

"If she had only waited a few more days I could have shown her that Colonel Warlow's son was not the poor homesteader—that pariah of the cattle-king—which she seems to consider me in her high pride. But no ; she must throw cold water on a poor devil before he has made too big a fool of himself to offend her pride by a declaration of his folly.

"But she has all the refined instincts of her class at any rate, and can send a disheartened, despairing wretch like me on a life-long journey of dreary longing, with a sweet graciousness that I must admire, though I curse it ever so bitterly!" Then, as there rose vividly to his mind a picture of that proud but vivacious face, lit by eyes of violet-blue, and framed by the mass of raven, wavy hair ; the coral, tender lips and creamy, dimpled cheeks so soft and tinted; the graceful form, in its filmy, flower-wrought robe of white,—he leaned against the elm-tree, and covered his face with his hands as though to shut the lovely vision from his sight, and murmured in tones of deepest agony : —

"Oh, Mora, Mora, my lost love ! how can I give you up?" It seems as if I have loved you from eternity ; and to lose you now is like the pangs of death !"

Rousing himself as the sound of retreating wheels was heard below the terrace, Clifford walked back to the hall-way, where he met several depart-

ing guests; and as he came into the hall, with a
slow leaden step, he saw, with a start, that Miss
Estill was standing alone by the stairs, where she
had turned after bidding some of the guests good-
night! When she saw his face, with its look of
white, tense misery, she said quickly : —

"Oh, Mr. Warlow! I have missed you for an
hour. You are ill, I fear."

"Yes, Miss Estill, I am—sick of the world; but
it is a very slight matter—only a broken heart,"
young Warlow replied, in a low, husky tone, while
his eyes flashed like purple amethysts.

She turned deadly white, and gave him a look
wherein he read a proud pity, that sent a flash of
hot indignation to his face; then he bowed and
walked away without glancing back.

As he came into the glare of the lighted parlor,
Maud met him, and, after giving him a glance of
deep sympathy, she said with her accustomed tact: —

"Clifford, you are no better, I fear; so let's return home. Most of the guests are starting already,
although it is only nine; but we have, like them,
also a long drive before us to-night."

So, bidding their hostess good-night, the Warlow and Moreland party started toward the hall;
but at the door Miss Estill met them, looking pale
and *distrait*, though regretful at their early departure.

She tarried a moment at the door, talking to
Maud and Grace regarding the details of the picnic;
and as she stood under the full light of a large lamp,
held by a marble statue of Mercury, the wonderful
grace and beauty of her creole face came into daz-

zling relief, and Clifford paused with a look of hungry longing on his face, while the remainder of the group hurried on to where the carriage waited, leaving him alone with Mora.

"I will say farewell here, Miss Estill. We shall meet at the picnic, Friday, but there will be little chance to bid you adieu there. I start for South America the next morning to stay indefinitely; so good-bye—forever!"

Even now in this trying moment, while his heart turned cold with an agony that not even death could equal, Clifford was true to the instincts of a gentleman, and waited immovably for her to offer her hand; but she only stood and toyed with her dainty fan, saying with the same cold, proud look that she had given him once before that evening:—

"This is very sudden. Indeed you can not be in earnest; so I shall reserve my adieus until the very last. I will try at the picnic to persuade you to abandon such an unkind course, and remain with us."

"Very well, Miss Estill, but I had forgotten to tell you that I have a disclosure to make at the picnic—one of grave import to you—and beg for an hour of your time while there. I would prefer the morning, if you please.

"With pleasure, certainly," she replied; but their talk was interrupted by some guests preparing to depart; so young Warlow hurriedly said good-night, and joined Maud and the others in the carriage.

Soon they were rapidly whirling homeward up

the level, winding road; but as no one seemed to
be in a talking mood, the journey was rather a silent one, the monotony only relieved by a scurrying
flock of wild-grouse or the dim and retreating form
of a startled jack-rabbit, looming large and indistinct upon the level prairie.   In places the tall
blue-stem moved in the wind with a rolling, wave-
like motion; then again giving place to vistas of
open glades, carpeted by the buffalo-grass, that the
rains and sun had bleached almost white.

A forecast of autumn was felt in the rising gales,
which moaned through the tall cottonwoods along
the stream; the water flashed cold and bright under
the starlight, and the buffalo-birds—our Western
whip-poor-will—swooped down with a bellowing
roar close to the heads of our friends as they drove
by, indicating that a rain was near at hand.

Chapter XIX.

A STRANGE THEORY.

"OUR BODIES MAY BE TENANTED BY SOULS THAT HAVE LIVED BEFORE."

A POURING rain from a vapor-laden sky, dull and gray, saluted Clifford the next morning with a chill welcome; but still the general gloom that pervaded all nature was in such perfect harmony with his mood that he felt a grim satisfaction, in a cold, lethargic way, at the sympathy of the elements.

"I am growing tired of this monotonous life," he said at breakfast, "and have decided to commute my homestead and knock around in the world awhile; so if Mr. Moreland, Ralph, and you, father, are willing to go to Abilene as my witnesses, we will start Saturday morning. I can take the train from there, and save another trip;" then seeing Maud's and his mother's look of distress, he added: "I may not be gone long, so I'll leave every thing as it is untill my return."

"Why, Clifford, my boy, what has come over you? This is wholly unlike your nature. I had always felt so glad that you were not of a roving disposition, and now you fly off at a tangent, and when we were not looking for any thing of the kind either. It is very strange, indeed!"

Clifford made no reply, but rose from the table,

followed by Rob, whose face was momentarily growing longer and more doleful in its expression, while Maud shot a warning look at her parents, and as the boy's retreating footsteps grew fainter, she answered their questioning looks by saying:—

"Poor Clifford! he is passing through that course of true love which is said to never run smooth, and it is best not to interfere; but I hope at the picnic to see him on better terms with Mora, which may change his plans at once."

"Only a lovers' quarrel?" said Mrs. Warlow, with a troubled smile.

"No; I fear it is not so tangible as that," Maud replied. "Clifford seems to have caught the impression, some way, that Mora regards him as a mere fortune hunter, or looks down on him for his poverty; you know that she will be equal heir with Hugh in the immense Estill estate, which is said to be worth half a million, she being their only other child," she added, while narrowly watching her parents' faces; but to her wonder, her father and mother betrayed no surprise at this last remark, which caused a doubt to enter her mind that they were aware of the great discovery that Mora was the daughter of Bruce and Ivarene, which she had until this moment believed was a fact revealed to them when the Estills made their visit, more than a week before.

"Can it be that they are still ignorant of that fact?" Maud mentally asked herself; and then she began to wonder why the Estills had shown the locket, with its pictures of Bruce and his wife, and withheld from her parents the more important secret that Mora was also the daughter of those ill-fated friends; but her reflections were cut short by her father saying, with a weary sigh :—

"Ah! this is the sting of poverty indeed! Oh, why should I have been so ill-fated as to lose two fortunes in succession?"

"George, do not grieve over the past; that's beyond recall," Mrs. Warlow said gently; then she added: "It is better that my children should confine themselves to their own sphere; for you can see that if Miss Estill loved my boy, as well she might, for himself alone, she would never think of the difference in their wealth. It may save them a life-time of misery; for without mutual love, matrimony would be a state of abject servitude."

"Well, if Clifford sees fit to take a change of scene, it will serve to cure him of his—attachment; and if Mora, in the meantime, discovers her mistake in undervaluing Clifford—a fellow that any girl under the sun might be proud of—why, it may all come out right yet," said Maud as she rose from the table and began to polish and clean the great silver coffee-urn, another relic of old plantation glory, but which had never been considered too good for every-day service.

All day Clifford worked with a fever of energy to prepare for his journey, which he was compelled to do; for the picnic was set for the coming day, Friday, and he had to see the Morelands to secure their attendance with him at the land-office as witnesses to prove his actual residence and cultivation

upon his homestead, which he had concluded to
commute, or in other words, pay the sum of two
hundred dollars to the government in lieu of five
years of residence and cultivation thereon. Having secured their testimony, or their willing promise to accompany him to Abilene and there testify
to his good faith, etc., he made everything ready
for his departure the next morning after the picnic.

When Maud and his mother questioned him
regarding the destination and duration of his trip,
he said he would go South awhile, but evaded telling them that he had determined to go to Buenos
Ayres and remain until he had made a fortune that
would cause Miss Estill to regard him as an equal.

He noticed the sadness, however, of the family,
and when he met Rob's look of grief his fortitude
was sorely tried, and he regretted having formed
such a hasty resolution. But it was too late now to
retreat, he foolishly concluded; so, choking down a
lump in his throat, he walked out to take a last
view of his farm. As he sauntered along in a list-
less way, looking at the fields, every furrow of
which he had turned over in the past with such a
deep pride of ownership; at the trees and deep
pools, that greeted him with the air of old friendship, he began to realize how dear the place had
become, and he wondered, in a self-pitying way, how
he could bear the existence that awaited him out
on the sky-begirt level and lonely pampas of the
Rio La Plata.

When he came to the gothic dwelling, the circle
of roses and trellises of luxuriant vines, the slop-

ing orchard and vineyard, they all seemed to be
still imbued with the strange thought which had
ever haunted him while he was busied there.
" Here for the first time since eternity began, I
found a true home. All this is mine, and on this
spot I shall pass my life. What events will transpire here in the unknown future! I shall know
joy and sorrow here, but who will share it all with
me?" As these visions recurred, he thought bitterly that he never had counted upon an hour of
trial like the present. Then, throwing himself
down in the shade of the old wall, he cried aloud in
anguish, as he buried his face in the soft, matted
buffalo-grass: " Oh, it is hard to part from all this—
and only for a woman who cares nothing for me!"
But at length he became calmer, and as a feeling of
resentment towards the proud heiress began to possess
him, he arose and went into the house: then, after
taking the usual precautions against surprise, he
raised the trap-door and unlocked the treasure-chest.

On glancing at the heap of red gold mingled
with the dazzling gems, he took from the compartment the paper which he had almost forgotten having never read; then breaking the seal, he found
that it was the wills of both Bruce and his wife on
separate sheets of vellum, executed at Santa Fe,
devising all their estate each to the other, in case
of either dying during the long journey on which
they were about starting.

" I will bring her here to-morrow. She shall
read the pathetic Journal of Ivarene and this will.
I shall tell her of the long search after the treas-

ure, and her right to all this wealth; then, after restoring both her name and fortune, there will be little left for me to do but to slink away, while some long-necked aristocrat will step to the foreground and carry off the prize," soliloquized our hero with bitter sarcasm, as he placed the papers in an inner pocket of his drab coat, and closed the chest with a vicious snap.

The rain had ceased long since, and a band of crimson and rose on the western horizon gave a promise of fair weather on the morrow; but Clifford lingered about the beloved place, feeling that this was his farewell to a spot that had grown dear as life to him in the last year. He found it hard to tear himself away; so he seated himself upon a travel-worn ridge in the old trail, worn years ago by the wheels of the freight wagons, but now carpeted thickly with the buffalo-grass, which seems to delight in hiding just such an unsightly, trampled place with its pale-green tendrils. As the shadows darkened among the trees, and the gloom of a starless, fog-ladened night settled down with a palpable silence, young Warlow became lost in thought.

The scene which followed was always a mystery to him; for he never knew whether he had witnessed a supernatural sight or not. He often tried to persuade himself that he had lapsed into a fit of transient slumber, and the whole spectacle was only a vivid dream.

The time passed by unheeded, and it was near the hour of ten when his fit of abstraction was broken by seeing a group of fire-flies flashing about in an unnatural manner. He remembered, dimly, seeing great numbers of these luminous insects congregating around the long grave, not fifty paces away; and his blood grew cold as he saw, with a thrill of horror, that the flashing, mazy clouds began to slowly resolve themselves into the semblance of human forms, that leaped and danced in fiendish glee; now bounding high into the murky air, or again brandishing weapons, that resembled warclubs and tomahawks, in a threatening and heartsickening manner.

While these mysterious forms gyrated about in their unearthly war-dance, Clifford stood petrified with horror and astonishment, not unmixed with a strange curiosity to see how it would terminate; and when the luminous figures joined hands, and slowly paced about the grave, as though to the chant of some wild and savage death-song, a dim and glimmering circle of phantom warriors, Clifford could bear it no longer, but sprang to his feet with a cry of horror, that was echoed by a shriek which he instantly recognized as being the voice of Rob. As the skurrying hoofs went tearing away, he shouted quickly: —

"Rob! Rob! wait,—it is Cliff! Come back like a man, and let's investigate;" but he saw that at the first sound of their voices the figures had flashed asunder like thistle-down before a breath, and now were whirling and weaving in a bewildering maze of light that melted away as he gazed, and separated into the innocent flitting forms of fire-flies that were hieing off to the dark nooks along the stream.

As Rob came back, riding slowly and in an uncertain manner, Clifford emerged from the gloom of the trees into the less ebon darkness of the open ground; then Rob halted and said, in a shaky voice:—

"I thought that I had run afoul of the old devil himself when you yelled so! What is the matter, anyway?"

Briefly as possible Clifford told of the strange sight which he had just witnessed—a scene which he then thought was more like a fevered dream than a reality.

"But how does it happen you were here?" he added.

"Why, we were uneasy about you, and I had come in search. I knew you would be up here, for I saw you walking this way. I had just got here, and was going to call you, when you yelled like a catamount down by the old grave. What does it mean, Cliff? It makes me cold yet!" he added, with chattering teeth.

"Well, it's something that can not be explained away," said Clifford, while walking back beside Rob, who, too well bred to ride while another walked, had dismounted, and was leading his horse. "There is only one view that I can take of it, and that is a supernatural one," he continued, as Rob linked his arm within his own, and they struck the road homeward. "There is a belief gaining ground, Rob, that the spirit—or the life principle, animation, or whatever it may be which we call soul—after it is disembodied by death, may yet linger about in some subtle, invisible form akin to electricity, and may become embodied again by entering into the being of a new-born child,—which, if true, may account for the strange resemblance we often see peering out of the eyes and face of an infant that recalls some long-dead friend or ancestor. It may be that the power which mind wields over matter would enable the strong, magnetic spirits of those savage warriors, who, no doubt, died terrible deaths of violence on this tragedy-haunted spot, to attract the fire-flies, and mold them into a semblance of their former bodies, or, at least, imprison them for a time within the spirit outline of their former selves. This, alone, would enable them to become visible to our eyes, proving what we already know, that without matter of a living nature the spirit— or magnetism, which we call soul—would be always as invisible as the air."

"Why, Cliff, you talk like a heathen!" replied Rob, vehemently, who, though addicted to the vice of swimming on the Sabbath, 'hooking' water-melons from the Mennonites, and hiding Easter eggs, was still strictly orthodox to his boot-heels. "So you think," he continued, "that a human soul may take the form of a panther or a pauper—whichever the spirit most resembles—and be cast and recast over and over again, like an old piece of boiler-iron, until at last it becomes—well, just what, I'd like to know?"

"A good Christian being that progresses towards perfection, and learns wisdom from his former mistakes, I guess," replied Clifford, as they turned the horse into the pasture and sought the house. As they came into the yard, he added: "If there is one spot on the continent that should be haunted, it certainly is the old Stone Corral and the near-by crossing of the Santa Fe and Abilene Trails; for there has been more crime and cruel deviltry committed there than upon any other square mile in the Western world."

The next morning broke with a cloudless sky, balmy and serene. A light wind from the southwest lifted the ribbon of vapor along the Cottonwood, and wafted the fresh and perfumed odors of wild hop-vine and water-mint, desert-sage and sand-plum, over the garden and into the Warlow breakfast-room, where Clifford was narrating to his horrified parents and sister the particulars of that unreal and mystery-wrapped scene which he had witnessed the night before.

"It all looks so unreal in this clear daylight that I am almost ashamed to repeat it," said Clifford, with a nervous laugh; but the hearers knew by the look of earnest gravity on his face that there could have been no mistake or deception as to his witnessing a sight that ever was a mystery to all.

"Well, this is a strange story indeed," said the colonel; "but, my boy, you must have been asleep unconsciously, and when you awoke your mind was in that abnormal state in which an optical illusion would have seemed like reality. An illusion of this nature is very hard to combat, from its very uncertainty; and we can only reason, from general principles, that it was a half-waking dream."

The preparations for the picnic put an end to any further discussion, and at ten the grounds were enlivened by a throng of people, all in their happiest mood and best attire.

When the Estill carriage came on the ground, Clifford hurried forward and assisted Miss Estill to alight; then, after shaking hands with Mrs. Estill, who excused her husband's absence by saying that he had not returned from the Comanche Pool, whither he had gone a week before, he found a seat for the elder lady, and disappeared with Mora on the pretext of boat-riding.

They walked in silence to where his boat was tied to the trunk of a weeping elm. As Clifford helped her into the seat, her warm clasp sent a thrill to his heart that caused a hot flush to mount to his face; but it soon receded, leaving him paler and more care-worn than ever. But Mora noticed that his cravat of dainty lawn was tied with that precision only attained by a thorough man of fashion, and the spray of snowy elder-bloom, late but fragrant, combined with a solitary pansy-shaped flower, pale blue with a fleck of gold at the heart, into a *boutonniére* that denoted a taste refined and fastidious in its wearer.

They shot out into the narrow stream under Clifford's vigorous strokes, and skimmed lightly along through the silver-linked pools, shaded by trees that were smothered by poison-ivy and wild-

22

grape vines, that trailed in the water with their purple-laden tendrils of ripening fruit. At length they reached the bank near young Warlow's dwelling, after a journey which he thought had lasted for an age, but which, to be correct, was just four minutes in duration. There had been an attempt on her part at conversation, but seeing the far-away look in his eyes and the expression of haggard misery on his white, handsome face, she became more cold and reserved than ever, and sat with averted face, trailing a gaudy cardinal-flower through the water.

On landing, he again encountered her hand, which did not fail to send an electric shock through him, as he assisted her ashore, and for a moment he thought that she held his hand longer than the occasion required, and he raised his eyes to her face with a quick flash of joy; but the downcast look and pale cheeks which he saw, sent the blood back to his heart with a sickening chill, and they walked together in silence up toward his dwelling.

When they reached the house he led the way to the spring and motioning her to a seat under the shade of that giant elm, he drew the wills forth and handed them to her saying:—

"Here, Miss Estill, is what makes you the greatest heiress in this western land!" then, as she silently read them through and lifted a puzzled face to his, he handed her the Journal of Ivarene, and watched breathlessly, while she became flushed and pale by turns while perusing the faded and time-worn paper.

"Ah! poor, ill-fated Ivarene! what could have

become of her and that helpless infant,—and brave Bruce too?" she cried, with tears in her eyes.

"The parents were murdered, no doubt, by that mad hunter, and the child was stolen and left at Estill's ranch along with a locket containing the name of Morelia and the pictures of Bruce and Ivarene. The mysterious kinsman buried on the hill-top was Olin Estill, who was only the mad hunter in disguise, who stole that blue-eyed, dark-haired daughter, named Morelia."

"Ah! you believe me to be the daughter of Bruce and his lovely wife!" said Mora, springing to her feet, while tears rained from her eyes, and her hands were wrung with deep emotion.

"Yes, I am certain that you are Morelia Wal-raven. I had suspected this from the hour that father called you Ivarene, and I set to work earnestly to recover the lost fortune, which I believed was buried near this spot. I worked faithfully, Miss Estill, to restore it all to you, knowing full well, all the while, that when found it would only widen the gulf between me and the cattle-king's daughter an hundred-fold. I will not dwell on the horrors of that fortune hunt, nor its perils, when I fought that gray-robed demon, which glared at you upon the grave-capped hill; how I struggled with that murderous spectre in the darkness of midnight, after being greeted in a noisome pit by a gigantic rattlesnake, which I slew as it writhed at my feet, with certain death in its fangs; nor the horror I felt when it was dead, at length, to grasp a human skull, that mocked me with eyeless sockets and

grinning teeth when I snatched it from the buried
cask—hoping I had found the casket of gems.

"But come with me, and I will show you that
the Warlow honor and pride is no vain boast;
that the poor planter's son can face danger and
death for the sake of right alone."

Then, as she followed, pale and trembling, into
the room, he threw back the lid of the treasure-
chest, and the red gold, the glorious rays from frosty
pearls, sparkling diamonds, blood-red rubies, and
strange green emeralds mingled, in a dazzling glare,
with the sheen of fire-opals and the glint of amethysts of purple, lilac, and rose.

" Here, Morelia Walraven, is your lost treasure,
your million of gems and gold, your proud name
and ancestral hall, which I restore," as he handed
her the deed of Monteluma. "To-morrow I shall
leave home and country, friends dearer than life, to
prove—to prove to you I am not that vile thing
which you take me for—a Fortune Hunter!"

She merely glanced at the pile of dazzling
wealth; then raised her eyes that glittered through
her tears like the turquois among the gold, and
while he poured forth a torrent of hot words that
seemed to come from his very soul, her color came
and went until a burning blush spread over her face,
and in a choking gasp she essayed to speak. When
he had ceased, she gazed a moment up into his face,
seamed and drawn in lines of white agony, then she
cried out:—

"Oh! what do I care for all this dross, whose
daughter I may be, or my pride of ancestry?

Clifford—oh, Clifford!—you shall never leave me.
I will die if you do. I love you! Oh, will I have
to say it?—yes, I love you better than all the
world beside. No, no! you shall never leave me!"
she said, with her white arms about his neck and
her soft, warm cheek pressed close to his; and—
and—well, I just skipped out there, leaving them
alone with a scene that was growing too unutterably
" rich for my blood," to use a Western phrase; but
half an hour later, as they strolled back to the boat
I overheard him say :—

" But why, my love, did you look so proud and
cold in the hall when I came in at your house only
the other night ?"

"Proud and cold, indeed," she replied, with a
gay laugh, as she shot a look of mingled love and
amazement into his beaming eyes. " Now, that
shows how well you can read a woman's heart, sir.
Dear Clifford," she added, tearfully, " do you know,
you dear blind boy, that at that very time I was
wretched and miserable, and longed to kiss you and
say that I had waited for years for just such an ideal
as you are ?"

" It is not too late now for that !" he cried rapturously, as they passed under the boughs of a
drooping tree, then followed a sound so explosive
that I beat a hasty retreat from such a danger-
fraught vicinity, and never came near again until
their boat touched shore. Maud came to them as
they landed, and said :—

" Where have you been, truants? I have missed
you for an hour."

"In paradise," replied Clifford, with such a look of happy abandon that Maud started joyfully; then Mora said, with a blush, as she clasped her arms about the form of delighted Maud :—

"Yes, I have coaxed him to stay forever; but I had to propose to the selfish being before he would promise at all."

Then Maud, seeing the tears of earnestness that began to start, kissed her new sister and Clifford very tenderly, saying, between her smiles and tears :—

"Oh, this is happiness indeed !" which sentiment seemed to be fully shared by the radiant couple whom she addressed.

Maud was not long in finding an excuse to leave the lovers to themselves; and when she had disappeared among the throng, they sauntered on to a secluded seat, under a vine-canopied tree, where the trailing bitter-sweet swept the closely-cropped grass with its graceful tendrils, loaded with a burden of orange and pink berries. Here, secure from intrusion, they could see the crowd of well-dressed people loitering about in detached groups, but were far enough removed from them to talk in that confidential strain peculiar to newly-mated young people, with no fear of interruption.

"When shall we reveal to your parents the discoveries which I disclosed to you to-day, Mora?" said Clifford, in a low tone.

"Let us be in no haste, Clifford," she replied; "for father is away, and mother would be unnerved and agitated at the revelation. Then we will have several guests to entertain for the next week, as Mrs. Potter and Miss Hanford will remain with us after the picnic. So I believe it would be best to defer it for a week or two."

"But what shall be done in the meantime with the treasure, Mora dear? There is a million dollars in gold and gems lying there in that chest. I tremble to think what the result might be if its existence were suspected in such an unprotected spot."

"Well, sir, you must nerve yourself to the task of not only caring for it, but of me also in the future," she replied, with a furtive caress; and, judging from his looks, he appeared to be equal to the latter responsibility at least.

"I have made arrangements to start to Abilene in the morning to commute my homestead and secure a title to it before the great sale of public lands Monday, which, it is said, will be sold at a very low figure," he replied, returning her caress with compound interest.

"Clifford, it looks mercenary and not at all sentimental for us to talk of business at such a time; but still we can love one another no less for that. The time is very short before that sale. It is a critical moment. I advise you to buy all the land that you can Monday; it will be very valuable soon," she said, with that mingling of sentiment and business peculiar to Western women.

"I shall invest what little I possess in that way, Mora; it is secure at least. I have always longed to own more of the land to the north of the corral; and this is, as you say, a golden opportunity to acquire it."

Then there was silence for a moment as Clifford sadly thought how little he really had for investment compared to the hoard that was lying useless in the chest. His father's gold was there still, but he had no real claim upon it ("I must deliver it to-night," he mentally concluded); and an involuntary sigh escaped him at the thought that strangers yet might control all that rolling, fertile prairie to the north, which he had vainly dreamed of owning.

As if divining his thoughts, Mora quickly said, as her hand sought his own with a gentle clasp:—

"Why not use some of that idle treasure for this purpose, Clifford? If it is mine, as it really seems to be, there will be no harm in investing part of it in that way. The emergency is great for decision and swift action, so I really believe you should take a large sum along for that purpose, not less than fifty thousand dollars of the recovered treasure, at least."

"You dear, clear-headed little woman!" he replied radiantly; "that is a capital plan indeed; so, if you think it best, I will take that sum with me, and invest it in land for your benefit."

"No, no; you misunderstand me, Clifford; it is for your benefit that I made the suggestion. You may take it as a loan, and repay me some time in the future," she added, demurely.

He was on the point of making some laughing rejoinder, when he started at the recollection that it seemed like fate when he recalled the loan of exactly fifty thousand dollars which Ivarene had

tendered his father, of which Mora was in total
ignorance. Then, in a low tone, he told her of the
strange coincidence, where history was repeating
itself; but he had not finished the story when a
summons to dinner was heard, and he accompanied
Mora to the Estill carriage, finishing the recital as
they walked slowly thither.

There were several guests clustered about the
carriage, and Clifford accepted an invitation to remain for dinner, which Mrs. Estill gave him, and
with Mora and young Downels, Miss Hanford and
Mrs. Potter, Clifford was soon busy helping to
spread the dinner on the snowy cloth beneath the
shade of a dense-foliaged elm. When the hampers
were unpacked and they were all seated upon the
grass about the cloth, it was evident that the Estills
could not be taxed with the sin of inhospitality, for
they had brought enough in their hampers for an
extra dozen guests.

There was boned turkey, hinting of sweet mar-
joram, garnished with quivering moulds of cherry-
jelly; chicken salad, with sprays of parsley; tank-
ards of silver and glass, filled with creamy milk;
tall glasses of jelly—pink, amber, and crimson;
pyramids of cake, bronzed and frosty, that conveyed a faint suspicion they were only meant for
show; great baskets of silver, marvels of frostwork
on flower and vine, piled high with purple grapes,
peaches of white and crimson, and golden oranges,—
all of which, alas! were the contribution of far-off
California.

Young Downels sat near Mora, who was as

fascinating and gracious as ever; but Clifford felt
a contentment and trust too deep for jealousy, and
was gay and witty to such a degree that Downels
began to have a suspicion of the true situation,
which was in no wise allayed when he saw their
eyes meet in a quick flash of love and admiration;
so he speedily transferred his attentions to Miss
Hanford, who seemed not at all averse to receiving
them *"ad infinitum."*

An afternoon of unalloyed bliss followed, and
when our hero placed Mora in the carriage, he
had given her a promise to ride down on his
return from Abilene, the following week; then, as
the stately barouche rolled away, he hurried homeward to complete his preparations for to-morrow's
journey.

At the supper-table, which was spread at a later
hour than usual, Colonel Warlow looked grave and
care-worn, while his wife was sad and thoughtful,
remembering that Clifford was to leave them, perhaps forever, and this was his last night under the
home-roof, a delusion which he was soon to dispel.   Maud's face wore a look of cheerfulness
which puzzled her parents, who had not witnessed
their son's manuevres during the day; and Rob's
eyes fairly danced with suppressed excitement.

Chapter X X.

"MY boy, it is a sad day for us all when you leave the home nest. We shall miss you more than I can express," said the colonel at length. "Ah! I had hoped to see you settled near us in our old age in this grand country. Clifford, I have seen a great many regions on this continent famous for their beauty and fertility, but this is the only place that I have ever seen where I would be perfectly content to live and die. You have yet to learn that 'distant hills' are no greener than those of home, and you will travel the wide world over and find no other place to compare with this, my son. I have been thinking to-day, Clifford," continued his father, as he pushed his plate of untasted food back on the table and folded his napkin—"that if I had only a tithe of the fortune that I once lost on this spot, it might be enhanced an hundred-fold at the great land-sale Monday; for I learn by to-day's *Times* that the Mastodon Bank has failed, carrying down in its collapse all the parties who had the lands condemned for sale, so now they are unable to bid at the auction, and hundreds of thousands of acres will be sold at a few cents an acre without competition. Oh, I realize that it is bitter, indeed, to be poor, my boy, for it is only your ambition that drives you from us," and, rising, he paced back and forth with bowed head, while Mrs.

Warlow's tears flowed unchecked as she thought of the long, dreary years that might drag on before her beloved boy returned.

The Warlow family were never demonstrative. There was always a matter-of-fact regard for each other; but this moment of sorrow brought to the surface a depth of family affection of which Clifford had never dreamed, and, as his father proceeded, he became more deeply affected than he ever had been before.

He thought, "The old days of trial and poverty are over forever," and as the realization of the great change, and his narrow escape from the misery. of self-exile flashed upon him, he leaned his head upon his hands, and a great sob shook his frame, while hot tears—yes, tears, which danger and the despair of a hopeless love had failed to wring—now fell in a torrent, as the storm of emotion, new and strange, surged in his breast.

"Oh, Clifford—Clifford! I thought you were not going," cried Maud, white with anguish.

"Cliff, I can't bear to see you leave," sobbed Robbie, while he clung to Clifford with the desperation born of his grief at the very thought of parting with his only brother.

"Clifford, what does this mean?" said Maud, seized by a nameless dread; but Clifford only answered by pushing back the table, the cover of which swept the floor and had concealed the object that was now revealed in the lamp-light.

"Gold! gold!" cried Maud in amazement, as

her eyes caught the glitter of doubloons heaped upon the floor.

"Oh God!—my lost fortune!" said the colonel in a hoarse whisper, as he knelt beside the half-emptied sacks, which he remembered at a glance.

"My brother—Clifford—you are a grand hero," shrieked Maud, wild with excitement and relief, and then ensued a contest between herself and mother who should first strangle our young friend in their embraces.

"Hero, nothing!" said Rob, who had just blown his nose upon the table-cloth with a snort like a porpoise, and who was still blubbering in a suspicious manner; "heroes do n't drip at the nose like a hydrant; but all the same he is a damn good fellow," he added, with a vigorous slap on his brother's back.

"I have something else to show you over at my dwelling," said Clifford, recovering from his emotion, and smiling up at Rob; "and, if you will drive around there, I will row ahead and light the lamps;" then, without waiting to explain, he hurried out into the night. Although they were devoured by curiosity, they soon concealed the gold, and were driven rapidly up to the corral.

"I bet my boot-heels that Cliff has got that old spook chained up here, feeding him like a pauper," said Rob, in a tone of confidence, to Maud—a remark which elicited no reply, however, for she was puzzling over the strange discovery which she knew Clifford had made.

When they arrived at his dwelling he met them at the door, which he closely locked behind them; then, going to the sunken chest, he threw back the lid, and a wavering glare of gems and red gold flashed out with a splendor which dazzled and almost blinded the astonished group.

"The treasure of Monteluma!" exclaimed the colonel, in a tone of deep emotion.

"Oh, those frosty, glimmering pearls!" said Maud, exulting in the splendor of the jewels that she loved so well, and had always dreamed of owning.

"What a pile of lucre!" cried Rob, dancing about in delight. "Lordy! if I owned all this tin, I'd make the shekels fly for awhile, you bet! First, I'd swap that slow, flea-bitten broncho for Ed Porter's white pony, if I had to give even *twenty dollars* to boot; then next I'd have me a brand-new hat—a broad brim, too—none of your flimsy old wool things, but an eight-dollar sombrero, thick as a board, with a leather band an inch wide; then two cravats—and—"

"And?" said Clifford with a quizzical smile, as Rob began to show signs of an embarrassment of riches.

"Well, that's all, unless it is a pair of high-top boots, like Johnnie Russell's—with stars and new moons of red and yellow leather on 'em."

"You are a reckless spenthrift, Rob. Thirty-five dollars gone already!" said Clifford, laughingly, as his young brother's eyes continued to gloat over the million of heaped-up riches in the chest.

"Clifford, my son, how did you find all this

treasure? It seems like enchantment," Mrs. Warlow asked, in an anxious tone.

"Mother, it is too long a story to relate now;
but when I return from Abilene I'll give all the
particulars. It is ten now," he said, glancing at his
watch, "and we must start at six sharp, in the
morning, so there is but little time to spare."

"Yes," said the colonel, recovering from the
stupor of amazement into which he had fallen, "we
will start to the land-office early in the morning;
for I have determined to invest twenty thousand of
our new-found money in land; it seems providential
that it should come just now. I had been griev-
ing so much of late that this golden opportunity
would pass by; but, thank God! it will come out
right yet."

Maud, ever tactful and alert, seeing that Clifford
was unwilling to explain the particulars of the discovery, hurried their departure for home. When
they had all driven away, young Warlow filled one
of the sacks with coin, and placed it in a trunk of
clothing that was ready packed, locked the door behind, and slowly rowed down; but he had delayed
long enough to be certain of finding that they had
all retired when he arrived home.

In the morning Colonel Warlow was too unwell
to appear at the breakfast-table, and finding that his
indisposition was of too serious a nature to admit of
his traveling that day, Clifford received twenty thousand dollars—nearly thirteen hundred Mexican doubloons—from his father, with the instruction to invest
it in land at his discretion. The colonel told Clif-

ford at parting to consider half of the money as his
own; so with a light heart the youth started out on
his third essay at "fortune hunting."

Accompanied by Squire Moreland and Ralph,
who had unconsciously helped to load the Warlow
carriage with more than seventy thousand dollars in
gold, secreted in two innocent-looking trunks, Clifford took the winding trail for Abilene just as the
sun appeared above the rim of the eastern hills.   It
was a cool, dry July morning, very favorable for
producing that Western phenomenon, the mirage;
and as they emerged from the corn-fields and tall
thickets of blue-stem of the valley onto the rolling
uplands, carpeted with buffalo-grass, a scene of
mysterious grandeur burst upon their sight.

Objects that were miles away appeared close at
hand, plain and distinct in the pure, clear air; and
although a lofty ridge twenty miles wide inter-
posed, all the valley of the Smoky Hill was rolled
out like a map before them.   The winding river,
fringed by trees and groves; the wide prairie valley,
flecked with white villages; a long train on the
Union Pacific, "fleeing like a dragon through the
level fields and leaving a breath of smoke behind,"
seemed but a few miles away.

The Iron Mound, sixty miles distant, loomed off
to the north-west, and far beyond appeared the faint
outline of the Soldier's Cap—a towering headland,
that, like a giant's helmet, seemed to guard all the
Saline Valley, but now dwarfed, by the hundred
miles which intervened, to a mere dot upon the
horizon.

The Smoky Hills flamed up in a long line of purple, jagged buttes on the west, while to the south stretched away the fat prairies of the Russian Mennonite colony, their quaint, old-world villages of thatch and white-plastered adobe clustering thickly over the level plain that was begemmed by lakes of waving water, or what appeared to be such, but which in reality was only an optical illusion caused by a glare of rarefied atmosphere. Soon these phantom lakes began to flood the prairie with a wavering shimmer. Broad rivers became momentarily wider, until all the landscape was submerged and the villages swam in a sea of water a moment, sinking down at length like foundered ships, the white buildings towering up strangely like masts, which, at last, all sank from sight, leaving only a glare of silver behind.

Soon nature resumed her wonted aspect, though it seemed strangely unreal to see the Iron Mound sink slowly as they ascended the ridge, until it was lost to view, and what had been the Smoky Valley but a moment before was now the rolling highland which they had to traverse for hours before reaching their destination. For a space of twenty miles square, not a solitary house was to be seen. In fact, after leaving the valley the only sign of life visible was a distant herd along some timber-fringed stream, by which the picturesque and fertile tract was threaded, or a long line of antelope, that would cautiously keep to the highest ridges as they loped away in single file.

The ridged and travel worn-trail, where in

23

former years the herds of Texas and New Mexico had been driven along to Abilene, was now disused and lonely, as the traffic had been transferred to more western points; so our friends were relieved on reaching their destination after a monotonous drive of half a day.

Driving to a bank, Clifford deposited the unsealed bags of gold within the safe of that institution, while his two companions were looking for a hotel; then, next, young Warlow wrote a long and carefully worded dispatch to the American minister at Mexico, inquiring for information concerning Bruce Walraven and his wife, Herr Von Brunn and his wife Labella, and also the status of Monteluma, with a request for an immediate reply, that was no doubt facilitated by the information which the banker telegraphed, at Clifford's request, for the privilege of reference.

Without difficulty Clifford perfected the title to his homestead before the land officers. Then, in a fever of restlessness, our hero passed the intervening time until Monday morning, when he received a dispatch from the minister at the City of Mexico, stating that no trace could be found of either of the parties inquired for; that the old mansion of Monteluma had been confiscated during the "French invasion," but the estate was held by a wealthy foreign nobleman; that the agent of that nobleman was absent at Durango, so no further particulars could be learned until his return, etc.

"This is the last evidence in the proof that Mora is heiress to all the new-found treasure," men-

tally exclaimed young Warlow as he hurried into
the land-office and elbowed his way through the
dense throng of spectators to the desk, where the
receiver was gloomily saying, " that the sale would
be a failure, unless the agent of Lord Scholeigh
arrived, which was improbable now, owing to the
storm near St. Louis, that had prostrated the wires
and stopped travel."

"Proceed with the sale, if you please; I would
like to bid in a tract," said Clifford quietly. Then,
after several tracts in small bodies had been purchased by the bystanders, he began to bid in section
after section at fifty cents an acre; and when the
amount ran up to ten, twenty, and twenty-three
thousand acres, the crowd began to grow curious,
and jostled each other to get a better view of the
man who could bid in so quietly a six-mile square
tract without faltering; but the grave-faced and
gray-clad young ranchman, with no ornament about
him save a gold buckle to the collar of his brown
flannel shirt, kept steadily on, without any opposi-
tion, perfectly heedless of the scrutiny.

"He is a son of Colonel Warlow on the Cottonwood, who fell heir to a cool million from California, the other day," said a man, in a tone just
loud enough to reach Clifford's ears, and the receiver wondered what the handsome young man
found to smile at as he bid in the last section of
sixty-nine thousand acres; but how should he know
that Clifford was amused at the remark, thinking
that the small legacy had grown, like the story of
the " five black crows."

"Young man," said the receiver, in a tone of arrogant suspicion. "I shall insist on some proof of your ability to pay such a large sum before I proceed further."

"Very well, sir," replied Clifford, blowing a wreath of cigar-smoke into the official's face as he coolly handed him his certificate of deposit, subject to check of seventy thousand dollars, given Saturday evening after the banker had counted the gold. Then, young Warlow began to realize the prestige which wealth gives, as he saw the look of insolence on the officer's face quickly give place to respectful wonder, as he proceeded at once with the auction.

When the figures had reached a hundred thousand acres the crowd gave way to cheers, which swelled to a perfect tumult when six townships— nearly one hundred and thirty-nine thousand acres— were knocked down to the young bidder, who refused to bid any further, and the sale closed.

Clifford wrote out a check for the sum of sixty-nine thousand one hundred and twenty dollars, and received the receiver's certificate, which entitled the purchaser to a deed for the tract. As the officer closed the sale and the papers changed hands in the bank, a noted " wheat-king" hurried in and told Clifford that the New York agent of Lord Scholeigh was coming on a special train, fast as steam could carry him, and requested our young friend to await the arrival, as the agent had been detained by storms and wash-outs while *en route* to the sale ; and the kingly real estate agent further intimated that a fine profit on the purchase could be realized if Clifford was willing to sell.

So our hero consented to remain, and when the agent arrived he was almost stunned by the offer of double the price he had paid; the agent offering to take the entire tract at one dollar an acre. After some deliberation Clifford consummated a sale of seventy-five thousand acres, keeping a township, six miles square, for himself, and forty thousand acres for his father; and finding that he had seventy-five thousand dollars left. " Equal," the wheat-king said, " to the Dutchman's profit of ten per schent."

Clifford found it was an easy matter to induce the receiver to accept the agent's certified check on New York in exchange for his own. Then he arranged to leave the bag of doubloons, sealed, and only left for safety until he could return them to the chest; but the twenty-five thousand dollars of profit he deposited with the bank, subject to check. Having bought a heavy steel safe, with time-lock, and leaving orders for it to be delivered at once, he returned home on Tuesday morning, proud and happy over the result of his transaction.

When he arrived at home, he was met by Rob, who was pale and excited. When Clifford had hurriedly asked after his father's welfare, Rob replied that their parent was well, but a strange accident had occurred out near the secret cavern. He proceeded to tell how the gray-robed spectre had darted out from among the tall blue-stem, while one of their workmen was mowing near there. The apparition had so startled the horses that they became unmanageable, and when the strange figure, in a reckless manner, had sprung at their heads, they had whirled, throwing the crazied being under the sickle and mangling him so horribly that he only lived a moment. His body was carried to the cell, where it was now lying. This had occurred only a few hours before, and all the family were up there awaiting Clifford's return.

Mounting a fresh horse, Clifford galloped rapidly up the winding pathway, fearing—he hardly dared to think what. "Could it be that he would soon stand beside the mangled form of Bruce Walraven, Mora's father?" he was thinking as he dismounted at the well-remembered plum-thicket, and hitched his horse to a tree.

A moment later Maud flew out with a low cry of delight, and while embracing Clifford, she cried tearfully : —

"Oh, I am inexpressibly relieved. It is not Bruce, as we feared, but it's that blood-stained Eagle Beak, Olin Estill's partner in crime and final victim."

"Why, Maud! how do you know?" said he, breathless with suspense.

"They found a silver breastplate, such as were worn by chiefs in the early days, and on the medal was an engraving of the beak of an eagle; while on the reverse, now worn dim, was the name, 'Eagle Beak.' This large plate was hung about his neck by a heavy chain of silver, which was riveted so it is impossible to remove it without filing

it through, and the links have worn into the flesh—
oh, horrible!" she replied, with a shudder of
disgust.

With reluctant steps Clifford sought the cavern,
where his parents and the Moreland family were
grouped about the door; and after a few minutes
of greeting, he went in alone to where the corpse
was lying cold and still; and when he had removed
the white sheet from its face, he stood long and
silently regarding the revolting picture of depravity
and ferocious cunning that even yet showed on
every feature, frozen in the rigid calm of death.

"No, thank God! this is not the face of noble
Bruce; but still it is that of a white man—some
wretched desperado, who had fled from the aveng-
ing arm of justice, and had gained sway over a
band of savages as brutal and vicious, but less daring and cunning than himself," thought young
Warlow. "This certainly is a sermon on the
retribution which Providence holds in store for
those who perpetrate such crimes of inhuman
atrocity as this wretch is stained with," he said,
as Maud came into the cell.

They buried the remains upon a lofty hill near
by, the top of which was visible from their homes
in the valley; no ceremony was observed, but
the horrible details of burial were delegated to
a few workmen from the hay-field, and by three
that afternoon only a small mound of clay remained to tell of a life that had been but a fever
of bloody deeds.

Once—long years after—as Clifford stood in

the twilight with Maud, they heard the jabbering wail of a wolf on the grave-crowned hill, and Clifford said :—

"If the departed soul does hover about the grave after death, seeking re-embodiment, then Eagle Beak has surely been born again in the form of a wolf; for he was the very incarnation, no doubt, of such a beast during his existence here. I never pass by that thistle-grown and nettle-hidden grave without a shudder; and often in the dismal night, when just such a piercing howl resounds from that hill-top, I vaguely fancy it is the soul of Eagle Beak mourning because of the limited sphere of deviltry in which his 'wolf-life' constrains his savage spirit."

"Oh, Clifford! will you never outgrow such idle fancies?" Maud exclaimed.

"No, never so long as I meet foxes, jackals, and hyenas every day, that are only veiled by a human form—very thinly disguised often—and it is God's goodness, alone, that finally denies them that mask."

"Clifford, my brother, what a strange belief for 'Deacon' Warlow, pillar of the Church, and first in all good deeds of Christian charity and enterprise in his community, to entertain and express," she replied, with a look of strange interest dawning in her beautiful but matronly face.

"Well, Maud, I find abundant proof in the Bible to substantiate this faith," he answered, gravely, "while our lives teem with the evidence of its truth."

But I have digressed too long already, and will return to my theme.

As they drove back home from the death-haunted cell, Clifford told his parents of his search for the treasure; how, after discovering the gems, he had been convinced that the gold was also secreted near, and his ultimate success in discovering it buried in the grave that Roger Coble had noticed when he rescued his father after the massacre. The finding of Ivarene's Journal, his engagement to Mora, and discovery that she was the daughter of Bruce and his ill-fated wife, and the successful speculation in which he had figured with such great profit at Abilene, were left unrevealed, as Clifford thought his father was not strong enough to bear the strain of such excitement yet.

With Maud he was not so reticent, and after supper he told of the success at the land-office, and the use he had made at Mora's request of part of the recovered treasure.

After Maud had expressed her unbounded joy at the substantial results of that venture, Clifford noticed a shade of anxiety and sadness settle down on her face, and he hastened to say, while reaching up to gather a spray of trumpet-flowers that swung its blossoms of black, crimson, and salmon in heavy festoons over the latticed gateway: "Maud, you dear, unselfish creature, I know that you and Ralph are about to begin life together, and, when father offered me half of the twenty thousand dollars, I just mentally concluded to give you the benefit of it. It seems to me you ought to keep

24

the pot boiling with twenty thousand acres of good land."

While Maud hung about his neck, her tearful face hidden on his shoulder, her brother continued:—

"Poor Ralph will need a great deal of encouragement from you. I have been in that very kind of a boat myself lately, and know how to sympathize with him."

Soon he was galloping down to the Estill ranch; but I will not intrude upon the privacy of that meeting between himself and Mora, only leaving it all to the imagination of the reader. Mr. Estill had not returned yet, so they still deferred making any explanation of the strange discoveries made since his departure. It was agreed, however, to reveal all on his return. Plans for the future were discussed as they strolled out on the terrace; and before he left, young Warlow had won a promise that their wedding-day would be an early one—some time in September, Mora said.

"I have had such a strange dream, twice on successive nights, lately, Clifford. It seemed as though I was Ivarene, and that I led a dual sort of an existence, part of the time as myself, and at other times I was that ill-fated Mexican bride, longing to meet Bruce once more. Some way, Clifford, I never can reconcile myself to the belief that they are my parents, and the suspense of this uncertainty is growing unbearable."

Clifford was very thoughtful for a long while after this; but at length he begged her to await the return of Mr. Estill before they divulged the secret. Then, after a lingering parting, he returned home to begin, on the morrow, preparations for the new life that was before him.

Before leaving Abilene he had engaged a skillful stone-mason, who was to begin enlarging his dwelling at once with a large force of workmen at his command; and I will only briefly tell how soon the cottage grew into a many-gabled mansion of red sandstone, with bay-windows and long wings, terraces of stone, with balustrades of white magnesia, and marble vases filled with blooming plants, that trailed down their sides with blossoms of rose, creamy white and scarlet.

A thousand head of cattle were bought, and hurrying workmen were busy stacking vast ricks of prairie-hay near the large barn that was rising like magic under the trowels of a score of masons.

In these details I have anticipated somewhat, but will return to the thread of my story.

The suspicions of the colonel and Mrs. Warlow were at once aroused by seeing a force of workmen beginning to enlarge Clifford's dwelling; and on perceiving this, Clifford hastened to reveal all the discoveries and transactions of the past few weeks. The journal deeply afflicted his father, who at once came to the same conclusion which the younger members of the family had arrived at on reading that document,—that Bruce and his wife had been murdered by Olin Estill, who had stolen their child and had left it at the Estill ranch; that Mora was that child, and that the family had raised her as

their own daughter. When Clifford told of his
success in the land transaction and of wishing that
Maud should have the twenty thousand acres meant
for himself, his parents seemed both pleased and
proud of his course, although his father cautioned
him against using any more of the treasure until
Mr. Estill was made aware of the discovery.

" Did not the Estills tell you that Mora was the
daughter of Bruce and Ivarene when they made
their first visit here ?" said Clifford, in surprise.

" Why, no, indeed !" replied his father; " they
told us of the part which they feared their nephew
took in the massacre. They believed he murdered
the originals of the pictures which he left at their
house soon after that tragedy, but he appeared to
be insane and they never saw him alive again. It
was months after when his skeleton was found on
the prairie, barely recognizable, which they buried
on a hill near the ranch."

" And that was all ?" said Clifford, in a tone of
anxiety. " But do you not think that Mora is
Bruce's daughter ?"

" I have no doubt of it; for she is the perfect
counterpart of Ivarene in voice, face, and expression,
although her eyes are blue while those of Ivarene
were black. Still the same look is there that I
shall never forget. Why, when I meet her gaze, it
always seems that Ivarene is trying to speak to me
once more," said the colonel with deep emotion.

After this interview, Clifford lost no time in
hurrying down to the Estill ranch to seek an interview with Mora ; and after they had met, with all

the demonstrations peculiar to lovers, he noticed a strange look of trouble on her face, and when he tenderly asked its cause, she faltered a moment, then bursting into tears, and hiding her face on his breast, she confessed that the suspense of awaiting her father's return had become at last unendurable, and she had told her mother all the particulars of their engagement, the discovery of the treasure, their subsequent use of a portion of it, and their well-founded belief that she was the daughter of Bruce and Ivarene Walraven.

"She confessed, then, that it was true?" said Clifford, in a tone of suspense.

"No, stranger still!" said Mora, as she raised a tear-stained face to his—" no, Clifford, she seemed struck dumb with astonishment, and reiterated the assertion solemnly that I was her only daughter, born five years after that tragedy. I am convinced that it is true, Clifford; nothing can convince me that she is trying to deceive us, for she is too sincere to keep the truth from us now. Yes, I am an Estill; but she said that my strange resemblance to the picture in the locket had always perplexed her, and my father and they were very sensitive on the subject. She saw you were startled by my lack of resemblance to any one of the family, when you made your first visit here; but she is glad to know that you are to be her son at last, Clifford." Had a thunderbolt fallen at his feet, young Warlow could not have been more startled than he was at this announcement. Then, after a moment of silence, he said: "Ah! Mora darling, it does not matter whose daughter you may be, so your heart is mine; but how strange it is that we should have arrived at such a wrong conclusion!" Then, as he began to reflect, he found that her mysterious resemblance to Ivarene was their strongest proof that she was not an Estill.

An interview with Mrs. Estill followed, in which she gave a willing assent to the lovers' union; then she again asserted, with truth and sincerity stamped upon her face and tone, that Mora was her only daughter, born of her own flesh and blood, but that there was a mystery connected with her birth which she had never revealed to any one but her husband.

"Mother! mother! what is it?" said Mora in great agitation, while Clifford sprang up with a look of intense interest depicted upon his face.

"It is a strange and unreal thing to relate in this enlightened and skeptical age, and I should never divulge it but for the events of the last few days; but Mora's unaccountable resemblance to the face in the locket, which is that of Ivarene, is not the only mystery that surrounds her birth. In the autumn of 1849, September 16th—I remember the date perfectly—one of our herders came in at night very much terrified by a sight which he had just witnessed. He had seen two mysterious lights flitting about the base of Antelope Butte, several miles up the valley, where he had been looking after our cattle that had become scattered while we were at Fort Riley—driven to take refuge there from the Cheyenne Indians that were raiding the frontier settlements during August. Why I remember the date so distinctly is from the fact that we had only returned that day, finding our cabin in ashes.

"Fearing it might be some signal of lurking savages, Mr. Estill and myself ran with the herder to the bluff which overlooks the house on the north, and saw a sight that was full of mystery; and which, in fact, was never explained.

"There were two large blue lights, of such an unnatural color and appearance as to attract instant attention, flitting about up the valley. They would seem to skim along in long, undulating swells, like the flight of swallows, often rising hundreds of feet in the air, but always darting back to the base of the butte. We were relieved to know it was not Indians, and thinking it was one of those gaseous or igneous phenomena peculiar to water-courses, we did not investigate further, but only regarded their appearance with curiosity.

"Their visits finally reached our premises, and I was horrified to see them hovering about the house later in the season; but all our attempts to approach them were frustrated, for they would recede as we advanced; then we really began to feel how very unaccountable they were, and became perplexed with the mystery. This state of affairs continued until Christmas eve, 1852. As I was standing at a window with Hugh in my arms, I saw the two lights come flitting down the valley together. When they reached a point close to the house they halted, and, after hovering about together for a while, the larger light darted off eastward, and was never seen again.   The lesser one remained flitting about the house, or to and fro between here and Antelope Butte, until, one night in May, 1854, the light, after hovering near by, disappeared forever. *That very night Mora was born.* Seeing a resemblance in her childish face to that within the locket—a likeness that has increased with her age, until now she is the very image of poor, dead Ivarene—we named her Morelia (shortened to Mora by her friends), a name that was engraved and set with rubies upon the locket. We thought this the name, of course, of the female face within the locket, but from the Journal of Ivarene it is apparent that it was the name of her dead mother instead.

" This precious locket had been flung at my feet by Olin Estill, a renegade nephew of my husband, whom he had discarded on account of his vicious tendencies, and who had been leading a mysterious existence, connected, I now fear, with a band of outlaws that committed the massacre at the corral. He had been absent from our house several months, until the day after our return he suddenly appeared at the tent-door, and, after glaring at me a moment, had flung the locket at my feet, then, with a blood-chilling shriek, had fled away. We never saw him alive after that day ; but his skeleton, torn asunder by wolves and barely recognizable, was found months after, and buried upon a hill-top near here."

" Did you never search Antelope Butte ?" Clifford asked, with grave thoughtfulness depicted in his face.

"No; we never did, although we once talked of doing so, but forgot it soon in the anxiety and care of our life," she answered.

"I shall do so to-morrow," he said, "for I believe the mystery of their fate is hidden there. Yes, Bruce and Ivarene must have died some terrible death there at that bluff, and I shall never rest until the cloud that wraps their fate is dispelled."

On his return home he related to his parents the story which Mrs. Estill had told. When he had finished, his mother was pale with a strange excitement; and his father exclaimed in a hoarse voice of agitation :—

"Clifford, you should make a careful search on Antelope Butte in the morning. I fear that Bruce and Ivarene perished there."

"My son, I never have told you that only a few months before you were born just such a light flashed into my room as the one that flitted about the Estill ranch," said Mrs. Warlow, pale and trembling with emotion. "It was on Christmas Eve, 1852, that I was sitting in the firelit room waiting your father's return, when I saw a pale blue haze dart past the window, hover a moment, then return ; and as I raised the sash I seemed to be smothered by a flash of thick, luminous fog, and fell prostrated as by a stroke of lightning. I did not lose consciousness, however, but called one of the negro women, who helped me to a lounge, and lit the lamp. I was nervous about the occurrence ; but your father explained the phenomenon as being only a collection of natural gas, generated in damp localities. The light flitted about for a few months; but on the night of your birth, Clifford, it disappeared, and was never seen again. How strange that one of those lights should disappear from her house that night, and appear at mine, hundreds of miles away! Then the similar circumstances under which those mysterious halos vanished—the very night, it appears, of your birth and that of Mora! She was born in May, 1854, so Mrs. Estill says."

"We must search Antelope Butte in the morning," said Clifford, trying to conceal his agitation and to speak calmly; "for I fear that the final tragedy of Bruce and Ivarene was enacted there. I dread the discovery that we may make, while, at the same time, I long to unravel the dark mystery which enwraps their fate." Then he hurriedly left the room and sought slumber in the quiet of his own bed-chamber; but it was in vain, for strange fancies kept him awake and thoughtful while the hours slowly dragged by.

Since the night when he had seen that weird and unearthly phantom war-dance around the long grave, Clifford had begun to entertain some strange fancies, which slowly grew upon him as he reviewed the stories which Mrs. Estill and his mother had told that evening, until finally he said, as the gray of morning began to tinge the eastern sky with its ashy pallor:—

"I am almost convinced that Bruce's theory is a true one. Father has long believed me to be the reincarnation of the spirit of Bruce Walraven. This, if true, will account for my strange resemblance to a man who died, in all probability, long before I was born, and will also account for the mysterious memories which always haunt me, like the glimpses of a former life. Can it be possible that the soul, at will, can take on a new body again after death, and profit by its past mistakes? That would be a resurrection, indeed! Can it be that all the air about us is peopled by the spiritual outlines of dead and half-forgotten friends, only waiting their time to be re-born, and we ourselves may be but bodies that are inhabited by the souls of people who have lived before? If this theory is as correct as it is comforting, then death has lost all its terrors; for what could inspire more delight in the heart of an aged and care-worn person than the knowledge that, after he had cast off his faded and wrinkled body, by that process which we call death, he could walk again in all the freshness of youth and beauty on earth, which, say what we may, is dearer than any other place can ever be.

"This theory I shall put to the test to-day," our hero said; "for if the remains of Bruce and Ivarene are found near Antelope Butte—as I am convinced that they will be—then my conjectures are confirmed and the mystery of eternity, which has mocked and puzzled man from his creation, is revealed. It will prove that those mysterious lights were their spirits still hovering about their grave, waiting their opportunity to be re-born. This looks no more improbable than many of the mysteries of science did a few years ago. But, then, life itself would still remain a grand mystery, as would sight, sound, and hearing."

By this time he had arisen, and, after dressing, he seated himself before the tall mirror.

"This strange belief has been growing upon me since I heard Mrs. Estill's and mother's revelations until it has become almost conviction, and if we find that on Antelope Butte, which I feel we will—then it will convince me that Mora is—God how strange that sounds!—Ivarene born again to enjoy the happiness which her untimely fate prevented her securing in her brief life."

As he scanned his own reflection in the mirror, by the sunlight, which now was flooding the eastern hills in its golden mantle, while a look of growing wonder and strange curiosity came over his face, he exclaimed, with a start: "Then Bruce Walraven is—myself!"

After a moment of serious reflection, he continued: "Well, there is nothing so very improbable or uncanny in the thought, at last; for it is just as probable that God may have given me a soul that had lived before, as one that had not. No; human nature has too much wisdom to ever have gained it by one life."

If our hero's theory was true, then Bruce could not have asked a better fate than to live his life again as the handsome youth reflected there, with his crisp golden hair, eyes of pansy blue, and the flush of young manhood on his glossy cheeks.

Chapter XXI.

AN hour later found the Warlow family at the foot of Antelope Butte, whither they had all driven to make a search for—what they shrank from saying. They had been there only a short time when they saw the Estill carriage coming. When it drew near they discovered that it was Mrs. Estill and Mora, who, when they were assisted to alight, said they had seen the Warlow carriage with their field-glass, and suspecting the meaning of its visit to the butte, they had hurried up to join the search with their friends.

As Clifford, Rob, and Ralph were carefully searching the face of the declivity, Mrs. Warlow told Mrs. Estill of the remarkable fact that she had also seen that mystic light on the night it had disappeared from Estill Ranch; then, as Mora drew near, she gave a circumstantial account of the event, which caused her hearers to exchange looks of perplexed amazement.

Mora became thoughtfully silent, and, leaving the others, she wandered restlessly back and forth at the foot of the bluff, watching the searchers intently.

She was startled at length by a cry of astonishment from Clifford, and with the others she hastened up the steep acclivity to where he stood in a recess of the cliff. When she reached his side he was leaning heavily against the rocky wall, white and trembling.

"Oh, Clifford! speak! what is it?" she cried, breathless with a strange dread.

He could only point to the face of the rock with an unsteady finger, while the sweat-drops rained down from his white face, wrung by an agony of emotion which he vainly strove to repress.

Sinking down upon the sloping mound, matted with grass, and kneeling there at the foot of the cliff she read with a startled gaze the inscription which was carved in faint, moss-grown letters, upon the magnesian stone:—

"My Ivarene, my lost love, lies dead beside me with our little child, cold and still, on her breast. I am wounded and dying; but death is sweet now. We were coming here to watch for the trains when we were assaulted by the strange hunter, who shot us both. My love only breathed one breath. I carried her here. The child was pierced by the same shot. My eyes are growing dim; but I welcome death. Oh, farewell, bright world! I feel my life ebbing fast away, but would not stay without my darling. I go to meet her where there will be no more parting. Oh, the joy and bliss to see her smile again! It makes me long for death. We shall live again! Bru—"

With a wild cry of agonized grief, Mora covered her face, while the others read, with streaming eyes, that last message from the tomb. Then, as they drew back and waited with broken sobs and smothered weeping, Ralph and Robbie began tenderly to remove the *débris* and soil which time had formed into a mound below the inscription.

When, at last, there was revealed two skeletons, locked together in the last clasp of love, which even death could not sever, Maud cried aloud with a wail of anguish :—

"Oh, *can this be the last* of beautiful Ivarene and dear, brave Bruce?"

Choking back their sobs, they all knelt in a circle, while Mrs. Warlow's voice rose in a passionate, fervid prayer; then tenderly, with loving care, they carried the remains down to the Warlow carriage, leaving Mora and Clifford still lingering by the vacant mound.

They stood in silence a moment, the only sound the soft rustle of wild-ivy that half draped the cliff in its mottled foliage of crimson, green, and bronze; the radiant sunlight from the cloudless sky lit up the sunflowers and gentian that grew in stunted clusters on the hillside, while the sumac flaunted its plumes of scarlet, gold, and purple along the rifts of the white, rocky wall.

Lifting their gaze from the open grave, their eyes met in a swift flash of joy, while a half-puzzled look of delight and recognition struggled over their faces; then, bounding lightly over the open grave, Clifford whispered in a tone of unspeakable love and yearning:—

"Oh, Ivarene, my sweetheart of long ago, we meet at last!"

"Then it is as I have dreamed—and you are

Bruce!" she answered, with a sob of joy, while springing into his outstretched arms.

"Yes, love, I am convinced that we meet again after all these years of waiting. Though to the world we may be only Mora and Clifford, yet, darling, to each other we will ever be Ivarene and Bruce," he replied, while raining kisses upon her upturned, radiant face.

Ah! how can I tell of the serene wedding morn that marked that happy day when Clifford and Mora paced back and forth on the sunlighted terrace at the Stone Corral, now no longer a modest cottage, but a stately though quaint mansion of red sandstone. The tender, blue haze of Indian summer brooded over the valley, where the fields of wheat shone dewy and green, and the newly-mown meadows stretched away like a verdant carpet far out onto the highlands, miles upon miles—all their own. The marble fountain threw a glittering sheen of silver high in the air, while the breeze swept the blossom-laden tendrils that trailed down the snowy vases, and swayed the limbs of the old elm to and fro about the gables of the elegant home.

"Oh, Ivarene, dear love! how strange it is to take up the thread of our happiness on the spot, almost where our lives went out in such black despair just twenty-six years ago! I know why you wish to have our bridal here, darling; for it was here, at the Old Corral, that our former trials overwhelmed us, and it is doubly sweet to begin happiness again on this spot."

"Bruce, my darling, I can remember nothing of

the old life and its trials, that ended at our grave on Antelope Butte; but my love for you—ah! that can never perish. It has survived even the horrors of that lonesome tomb. It is strange we only recognized each other at that empty grave; but I had always felt such a longing to meet some one, that now I know it was the spirit within me crying dumbly for you; and oh! the unutterable content when at length I met you, and the joy of only being with you now,—it is more than Eden!"

"Sweet Ivarene, do you ever ponder on what eternity means for us, now we have its secret?—a limitless succession of life in all its phases; that the grave is only the door to life again, when we can choose another birth—passing through all the freshening scenes of infancy and youth; growing up again as boy and girl; seeking each other out for another union like this, where we shall always recognize each other, but forget the old life,—it is *this* which gives hope and zest to this happy day; for we know that we shall really never be separated."

"We will pass a happy life together, my love; and from out our abundance we can sweeten the lives of many others who have not been blessed with great riches," he continued, in a tender tone.

"Yes, dear Bruce, and the treasure of Monteluma should be dedicated to charity alone, for we have enough without it," she replied; then, pointing to a newly-sodded grave at the foot of the lawn—a mound that was marked by a marble slab on which only was engraved,

"BRUCE AND IVARENE,"

she continued, with a smile of ineffable peace on her beaming face: "That is for the eyes of the world, dear Bruce; but we know that we are they, only masquerading under the names of Mora and Clifford."

At that moment Maud, Ralph, Hugh, and Grace came on to the terrace above, and Hugh, in a voice husky with emotion, said:—

"Come, Mora and Clifford, the minister waits."

Tarrying a moment, while the others moved on along the terrace, the happy pair stood gazing out over the tranquil valley, then, drawing aside her veil, which trailed liked a mist down over her robe of glistening satin, white as a snow-drift, she raised a radiant face to his, and said:—

"My Bruce, we live again—we live again!"

Stooping, while their lips met, he murmured:—

"Yes, Ivarene, dear bride, and this—oh! this is heaven!"

A moment more, and they had disappeared within the flower-wreathed doorway.

THE END.